"A vigilante detective in the manly-man mode . . . a rat-a-tat tone."　　—*The Washington Post Book World*

"Fast pacing and an involving mystery."　　—*Booklist*

Two Dollar Bill

"A smooth and solid thriller."
　　—*News-Leader* (Springfield, MO)

Reckless Abandon

"Fast action, catchy plot, and spicy dialogue."
　　—*The Calgary Sun*

"[An] amusing, full-throttle sex-and-crime romp."
　　—*Publishers Weekly*

Dirty Work

"High on the stylish suspense."
　　—*The Sante Fe New Mexican*

"Sleek and engaging."　　—*Publishers Weekly*

The Short Forever

"A tight mystery right up to the end . . . good-guy charm."　　—*The Palm Beach Post*

Cold Paradise

"A delightful tale of sex and violence . . . *Sopranos*-style . . . slick, sophisticated fun."　　—*The Washington Post*

"Woods delivers his most riveting and glamorous Barrington novel yet."　　—*Vero Beach Press Journal* (FL)

BOOKS BY STUART WOODS

T.

In the Bel-Air district of Los Angeles, one of America's wealthiest and most star-infested communities, Stone Barrington comes face-to-face with his past. . . .

A beautiful Bel-Air widow, already one of the wealthiest women in America, needs Stone's help to become even more cash-rich. At stake is the sale of her investment in—and the resulting dissolution of—Hollywood's world-famous Centurion Studios. Stone is no stranger to the stylish and lucrative world of Centurion, and he has more than a passing acquaintance with the lady herself.

But when he arrives in Bel-Air to finalize the sale, the tranquillity of that famous neighborhood turns out to be no more than a facade. One of L.A.'s most rapacious power brokers has Centurion and its unique real estate in his sights, and he will not be denied. Stone finds himself dragged into a surprisingly complex and high-stakes game, the kind only the truly rich and dangerously ambitious can play—and survive.

PRAISE FOR THE NOVELS OF STUART WOODS

Strategic Moves

"Fans of the Barrington saga will enjoy his latest entry. . . . The action never slows from the start."
—*Midwest Book Review*

Lucid Intervals

"Woods's Stone Barrington is a guilty pleasure. . . . He's also an addiction that's harder to kick than heroin."
—*Contra Costa Times*

"Smooth. . . . Woods mixes danger and humor into a racy concoction that will leave readers thirsty for more."
—*Publishers Weekly*

continued . . .

"In *Lucid Intervals*, [Woods's] blend of booze, broads, and bullets remains a winning formula. In an ever-changing world, it's nice to have reliables such as Woods and his characters on which to depend."
—*Bangor Daily News*

"Fans of Woods's long-running series will not be disappointed by this romp, which is peppered with plenty of humor."
—*Booklist*

"[A] first-class page-turner." —*Albuquerque Journal*

Kisser

"POW!!! He's back with more twists and trysts."
—The Mystery Reader

"A fun, breezy page-turner." —*Booklist*

Loitering with Intent

"Have a margarita handy when you read this fun page-turner." —*Southern Living*

"[A] solid, action-packed thriller."
—*The Globe and Mail* (Canada)

Hot Mahogany

"[A] fun ride from Stuart Woods." —*Bangor Daily News*

"Series fans will find all their expectations nicely fulfilled."
—*Publishers Weekly*

Shoot Him If He Runs

"Fast-paced . . . with a whole lot of style."
—*Bangor Daily News*

"Woods certainly knows how to keep the pages turning."
—*Booklist*

Fresh Disasters

"Fast-paced, hilarious, and tragic."—*Albuquerque Journal*

"Good fun." —*Publishers Weekly*

STUART WOODS

BEL-AIR DEAD

A STONE BARRINGTON NOVEL

A SIGNET BOOK

SIGNET
Published by New American Library, a division of
Penguin Group (USA) Inc., 375 Hudson Street,
New York, New York 10014, USA
Penguin Group (Canada), 90 Eglinton Avenue East, Suite 700, Toronto,
Ontario M4P 2Y3, Canada (a division of Pearson Penguin Canada Inc.)
Penguin Books Ltd., 80 Strand, London WC2R 0RL, England
Penguin Ireland, 25 St. Stephen's Green, Dublin 2,
Ireland (a division of Penguin Books Ltd.)
Penguin Group (Australia), 250 Camberwell Road, Camberwell, Victoria 3124,
Australia (a division of Pearson Australia Group Pty. Ltd.)
Penguin Books India Pvt. Ltd., 11 Community Centre, Panchsheel Park,
New Delhi - 110 017, India
Penguin Group (NZ), 67 Apollo Drive, Rosedale, Auckland 0632,
New Zealand (a division of Pearson New Zealand Ltd.)
Penguin Books (South Africa) (Pty.) Ltd., 24 Sturdee Avenue,
Rosebank, Johannesburg 2196, South Africa

Penguin Books Ltd., Registered Offices:
80 Strand, London WC2R 0RL, England

Published by Signet, an imprint of New American Library, a division of Penguin
Group (USA) Inc. Previously published in a G. P. Putnam's Sons edition.

First Signet Printing, December 2011
10 9 8 7 6 5 4 3 2 1

In memory of Elaine Kaufman (1929–2010),
who loved writers

1

Elaine's, late.

Stone Barrington sat with his client, Mike Freeman, of Strategic Services, and his former partner from his NYPD days, Dino Bacchetti, over the ruins of dinner and a bottle of excellent Cabernet.

"That was good," Mike said. "I never knew how good the food was here, until you started bringing me."

"Comfort food," Dino said.

Elaine sat herself down in the spare chair. "Comfort food?" she asked. "Is that some kind of crack?"

"It's high praise," Stone said quickly, not wanting to get her started. Elaine's did not enjoy a high reputation with the food critics of the local media, because they didn't come often enough to get the good tables, but the regulars knew how good the food was, and that was all she really cared about.

"I'll take high praise," Elaine said.

Stone's cell phone hummed on his belt, and he dug it out of its holster. "Stone Barrington."

"Stone, it's Arrington," she said. Stone and Arrington had once been a very big item, to the extent of his having fathered a son by her.

"Well, hello there," he said. "I thought I'd never hear from you again." They had spent one night together in his Maine house, on Islesboro, at Dark Harbor, and then she had taken her leave, saying it was over.

"I want to hire you," she said.

"I'm for hire. How's Peter?"

"He misses his father," she said.

Stone wondered which father she meant, himself or her late husband, movie megastar Vance Calder, whose son the world believed Peter to be. Stone didn't know what to say.

"I mean Vance," she said. "He hardly knows you."

"All right," Stone said. "Why do you want to hire me?"

"I'm going to say this fast, because I'm sleepy, and I want to go to bed. I know you're at Elaine's at this hour, but I'm not."

"So, say it fast."

"You remember Centurion Studios? A large Hollywood film factory."

"I believe so."

"You remember that Vance owned a third of the shares when he died?"

"I didn't know it was that much."

"He'd been buying the stock for many years, every time somebody died and some shares became available."

"Got it."

"There's a stockholders' meeting coming up, and there will be a vote on whether to sell the studio. It has always been closely held, and Vance wanted to keep it that way."

"Who's buying?"

"I don't know, some corporation or other. They'll sell the property to developers, and the studio will just be a letterhead."

"And what do you want me to do?"

"Vote my shares against the sale, and do what you can to get the other stockholders to vote against it."

"How many are there?"

"A couple of dozen, maybe. I'll send you a list, along with my signed proxy, to the Bel-Air house. You can have the guesthouse, as usual. Manolo and Carmen will take good care of you."

Manolo and Carmen were the Filipino houseman

and his wife who ran the place. Stone knew he would be taken care of very well indeed. "All right, I guess I can manage that."

"Can you get there tomorrow?"

"Or the day after," Stone said. He wanted to fly himself in his new airplane.

"I guess that will be all right," she answered. "You remember Rick Barron?"

"Yes. I met him and his wife at Vance's burial."

"That's right. Call him as soon as you get there, and take him and his wife, Glenna, to dinner. Rick is in his nineties now, but he's sharp as a straight razor, and he's leading the fight to keep the studio closely held."

"I'll be glad to do that."

"In fact, invite them to the house, and let Manolo and Carmen do the dinner. They know all the Barrons' favorite dishes."

"All right."

"Call me when you get there?"

"Will do."

"Say hello to Elaine and Dino."

"Will do."

"Goodbye." She hung up.

Stone put away his phone. "Arrington says hello to both of you," he said to them.

"How is she?" Elaine asked.

"Sleepy," Stone replied. "Dino, you want to spend a few days in L.A.?"

"On whose nickel?" Dino asked.

"Transportation is free, and we'll be staying in Arrington's guesthouse."

"I'm in," Dino said.

Mike spoke up. "Can you just walk away from the NYPD that way?"

"I get time off, just like everybody," Dino said, "but I get to approve when, and I approve this one."

"Okay," Mike said.

"Mike," Stone said, "Dino has the NYPD by the ear, didn't you know? He's a law unto himself over there. The new commissioner, who doesn't know him very well, loves him."

"He'd love me more, if he knew me better," Dino said.

Elaine pinched Dino's cheek. "To know him is to love him," she said, planting a big kiss on his forehead. She got up and made her move to the next table of regulars.

Dino rubbed his cheek. "I hope she didn't make a bruise."

"With that five o'clock shadow, who could tell?" Stone asked.

"You guys have the life," Mike said. "And I'll bet you're going to fly the Mustang out there."

"You betcha," Stone replied.

"Hey, wait a minute," Dino said. "I didn't volunteer for suicide."

"It's time you had your first flight in the Citation Mustang," Stone said.

"He's right, Dino," Mike echoed. "You'll love it."

Dino looked doubtful. "I just don't know if God intended Stone to be put in charge of a jet airplane."

"You liked my old airplane well enough," Stone said.

"Yeah, but it had a propeller up front that made it go, and I took comfort in that."

"The Mustang has two engines, Dino," Mike said, "and they're fan jets. Twice the safety."

"No propellers, though."

"Propellers would just slow it down," Stone said.

"Mike, you think I should do this?"

"I've flown with him, Dino; he'll get you there."

"Well, okay, if you say so."

"You get a choice of seats," Stone said. "Up front with me, or you can lounge in the back and sleep all the way."

"How could I sleep with you at the controls?" Dino asked. "I'll take my chances up front, where I can do something, if I have to."

"I'll teach you to fly the airplane, Dino," Stone said.

"Hey, that's a good idea. That way when you turn blue and clutch your chest, I can save myself."

"I wish I could be alive to see that," Stone replied.

2

Stone rose the following morning, showered, shaved, packed and took his luggage down to the garage in the elevator. He put his bags in the trunk of his car and went to his office.

His secretary, Joan Robertson, put some papers on his desk. "Sign these," she said.

Stone signed them.

She picked them up. "Thank you."

"What were those?" Stone asked.

"Just a complete power of attorney and assignment of all your assets to me, personally, with immediate effect."

"Oh, okay," he said absently. "I'm going to L.A. for a few days," he said.

"Another vacation?" she asked.

"You know I never take vacations, unless there's work involved."

"What's the work?"

"Voting some shares at a stockholders' meeting for Arrington Calder."

"Sounds simple enough."

"No, I have to persuade others to vote with me."

"If there are any women in the group, you'll succeed," she said.

Stone brightened. "That's a thought," he said.

"When will you be back?"

"I don't know—give me a week."

"It's not as though you're needed here," she said. "I can handle whatever comes along."

Stone knew that was close to the truth. "Try not to practice any law," he said. "You'll get arrested."

"Don't worry. There won't be any of my fingerprints on anything." She flounced back to her office.

At Teterboro Airport, Stone did his walk-around preflight inspection of the airplane while Dino stowed their luggage in the forward compartment. When he finished, Dino was standing, staring at the airplane. It was the first time he'd seen it, Stone reflected.

"Well, I like the paint job," Dino said.

"Is that it?"

"The airplane is kind of pretty; it looks like it could fly, if it had to."

Stone pushed him aboard and settled him in the copilot's seat, then pulled up the stairs and closed the door. He got into the pilot's seat, ran through the checklist, and started the engines. Then he called Teterboro Clearance and got his IFR clearance for his first leg.

"How many times do we have to stop?" Dino asked.

"Twice, if we're lucky. There'll be very little in the way of headwinds today, maybe even a little tailwind. That's unusual."

"I'll take what I can get," Dino said.

Stone radioed Ground Control and got permission to taxi. Shortly, they were ready for takeoff.

Stone looked at Dino and saw a film of sweat on his forehead. "I turned on the air-conditioning," he said. "Are you still hot?"

"I'll be okay," Dino said, mopping his brow.

It occurred to Stone that Dino might really be nervous about flying in the jet. "I'll give you something to look at," he said, pointing to the copilot's Primary Flight Display. He pressed a button on the throttle and a wide, magenta V popped up on the screen. "When we take off, all I have to do is to keep the yellow V, which represents the airplane, nestled up against the magenta V, which represents our climb angle and course. As long as the two are together, we're fine."

"Okay," Dino said, tightening his seat belt.

The tower called and cleared them for takeoff. Stone taxied onto Runway One, stopped the airplane, centered the heading control, and, with the brakes on, shoved the throttles all the way forward. The engines ran up, and he released the brakes. The little jet shot down the runway, and, at ninety knots, Stone rotated, pulling the yellow V up into the magenta V. He raised the landing gear and flaps; then, at 700 feet, he pressed the autopilot button and turned the heading bug to 040. At 1,500 feet, following the departure procedure, he turned to 280 and climbed to 2,000 feet; then the controller gave him 10,000 feet, and they were on their way.

Dino was staring at the PFD.

"It's okay to look out the window now," Stone said. "The autopilot is flying the airplane, and it is a better pilot than I."

Dino looked around. "This isn't bad," he said. "It's quieter than your old airplane, and smoother, too."

"That's the idea," Stone said. The controller handed them off to New York Center, and they climbed to their final altitude of Flight Level 340, or 34,000 feet. Stone reduced power to the cruise détente on the throttles. "That's it," he said. "Now the airplane flies us to Wichita."

Dino looked at the chart on the big panel display. "That looks like a long way."

"See these two rings?" Stone said, pointing. "The dotted one is the distance we can fly and still have a forty-five-minute fuel reserve, and it falls beyond Wichita. The solid ring is the distance we can fly before dry tanks."

"Let's not fly that far," Dino said.

"And we even have a little tailwind," Stone said, pointing at the indicator.

They refueled at Wichita and took off again.

Dino handed Stone a sandwich and a Diet Coke from the ice drawer. "Where's our next stop?"

"Santa Fe."

"Why that far south?"

"We could refuel in Denver, but look," he said, pointing at the display. "The Nexrad shows some thunderstorms over the Rockies, so we'll go south of them to Santa Fe, then on to Santa Monica. The weather along that route is clear all the way."

"Got it."

They picked up three hours with the time change, and as they made their final turn on approach to Santa Monica, the sun was setting before them like a big red ball into the Pacific.

Stone left a refueling order. Then their rental car was brought out to the airplane, and they drove to Vance Calder's home in Bel-Air.

"This is possibly the ritziest neighborhood in Greater Los Angeles," Stone said, "and Vance owned eight acres of it." They drove through the open gates and pulled up in front of the house.

Manolo awaited them with a luggage cart. His greeting was warm, and he led them through the house to the back garden, where the sumptuous guesthouse awaited them by the pool.

Stone and Dino had both stayed here before, and they settled in quickly.

"What time would you like dinner?" Manolo asked.

"Well, it's three hours earlier here than in New York. How about nine?"

"Of course," Manolo said, then left them to unpack.

They dined by the pool. The evening was cool and pleasant and the food delicious.

Stone's cell phone went off. "Hello?"

"It's Arrington," she said. "There's been a change of plans."

3

Stone sighed. "What do you mean, a change in plans?"

"I want you to vote my shares for the sale of the studio."

"I guess I'm tired after the flight," Stone said. "I thought you just said you wanted me to vote your shares *for* the sale of the studio."

"That's exactly what I said."

"But what about Vance's wishes?" Stone asked. "You said he had always wanted the studio to be closely held, not sold to some developer."

"I wish I could follow his wishes, but I can't," Arrington said.

"What's wrong, Arrington? Why the about-face?"

"I need the money."

Stone was astounded. Arrington had been left a *very* wealthy woman at Vance's death. "Arrington, I really am very tired after a long flight. Can I call you in the morning, and then we'll find the best way to do this?"

"All right, but I'm not changing my mind again," she said. "Good night." She hung up.

Dino was looking at him. "She flip-flopped?"

"She flip-flopped."

"Oh, well, what do you care?"

"I'm too tired to care right now," Stone said. "I'm going to bed." Ten minutes later, he was asleep.

Stone woke the following morning in a strange, sunlit room. It took him a moment to orient himself and to realize the phone was ringing. He struggled to sit up in bed and grab the receiver. "Hello?"

"Stone? It's Rick Barron," a voice said. He sounded a lot younger than his ninety-odd years.

"Good morning, Rick," Stone said. "It's been a long time."

"Too long. Arrington called me a couple of days ago and said you were winging your way west."

"Yes, and she suggested we have dinner. Would you and Glenna like to come here tonight?"

"We'd love that; I've always been a sucker for Carmen's cooking. May we bring a guest?"

"Of course. Seven o'clock?"

"I see you remember L.A. is an early town. That's perfect."

"I'll look forward to seeing you," Stone said. They said goodbye.

Someone rapped on Stone's window, and he looked up to see Dino outside, wearing a terry robe. "Come on," he shouted through the closed window. "Breakfast."

Stone brushed his teeth and took his vitamin pill, then got into the guest robe and his slippers and went outside.

"I ordered for you," Dino said, waving him to the seat on the other side of the table. "Man, you were out last night. Sleep well?"

"I think so; I don't remember," Stone said, taking a seat.

Manolo and Carmen were coming across the garden with trays. They set them before Stone and Dino and simultaneously took the covers away.

"Eggs Benedict!" Stone said. "My favorite."

"I knew that," Dino said.

"Oh, Manolo, Carmen: Rick and Glenna Barron are coming to dinner tonight at seven with another guest. I think you know the things they like."

"Oh, yes, Mr. Stone," Manolo said. "We will be ready for them." The couple returned to the kitchen.

"Who are Rick and Glenna Barron?" Dino asked.

"Rick is the chairman and CEO of Centurion Studios," Stone replied. "I think he's mostly confined himself to management for a while, now, but he still produces a picture now and then. His wife is Glenna Gleason."

"The old-time movie star? I love her!"

"Not as old as Rick, I think, but getting up there. I met them at Vance's burial a few years back. I'm supposed to plot with Rick about how to save the studio, but now Arrington has pulled this reversal, and I don't know what to do."

"What, exactly, is the deal about?" Dino asked.

"I think Rick is going to explain that to us tonight," Stone replied.

"And then you explain that Arrington is voting against him?"

"God, I hope not. I've got to talk seriously to Arrington."

An hour later, Stone called Arrington at her Virginia horse-country home.

"Hello?" She sounded sleepy.

"Did I wake you?"

"Not really. I sort of slept in this morning. I'm sorry I got you when you were so tired last night."

"I've recovered now, and I want you to explain to me why you need the money from the sale of your studio stock."

"Oh, Stone, this is going to sound crazy to you, but I learned yesterday that I have an opportunity to buy a neighboring horse farm and business."

"What kind of business?"

"Breeding and racing thoroughbreds," she replied. "Perhaps you've heard of it; it's called Virginia Champion Farms."

"Yes, I've heard of it; it's just about the biggest racing farm in the country, isn't it?"

"The biggest outside Kentucky, anyway. The owner, Rex Champion, who's a friend of mine, is getting on in years and is ready to sell. Horse farms are down in price right now, along with everything else, and this is a wonderful opportunity."

"How much?"

"I got him down to fifty million dollars."

Stone was struck dumb.

"Hello? Are you still there?"

"I'm still here; I'm just stunned."

"My financial adviser says it's worth sixty million, and that's what he was asking, but I got him down to fifty. I can't sell stocks right now, what with the market being the way it is, and my biggest asset is Centurion. This buyer has come along at just the right time."

"And that's all you can sell to raise the fifty million?"

"I'm afraid so. Oh, I'm sentimental about the

studio, Stone, but I've always wanted to be in racing."

"I thought your only interest in horses was hunting and dressage."

"Those things cost money; racing horses *makes* money."

"Arrington, you're not a businesswoman, and that's a big business."

"The beauty of it is that I get the whole thing intact, with a staff, a board of directors, and all the real estate and stock. In a better year, it would cost seventy-five million!"

"Arrington, let me look into all this. I'm having dinner with Rick Barron tonight, and I want to hear what he has to say, and I can look into Virginia Champion for you, too."

"Oh, all right, but I'm not going to change my mind about this, Stone. Remember, you're working for me, not yourself."

"I'll speak with you in a day or two," Stone said, and hung up.

4

Stone got dressed and called Bill Eggers. Eggers was the managing director of the law firm to which Stone was of counsel—meaning he handled the cases the firm did not wish to be seen to handle. This association gave him advice and backup when he needed it, and he needed it now.

Eggers came on the line. "Morning, Stone; what can I do you for?"

"You can do me some advice, Bill, and some other help."

"What have you got yourself into now?"

"Two very large business deals," Stone replied.

"That's a little out of your line, isn't it?"

"Bill, why do you think I'm calling you?"

"Oh, all right; what do you need?"

"I need these two deals looked at objectively,"

Stone said. "The first is the possible sale of Centurion Studios to some real estate developer. I know you have the contacts out here to put an ear to the ground. I want to know what's being said about the deal."

"I can do that; what's the other one?"

"Arrington Calder wants to buy Virginia Champion Farms for fifty million dollars. You know the company?"

"I do, and I know Rex Champion. He's a gentleman, but with a sharp edge."

"I want to know what the farms are worth in today's dollars—land, horses, other assets—and I want to know about the quality of the current management, and see the profit-and-loss statements for the past ten years or so."

"To find out all that I'm going to have to send a business appraiser outfit down there to rake the books and talk to the people. We can't do this surreptitiously."

"Of course not."

"And Arrington is going to pay for the assessment?"

"She will."

"I need a direct statement from her about that, not your opinion of what she'll do. This is going to cost in the low six figures and take a couple of weeks."

"I'll get her permission today."

"I'll make the call as soon as I hear from you. In the meantime, I'll make some calls about the Centurion deal. Are you in L.A.?"

"Yes, I'm here to vote Arrington's shares in Centurion."

"Okay. See you." Eggers hung up.

Stone called Arrington. "We have to send somebody to Virginia Champion to look the company over."

"Why? I trust Rex Champion."

"This is just due diligence, Arrington; it has to be done to protect you, and it's going to cost in the low six figures. Champion will understand; call him and tell him these people will be there tomorrow."

"Oh, all right, but this is embarrassing."

"It's business; Champion will understand that, and you have to learn not to be embarrassed about proper business requests."

Arrington hung up, and Stone called Eggers back to report the conversation. He was done for now, until he saw Rick Barron, anyway.

Stone and Dino were in the living room of the main house when Manolo ushered in Rick and Glenna Barron. They rose to greet their guests, and Stone introduced them to Dino.

"Our other guest will be along shortly," Rick

said, as they shook hands. His handshake was dry and firm, and his movements were not those of a very old man. Glenna, amazingly, looked a healthy sixty. Everyone ordered drinks.

"When did you arrive, Stone?" Rick asked as they sat down.

"Yesterday afternoon, late. I flew us out."

"Oh, in what?"

"A Cessna Citation Mustang, recently acquired."

"Beautiful little airplane," Rick said.

"I know that you flew off carriers in World War Two," Stone said.

"Yes, but I flew a lot more than that. My father owned a little FBO at Santa Monica Airport, and I flew charter flights for him for years. I still own the FBO. I've also been type rated in every jet Centurion has owned, including the current Citation Ten, though I haven't been pilot-in-command for years. I still have my medical certificate, too."

"I didn't know all that, Rick; you'll have to come and fly my airplane."

"I've already flown one, thanks. We're thinking of buying a smaller, shorter-range airplane for flying around the West."

The doorbell rang, and Manolo escorted in a tall, striking blonde. It took Stone a moment to recognize her.

"Stone!" she said, rushing toward him and planting a tender, juicy kiss on his lips.

Stone dabbed at his lips with a handkerchief, and it came away red. "Charlene, it's so good to see you," he said, then introduced her to Dino, who was flabbergasted to meet a bona fide movie star. Stone had had a brief fling with Charlene Joiner on a previous visit to L.A., just as she had had flings with numerous men, including a president.

They all sat down again, and Manolo served their drinks.

"Rick was telling us about his flying career," Stone said.

"I've flown with Rick, and he's a marvelous pilot," Charlene said.

Rick warmed to the conversation. "Stone, do you remember the movie actor Clete Barrow?"

"Of course," Stone said. "He swashed a lot of buckles in his time. Died in the war, didn't he?"

"That's right, he did. In September of 1939 I flew Clete, David Niven, and Clark Gable up to Oregon for some steelhead fishing on the Rogue River. We were up there when we heard Neville Chamberlain on the shortwave radio, announcing that a state of war existed between Britain and Germany. We returned to L.A. immediately, and before you knew it, Clete and Niven had left for England, where they joined their old regiments.

Niven had a splendid war record, and Clete died at Dunkirk, getting his men onto boats. After Clark's wife, Carole Lombard, was killed in an airplane crash while returning from a bond tour, Clark enlisted, too. So did I, but for a different reason."

"That was quite a moment in history," Stone said.

"Glenna got into it, too," Rick said. "I was serving aboard the aircraft carrier *Saratoga* when she came aboard with Artie Shaw's band for a show, and we got to have a very brief meeting."

"It was a remarkable experience," Glenna said. "Artie, the band, and I were lowered from the main deck into a huge area hangar belowdecks on an aircraft elevator, and three thousand sailors went wild. I've never heard such a sound, before or since."

Manolo came into the room. "Dinner is served," he said, and everyone followed him into the dining room.

Rick walked arm in arm with Stone and whispered, "We'll get down to business over coffee."

5

When the dishes had been taken away, Manolo approached the table. "Would you like to have coffee in the study, Mr. Stone?"

"Thank you, yes, Manolo," Stone replied, and stood.

Glenna looked across the table at Dino. "Dino, would you like to take a look at the gardens while they talk business?"

"Of course," Dino said, standing and offering her his arm.

Stone, Rick Barron, and Charlene Joiner settled in the comfortable library/study with coffee and brandy.

"Now, Stone," Rick said, "I want to tell you what's going on and where we stand."

"Thank you," Stone said.

"A private hedge fund called Prince Investments has made us two offers, both of which we rejected, the most recent one over the objections of nearly half our stockholders. Now they're coming back with a final offer, and I'm going to need fifty-one percent of the voting shares to keep us in business."

"What was the last offer?" Stone asked.

"Twenty-five hundred dollars a share," Rick said. "My sense of the other stockholders is that they'll sell at something near three thousand."

"How many stockholders?"

"Fifty-five. Arrington is the largest shareholder, with three hundred thirty-three thousand shares, I've got a hundred thousand shares—I've sold various blocks over the years to studio executives, to keep them—and Charlene has fifty thousand shares."

"How many shares extant?"

"One million. With Arrington's shares we've got four hundred thirty-three thousand, and I know of one other stockholder who will very likely vote with us—Eddie Harris, who was running the studio when I joined them, in 1938, had two daughters, one of whom died in her thirties. The other is Jennifer, who is in her midseventies now, and she holds twenty-five thousand shares, which can put us over the top."

"Tell me what will happen to the studio if the sale takes place."

"The studio was originally on two hundred acres, and we sold off fifty in the 1960s to build Centurion City, a mixed commercial/residential development. That money got us out of debt, and we've stayed that way. Prince's offer is for one hundred ten of the remaining one hundred fifty acres. That would consist of all of the back lot—our standing sets—our Western town, our small-town square sets, and numerous street sets, including our New York streets. It would rob us of five of our six soundstages, two of our three audio recording studios, and our set storage buildings. We would become, in essence, a small office park, including our admin buildings and the offices we rent to a couple of dozen independent producers who use our production facilities."

"And what would that do to your ability to make pictures and TV shows?"

"It would devastate us," Rick replied. "We would have to rent soundstages for our movie and TV productions, which would dramatically increase our production costs and cut our profits. Our hallmark has always been to make quality pictures and TV shows on moderate budgets. We simply could not continue our present production schedule, much less expand it. Centurion would become a shell, like too many of the remaining studios. I didn't spend two-thirds of my life in this business in order to see that happen to it."

"Who are the people who want to sell?"

"They're all studio employees or independent producers on the lot. They own, generally speaking, from as little as fifty shares to twenty thousand shares. Some of them are nearing retirement age, and they can sell us back their stock at a price determined by a formula, which would net them, maybe a third of what selling the studio would."

"So, some of them stand to make forty million to sixty million dollars if the studio is sold."

"Yes, and as you can see, that is a strong motive for selling."

"Yes, I can understand that. Any hope of getting some of them on your side?"

Rick shook his head. "I've been working on this for two months; we've boiled the list down to the four of us: Arrington, myself, Charlene, and Jennifer Harris."

"Rick, if you win this fight, how long will you be able to hang on to the studio?"

"I'm leaving my shares to my two grandchildren, and if Arrington hangs on to hers, then we can keep it going as it is for many years."

"I see," Stone said.

"Stone, do you understand the importance of

keeping Centurion as a working film studio? Not just to the stockholders, but to people everywhere who enjoy intelligent, quality entertainment?"

"I can certainly see why you feel that way," Stone said. "If I were a stockholder, that's what I'd want, too."

"Now we come to the crux of things, Stone," Rick said. "Jennifer Harris, Charlene, and I are on board. Everything depends on Arrington now. What is she going to do?"

"Has she expressed her intentions to you, Rick?"

"At first, she seemed to be with us, but the last couple of days I've sensed that she's wavering."

"She has to make some important business decisions not associated with the studio," Stone explained. "She won't be able to make a final decision until those have been resolved."

Rick suddenly looked closer to his age.

"I believe her heart is with you," Stone said, "and I will do everything I can to swing her shares to you. I'm afraid that's all I can say, at the moment."

"I see," Rick replied.

"Please don't be disheartened," Stone said. "This could still work out. When is the new offer expected?"

"Early next week."

"So we have a week or so to make it work."

"Yes, I suppose we do."

"Charlene, are you acquainted with any of the stockholders whom you might be able to swing our way?"

"I've pretty much done what I can," Charlene replied.

Somebody's cell phone rang. Rick Barron looked at his phone and stood up. "Excuse me for a moment," he said, then left the room.

Charlene turned her attention to Stone. "It's good to see you," she said. "I hope we can get together while you're here. It's been too long."

Stone knew from experience exactly what "get together" meant to Charlene, and he hoped his health was up to it. "It certainly has been too long," he said. "I'd like that."

Rick returned to the study and sat down heavily in his chair. "Jennifer Harris is dead," he said.

Stone and Charlene looked at him.

"How?" Charlene asked.

"I don't know; the police are at her house."

"Do you know what her will says about the stock?"

"No," Rick replied. "She seemed in perfect health."

Stone rose. "I think we'd better talk again, when you have more information. I hope we can get a grip on this."

Everybody went home, and Stone returned to the guesthouse, where Dino was watching television.

"Nothing's on at the right time out here," he said. "The TV schedule is crazy."

"That's not all that's crazy," Stone said.

6

Stone awoke to the hum of his cell phone on the bedside table. He tried to turn over to pick it up, but he was impeded by an arm across his chest. He looked that way to see a tousled head of blond hair on the pillow next to him.

His memories of the night before were hazy, involving arms, legs, and various other body parts in interesting, sometimes contorted positions and some loud noises. He lifted the arm and grabbed the phone.

"Hello," he croaked.

"God, you sound awful," Bill Eggers said.

"What time is it?"

"It's after nine . . . oh, I forgot, it's three hours earlier out there, isn't it?"

"Forgot, my ass," Stone said.

"Well, as long as you're up, want some news?"

"If you insist," Stone sighed, struggling to prop himself up with a pillow, in spite of the weight of Charlene's arm.

"I've had chats with a couple of people who are acquainted with Rex Champion's situation," Eggers said.

"Which is?"

"Depends on whom you believe. One of them says that Rex is flush with cash, but is old and tired and wants out; the other says he has bad cash-flow problems and that the stables are losing money hand over fist."

"And which one do you believe?"

"I'm stumped," Eggers said.

"You're a big help, Bill. You want to call me back when you have some indication of which way the truth lies?"

"Okay, go back to sleep." Eggers hung up.

Stone put down his phone and suddenly realized that Charlene's hand had migrated to his crotch. She gave a little squeeze.

"Oh," she said, "nice response."

"What did you expect?" Stone asked. He made to get out of bed, but she held on tightly.

"You appear to have me by the . . ."

"Yes, I do, don't I?"

"Charlene, I'm going to be here for at least a week; do you want to kill me the first day?"

"I know you better than that, Stone," she said, hoisting herself astride of him and slipping him inside her.

"I can't deny that," Stone said, "any more than I can extricate myself from your clutches."

She tightened a few muscles and accentuated the clutch.

"How do you do that?" Stone asked, breathing faster.

"Practice," she said, doing it again.

They continued in that fashion until they both came noisily. She gave him a wet kiss, then rolled off him.

"I still can't seem to move," Stone said, "but for entirely different reasons than before."

"Then I'll move first," she said, getting out of bed and padding, naked, toward the bathroom.

Stone watched the body that had graced dozens of movies float across the room. He was either a very lucky man or doomed—he wasn't sure which. He waited impatiently for her to get into the shower, then ran into the bathroom and, with a sigh of relief, let go.

"Join me?" she called from the shower.

He looked over at the half-misted glass door

and watched for a moment. "Oh, what the hell," he said, flushing, then opening the door and stepping in.

"Scrub my back?" she asked, handing him a brush.

He scrubbed her back.

"I'll do yours, too," she said, turning and reaching around him, pressing her body against his.

He marveled at how she could keep him interested, even after what they had just done in bed. He managed to extricate himself and found them robes.

"Breakfast?" he asked.

"Eggs Benedict, please."

Stone called Manolo and ordered the dish for both of them. They managed to get dressed before breakfast arrived, Charlene in a minidress she had tucked in her large handbag.

Dino joined them in the garden.

Charlene kissed him loudly on the ear. "Good morning, Dino," she said.

"What's that you say?" Dino asked, feigning deafness.

"Easy, you two," Stone said. "Charlene, tell me about this guy who runs the Prince hedge fund."

"His name is Prince," she said.

"Just one name, like the singer?"

"First name, Terry. There are rumors about how he got the money to start the fund."

"Tell me."

"You remember, some years ago, there was a guy named Prince running a huge drug business based in the Colombian jungle, way up the Amazon?"

"Yeah, the Colombian army raided it, didn't they?"

"Yes, and Prince was killed when he ran in front of a small airplane that was taking off."

"So it's not the same guy?"

"Terry is that guy's younger brother," she said. "Nobody's been able to prove it, but it's been talked around that his original money came out of that drug operation—a hundred million, or so. Then he got very lucky investing in films, two of them enormous worldwide hits that took in over half a billion each. He used his profits to start the hedge fund and got a lot of Hollywood money invested with him. I had a couple of million in the fund, but I took it out shortly before the last market crash."

"You're a smart girl," Stone said.

"No, I wasn't smart; I invested in two films that I expected big things of."

"How'd you do?"

"One made money, one flopped; I just about broke even."

"Tell me more about Prince."

"He started a hotel group and bought four or

five superluxury hostelries around the country. He was hot after the Bel-Air, where you've stayed, but he got outbid."

"What's the word on him now?"

"Well, he's left the drug money rumors behind him, and seems to be squeaky clean these days. He wants to put a new superhotel on the Centurion property, along with some houses and condos and office buildings, sort of like a bigger, fancier Centurion City."

"So he's not interested in the studio as a business?"

"Apparently, the production end has never excited him; he just wants to make money."

"Do you know him?" Stone asked.

"I didn't until he went after Centurion; then he made a point of meeting me and pitching for my shares. He's very charming and persuasive."

"Is he the sort of guy who might kill to get his hands on Centurion's property?"

Charlene stopped eating. "You mean like murdering Jennifer Harris to get her shares?"

"It crossed my mind."

Charlene shook her head. "He doesn't strike me as the type. I mean, if he doesn't get Centurion, he'll just move on to another project. He's a businessman."

"I hope you're right," Stone said. "That will make him easier to deal with."

Manolo brought Stone a phone.

Stone picked it up. "Hello?"

"Stone, it's Rick Barron. It's been a while since you were out here; I thought you might like to take a look at Centurion this morning."

"I'd like that, Rick," Stone replied. "Any news on the cause of death of Jennifer Harris?"

"We'll talk about that when I see you. Come to my office at eleven, and bring Dino; I'll buy you both lunch."

"See you then," Stone replied, then hung up. "Dino, we're invited to the studio by Rick Barron for a tour of the place and lunch. You available?"

"Do I look busy?" Dino asked.

7

The guard at Centurion's main gate took Stone's name, then placed a pass on the dashboard of his rented Mercedes and waved him through.

"How do we know where to meet Rick?" Dino asked.

"You forget, I've been here before," Stone said. "His office will be in the main administrative building." He made a turn, pulled into the parking lot, and left the car in a guest slot.

At the main reception desk they were directed to an elevator that opened into a paneled area and were met by a middle-aged woman in a smart business suit.

"Mr. Barrington? Mr. Bacchetti? I'm Grace Parsons, Mr. Barron's executive assistant. Please follow me."

They walked past half a dozen people working at desks and into a small sitting room, then through double doors into a large office, where Rick Barron was seated at his desk, talking on the telephone. He waved them to a seating area with comfortable chairs, finished his conversation, then joined them.

"Good morning, gentlemen," he said, sinking into an armchair. "I trust you slept well."

"*I* did," Dino replied. "I can't speak for Stone."

"Very well, thank you," Stone said, ignoring Dino.

"I was just on the phone with a homicide detective of my acquaintance," Rick said, "a Lieutenant Joe Rivera. Jennifer Harris's death is being treated as a natural one, but Joe is going to see that the medical examiner takes a closer look."

"I see we're on the same page," Stone said. "Do you think this Prince fellow is capable of murder to get what he wants?"

Rick shrugged. "Who knows?" He shifted positions and looked thoughtful. "I used to be a cop," he said. "I was a homicide detective, too, until I got busted by a captain whose niece I was seeing." He threw up his hands. "Oh, hell, whose niece I got pregnant. That's how I got into the movie business."

Stone frowned. "By getting a girl pregnant?"

"You might say that. It's what got me demoted to sergeant and put back in a patrol car. It was patrol duty that got me into the movie business."

"I'm not following," Stone said.

"Of course not," Rick said. "I was sitting in my patrol car one night in 1939, parked just off Sunset, trying to stay awake, when I heard the howl of the supercharger on a powerful automobile. I looked up just in time to see a Model A Ford coupe run a stop sign and start across Sunset, just in time for a Mercedes SS to plow into it and send it tumbling down the boulevard. The coupe came to rest upside down, and the Mercedes veered left into a high hedge.

"I checked the coupe first and found the female driver dead. Then I ran over and checked on the Mercedes. The driver had been thrown out and into the hedge, and I thought I recognized him. Then it came to me: his name was Clete Barrow, and he was Centurion's biggest star. He was conscious, but very drunk. He handed me a little black book and said, 'Call Eddie Harris.' I knew who Harris was, of course. I got him out of bed, and he told me to get Barrow out of there and to Centurion Studios before anybody else saw him.

"I got him into my car and turned the accident scene over to another sergeant who showed up and who knew the score with movie stars. I got Barrow to the studio, to his bungalow, where a doctor was waiting to examine him, and Harris showed up a few minutes later. The doctor pronounced Barrow well, except for a black eye, and he asked Eddie if he wanted a blood sample taken. Eddie said sure and told me to roll up my sleeve."

Stone and Dino burst out laughing.

"One thing led to another, and I found myself head of security for the studio, and everything grew from there."

"That's a hell of a story," Dino said.

"Nothing is stranger than real life," Rick said.

"And then you found yourself in the navy?" Stone asked.

"I didn't find myself there; I *fled* to the navy after murdering a man."

Stone and Dino were stunned into silence.

"His name was Chick Stompano, a mobster connected to Bugsy Siegel who liked to hurt women. He made the mistake of beating up Glenna. I had already talked to a naval recruiting officer, knowing that I'd have to go, and I'd had my physical. I went to Stompano's house, rang the bell, and when he came out I shot him in the head. I was at the door of the recruiting office when it opened that morning, and before noon I had been sworn in and was on a bus for Officer Candidate School in San Diego, thence to Pensacola, Florida, for flight training."

"There's nothing stranger than real life," Dino said.

"By the time I was invalided out, in '44, with a shot-up knee, the whole business had blown over."

"No repercussions?" Stone asked.

"Just one. When Glenna and I got married, a huge floral arrangement was delivered with a card from Ben Siegel, which I took as an overt threat. I don't know all the details, but I know that Eddie Harris made a call to a guy named Al, who owned a gun store and who was said to do contract killings on the side. A day or two later, Siegel was shot dead with a Browning Automatic Rifle, and the mob got the blame, because Siegel's girl had been stealing from them, and they held him responsible."

"Wow," Dino said softly.

Rick stood up. "Let's get some lunch," he said, leading the way out of his office and down to the parking lot, where they got into a golf cart. Rick drove them down studio streets, past the huge soundstages. People in the streets wearing odd costumes—cowboys, policemen, showgirls—made way for Rick's cart.

"This is what Prince wants to destroy, so that he can build a hotel," Rick said, waving an arm. "It took me and others more than half a century to build this, and if Prince wins, it will be gone in a month, and so will the movies that would have been made here."

He parked the cart outside the Studio Commissary and led them inside. The place was packed with producers and actors, some of them in costume. Stone, Dino, and Rick were seated at Rick's reserved corner table, and a waitress brought menus.

"I had heard of this fellow Prince," Rick said, "but I had never met him, until he came to see me one day. He didn't bother with the CEO, he came straight to me, and he told me he was going to buy this studio. He was brazen; he didn't ask me if we wanted to sell, he just told me, as if it were a fait accompli. I'm afraid I didn't react very well. I told him to get out of my office, or I'd have security throw him out."

"That's one way to begin a negotiation," Stone said.

"This isn't a negotiation," Rick replied.

"Everything is a negotiation," Stone said. "You and Prince were just staking out your opening positions."

"I suppose you could look at it that way," Rick said. "Maybe I'm getting too old to deal with something like this."

"It seems to me you're doing a pretty good job

of dealing with it," Stone said. "You haven't folded yet, and you may not have to."

"On the other hand . . ." Rick said.

"Let's not look at the other hand, until we have to," Stone said.

8

After lunch they got into Rick's electric cart, and he took them back via a different route, to show them more standing sets.

They passed down a tree-lined, small-town street, lined with comfortable houses.

"They're just facades," Rick said, "nothing behind them. If we did a shot of someone walking through a front door we then cut to a shot on a soundstage of him entering the living room."

They came to a small city square with a park in the middle and a courthouse facing it. The rest of the square was shops, a department store, and a corner drugstore with a lunch counter. Then Rick turned a corner, and they were in New York.

"Wow," Dino said, "this gives me chills; it's like

the beats I used to walk. You've got streetlamps, fireplugs, the works."

"The fireplugs operate, too," Rick said. "We have our own firehouse with two trucks."

Soon they were back at the admin building, standing next to Stone's rented Mercedes. "Thank you for lunch and the tour, Rick," Stone said.

Dino thanked him, too.

"What's your next move?" Rick asked Stone.

"I'm doing some due diligence on the investment Arrington is looking at, and I think I'd better meet Terrence Prince," he said.

"I'd give you an introduction," Rick said, "except that he and I are not really on speaking terms, and he might view you as my representative, instead of Arrington's."

"That's all right," Stone said, "I won't need an introduction."

They shook hands, and Stone and Dino got into the car.

"I know Joe Rivera at the LAPD," Dino said. "I gave him some help on the extradition of a fugitive a couple of years ago. You want me to talk to him about Jennifer Harris?"

"Good idea," Stone said. He got out his iPhone and Googled Prince Investments. "Wilshire Boulevard," Stone said. "Drop me there. Then you can have the car."

"How will you get back to Arrington's house?" Dino asked.

"I'll improvise," Stone replied. He made his way to Wilshire. It was easy to find Prince's offices, since the name was emblazoned at the top of the tall building. Stone got out, and Dino got behind the wheel. "See you later," Stone said, and walked into the building.

A large reception desk blocked access to the elevators, and it was manned by uniformed security officers. Stone noted that they were armed.

"May I help you?" a beefy officer asked.

"Yes, I'm here to see Terrence Prince; my name is Stone Barrington."

"Do you have an appointment?" the man asked.

"No, but Mr. Prince will see me. Let me speak to his secretary."

The officer dialed a number, then handed the phone to Stone.

"May I help you?" the woman asked in the voice reserved for handling nutcases.

"Yes, my name is Stone Barrington; I'm an attorney from New York, and I represent Arrington Calder. I'd like to see Mr. Prince, please."

"Does Mr. Prince know you?"

"Not yet," Stone replied. "Please tell him what I said."

"Please hold." She clicked off, and a string

quartet kept Stone company. She came back on. "Let me speak to the officer," she said.

Stone handed the phone to the man, who listened, then hung up. He would either get an appointment or the bum's rush.

"Please go to the fortieth floor," the man said, pointing at an elevator with a guard standing in front of it. "You'll be met." He waved to the guard.

Stone walked to the elevator and looked for a button to push, but there were no buttons. The door closed, and the elevator rose fast enough to nearly buckle his knees. When the door opened a tall, very beautiful blonde in a black suit stood waiting in an open, carpeted area.

"Mr. Barrington? I'm Carolyn Blaine. Please follow me."

"My pleasure," Stone replied. The view of her from behind was very good. As they crossed the open area, lighted from both ends by floor-to-ceiling windows, Stone reflected that Prince had devoted several hundred square feet of very expensive office space to impressing his visitors.

They passed a dozen offices with glass fronts and closed doors, then a large conference room where a dozen people sat around an acre of mahogany table. Somebody was exhibiting a large chart on a huge, flat-screen monitor. Finally they came to a pair of tall doors. Ms. Blaine placed her right palm on a glass plate and tapped a code into a keypad; then, with a click, one of the doors opened. Stone was faced with a pale mahogany partition containing a large Picasso from his Blue Period. Fifty to a hundred million, he thought. Blaine led him around the partition into a large room with a large desk, large windows, and large furniture. A large man in a pale yellow linen suit stood and began walking around the desk, talking, apparently to himself.

"I have to go," he said. "Get it done, then get back to me." He removed a clear plastic microphone boom from his ear and tossed it onto the desk; then he held out a hand. "Mr. Barrington," he said, "I wasn't expecting you, though I knew, of course, that you were in town." He was six-three or -four, of athletic build, and with a mop of blond hair that fell across his forehead. His hand was large and hard.

Stone shook it. "How do you do, Mr. Prince?"

"I do very well," Prince replied. "Please come and have a seat," he said, leading Stone toward a seating area, backed by a wall containing a single, very large Rothko oil, one of those that always reminded Stone of an atomic blast. "Would you like some refreshment?"

"Perhaps some iced tea," Stone replied.

"Of course. Carolyn? I'll have the same."

Stone watched Ms. Blaine walk toward a wet bar in the opposite room.

"She's quite something, isn't she?" Prince asked.

"Quite," Stone said.

"I think one should make a good first impression before making a first impression. What brings you to Los Angeles, Mr. Barrington?"

"Come now, Mr. Prince," Stone said. "You know why I'm here or you wouldn't have seen me without an appointment."

Prince nodded. "Quite so. Maybe not even *with* an appointment," he said. "How is Mrs. Calder these days?"

"Healthy," Stone replied.

"Is she considering my offer?"

"Anyone would consider a billion-dollar offer," Stone replied, "but she has other business interests that she must attend to as well."

"Ah, yes," Prince said, "Champion Farms. How is old Rex?"

Stone wondered exactly how he knew about the racing farm deal. "Never met the gentleman," he replied.

Their ice tea arrived, and Stone had the pleasure of watching Carolyn Blaine bend over to set it on the coffee table.

Prince raised his glass in a toasting motion. "Now to business," he said.

9

Stone took a sip of his iced tea. It was flavored with tropical fruit and delicious. "I'd like to know why you want to buy Centurion Studios," he said.

"I have no interest in Centurion," Prince replied, "only its land. From my time in Los Angeles I have observed that making a profit from the production of motion pictures is a very iffy way to invest one's money. One can make money from the movies, of course, but a better way to do it is to let the studios and the independent producers flail about judging scripts and putting together packages of directors and stars, then, when the projects are ready to go, deciding which ones to back. I have done very well that way."

"I understand your point of view," Stone said, "but without organizations like Centurion and the producers they have as partners, your choice of films in which to invest would be extremely limited."

"In that event, I can always invest in something else," Prince said. "I have no emotional involvement in motion pictures; I rarely even see one. I like investing in hotels, however. I've put together a group of some of the finest in cities across the country, and they make money. One makes more money, though, if one develops them, rather than paying a premium for the creations of someone else. The Centurion property will give me the kind of acreage to put a sumptuous hotel in a park, with enough land left over to develop offices and residences at the other end."

"How many of the acres would you devote to the hotel?" Stone asked.

"Perhaps only a dozen or fifteen," Prince replied. "There isn't enough acreage for a golf course—you need a couple of hundred for that—but I might get a par-three, nine-hole course in. That's about all a traveling businessman has time for anyway."

Stone looked around the room. "Why don't you have a model of what you want to build?" he asked.

Prince shrugged. "I don't have any trouble visualizing what I want, and since I'm using my own money, or that of my hedge fund, I don't need to convince people with no imagination to back me."

"Surely, you must have architect's plans."

"Nothing I'd care to show you," Prince replied.

"You understand that if Mrs. Calder decides not to sell you her shares, you won't get the property?"

Prince allowed himself a small smile. "I don't really think that's going to be a problem," he said.

Stone was stunned. This sort of confidence he had not expected, and there was nowhere for this conversation to go until he knew why Prince was not worried. He took another sip of his iced tea and set the glass on its coaster. "Well, I won't trouble you further, Mr. Prince," he said, rising and offering his hand.

"Thank you for seeing me on no notice."

Prince shook Stone's hand. "Any time at all," he replied. "Carolyn, would you please escort Mr. Barrington to the elevator?"

"Oh, I wonder if I might call a taxi," Stone said. "A friend dropped me here and took my car."

"Carolyn, call down for my car and have Mr. Barrington delivered to . . ." He raised his eyebrows.

"Bel-Air," Stone said. "That's very kind of you."

"It just sits in the garage until I need it," Prince said, "and I won't need it until this evening. If you have any shopping to do or other calls to make, please keep the car until seven, if you like."

"Thank you again," Stone said, then followed the gorgeous Carolyn out of the office and to the elevator. She stopped there.

"It will be only a moment," she said. "Do you have friends in L.A., Mr. Barrington?" she asked.

"A few."

"Would you like to have dinner with me while you're here?"

"That would be very pleasant," Stone replied, surprised; then he thought about it for a second. "Tell me," he said, "will this dinner be tax-deductible for Mr. Prince?"

She gave a little laugh. "No, this isn't business, just pleasure, and neither Mr. Prince nor I will be paying." She handed him a card. "This is my address; eight o'clock tonight?"

The elevator arrived, and Stone stepped aboard. "Book us into your favorite restaurant," he said. Then the doors closed and Stone left his stomach on a high floor as the car plummeted to the lobby.

He walked out of the skyscraper to find a bright, silver Bentley Mulsanne awaiting him. A man with a shaved head in a black suit and tie held the door open for him. The car had only recently been introduced and Stone hadn't seen one yet, so he had a good look around it before he got in.

The driver slid into the front seat and closed his door, sealing out all sound from Wilshire Boulevard. "Where may I take you, Mr. Barrington?" he asked.

Stone gave him the address of the Bel-Air house.

"No shopping?"

"I'm afraid I don't have time for shopping," Stone replied. "How do you like the car?"

"It's superb," the man replied. "Mr. Prince had an Arnage before, but this one is a considerable improvement in every way."

Stone electrically adjusted his seat and settled in for the ride. "What else does Mr. Prince drive?" he asked.

"He has an Aston-Martin DBS for the occasions when he drives himself," the man replied.

"He has good taste in cars," Stone said.

"In everything," the man replied.

As they approached the house, Stone gave the driver the code for the gate, and he was dropped at the front door. He thanked the driver and walked into the house, which seemed deserted, although he knew that Manolo was somewhere nearby. Dino was not back yet, and Stone changed into a swimsuit and took a plunge in the large pool. He swam a few laps, then put on a robe, and settled into a chaise longue, just as his phone buzzed.

"Hello?"

"It's Eggers," he said.

"Good afternoon," Stone replied. "You still at the office?"

"I never get out of here before seven," Eggers said.

"Do you have some news for me?"

"Do I! Rex Champion is close to bankruptcy. He's been selling off his breeding stock piecemeal to create enough cash flow to keep afloat until he can sell. And every time he sells another Derby winner, the value of the business drops."

"That's very interesting," Stone said. "Have you formed an opinion as to what the whole kaboodle might be worth?"

"Thirty-five million, tops," Eggers said. "That price would allow Rex to pay his debts and walk away free and clear, but I don't think he would have much left over. If Arrington wants to be generous, she could offer him thirty-eight million. In two or three years, if the economy bounces back and she can buy some good breeding stock, it could be worth half again as much."

"So you think it's a good investment for her?"

"If I didn't have to run this law firm, I'd put together some investors and buy it myself," Eggers said.

Dino appeared from the direction of the house, shucked off his coat, tossed his tie aside, and sat down. Manolo was right behind him with two tall drinks on a silver tray.

"Gotta run," Stone said. "Let me know if anything new comes up."

"Arrington is going to have to move pretty quickly to get the place before word gets out and the buzzards start circling," Eggers said. "Bye." He hung up.

Stone picked up his drink from where Manolo had set it, raised his glass to Dino, and took a gulp. "Welcome back," he said. "Did you learn anything scintillating?"

Dino took a similar swig and sighed. "Jennifer Harris died from something like an ice pick driven into her brain from the back of the neck, above the hairline," he said, pointing to his own neck. "Whoever did it was cool enough to wait for the blood to stop leaking before he placed her head on the pillow. Then he filled the tiny wound with spirit gum, so it wouldn't drain further."

"What's spirit gum?" Stone asked.

"It's a thick, gummy substance that actors use to create makeup, and undertakers use to fill indentations in a corpse. The ME might have overlooked the wound, since he wasn't expecting it, if Rivera hadn't asked him to be thorough."

"Well, we're in a whole new ball game, I think," Stone said.

10

Dino looked at Stone. "You look worried."

"I guess I am," Stone said.

"Something to do with Mr. Prince?"

"Yes," Stone said.

"What was he like?"

"Like Donald Trump, except with good taste and real money."

"I'm trying to get my mind around that," Dino said.

"He's a very slick article, and I came away impressed, until you told me about Jennifer Harris."

Stone's phone buzzed. "Hello?"

"It's Arrington. What are you doing out there?"

"Dino and I had lunch with Rick Barron today, and then I met with Terrence Prince."

"And how did that go?"

"Have you ever met or spoken to Mr. Prince, Arrington?"

"No, neither."

"He seems very cocksure about your selling your shares. Have you indicated to anyone that you intend doing so?"

"Nobody out there."

"How about at home?"

"My lawyer and accountant."

"Do you trust them both implicitly?"

"I guess. They're the same man."

"Does he have any special qualifications for managing your affairs?"

"I manage my own affairs; he's the old-line go-to guy, and he has a good reputation, locally, for giving sound advice."

"What is his name?"

"Howard Sharp."

"I think you should fire him at once."

"Why?"

"Because, if what you've told me is true, he's the only person who could have given Terrence Prince the assurance that you're going to sell your Centurion shares to him, and that is a serious ethical violation. It means you can't trust the man."

"And who should replace him, you?"

"No, I don't have all the skills required to advise you in a credible way. However, Woodman &

Weld does, and if you become their client, I can see that you get their best attention."

"What can they do for me that Howard Sharp can't?"

"They can keep your confidences, for a start. They can also tell you how much you should pay for Champion Farms."

"Will you ask them to offer an opinion on that?"

"They already have," Stone said. "Thirty-five million at the most, thirty-eight, if you're fond of Rex Champion and want to be generous with him."

"And how did they arrive at that number?"

"Through due diligence," Stone replied. "Something Mr. Sharp is not acquainted with, apparently. Tell me, did Mr. Sharp recommend that you pay fifty million for the farms?"

"Yes, he said it was a steal."

"Does he also represent Rex Champion?"

"I don't know—possibly."

"He sounds like trouble to me."

Arrington was silent for a moment. "Why does Woodman & Weld think Rex will sell for thirty-five million?"

"Because he's nearly bankrupt, and he's selling off his breeding stock for the cash to keep going."

"He assured me that both he and the business were doing well."

"Then he's desperate, and that has made him a liar."

"I don't relish looking him in the eye and offering him fifteen million less than he's asking, and I don't like putting his back against the wall."

"You shouldn't do that. You should let me or Bill Eggers do it, and, as Bill has suggested, if you want to be generous with him, you can offer him thirty-eight million."

Arrington thought about it for a moment. "Offer him thirty-six million," she said.

"Is that a firm price, or are you going to wiggle?"

"I'll go to thirty-seven million, if I have to."

"I think you should make him a take-it-or-leave-it offer, and walk away if he doesn't accept."

"All right, offer him thirty-seven million. If he accepts it, I'll hire Woodman & Weld, provided you supervise their work."

"Consider it done. In the meantime, don't fire Howard Sharp, and don't say anything to him that might make him think that you're not going to sell Terrence Prince your shares."

"All right, but I haven't changed my mind about selling Prince my shares. I still need the money to pay Rex for the farms."

"Here's my first piece of advice as your new attorney: don't sell a billion-dollar investment in order to raise thirty-seven million."

"Well, all right, but where am I going to get the money?"

"Do you have a financial statement?"

"Yes, current as of a couple of weeks ago. Howard Sharp helped me get it together."

"Fax it to me here, and give me your permission to share it with Woodman & Weld. We'll find a way for you to have your cake and eat it, too."

"I like the sound of that," she said.

"And remember, not a word to Sharp about anything. Make him think nothing has changed. If he presses you for an answer on selling your Centurion shares, tell him you're working on organizing things."

"Why do you think Howard Sharp is in Prince's pocket?"

"Because he's the only one who *could* betray you, and Prince has apparently bought him. Sharp has probably given him your financial statement."

"The son of a bitch," she said with some heat.

"Keep cool, and don't let on anything."

"I'll fax you the financial statement first thing in the morning; I'm on the way out to a dinner party now."

"That's fine," Stone said. He hung up the phone.

"You didn't tell her that the last person to refuse

to sell her Centurion shares to Prince was mur- dered," Dino pointed out.

"I didn't want to panic her," Stone said, "and she's in no danger as long as Prince thinks she will sell."

"I hope you're right about that," Dino said.

11

Stone found Carolyn Blaine's house easily enough, on Camden Drive, off Sunset. From its generous size he reckoned that either she had family money or she had had a good divorce. No ordinary executive assistant could pay the property taxes out of her salary, he thought.

Carolyn didn't ask him in; she came to the door with her purse and a shawl in her hand. "Let's have our first drink at the restaurant," she said.

Stone installed her in the Mercedes. "Where to?"

"Is Spago Beverly Hills all right?"

"One of my favorites," Stone said.

"I managed to get a table in the garden," she said.

Ten minutes later they were being seated among L.A.'s filmland glitterati, including a pair of movie stars and several faces familiar from television. Carolyn ordered a martini and Stone stuck with his usual Knob Creek.

"What's Knob Creek?" Carolyn asked.

"My favorite bourbon."

"The brown stuff?"

"American corn whiskey, this one aged for nine years. It's the patriotic thing to drink, instead of all that foreign swill. Abraham Lincoln lived in a log cabin on Knob Creek, in Kentucky."

Their drinks arrived, and she tasted his bourbon. "Not bad," she said. "I like it better than scotch."

"Smart woman," Stone said. They clinked glasses and drank.

"So, was our having dinner Terrence Prince's idea?" he asked.

"It was entirely mine," she replied. "He doesn't know about it." She looked around. "Of course, he knows a lot of the people here, so it won't be a secret for long."

"I don't care if he knows," Stone said. "It won't affect the business we have to do."

"Why not?"

"Aha, that's what Mr. Prince would ask."

"I'm curious about this transaction, but purely on a personal basis," she said.

"Prince wants to buy most of the land owned by

Centurion Studios, so that he can build a hotel and some office buildings and condos."

"Funny," she said, "I haven't seen the plans for that."

"How about a model?"

She shook her head. "Terry only uses models when he has to educate investors. How much is he offering?"

"That's not final, yet; somewhere between two and three billion dollars."

"He can do that with a combination of personal and hedge fund money. He'll finance a big chunk, too. He has excellent banking connections."

"Good for him."

"Is your client going to sell?"

"That is undetermined," Stone replied.

"And if you knew, you wouldn't tell me."

"I couldn't tell you," he replied. "Client confidentiality. Of course, Prince has already pierced that veil."

"You let him do that?"

"Nothing to do with me; he's bought my client's local attorney, in Virginia." Stone didn't mind if Prince knew he knew.

"Did you tell me that because you think I'll tell Terry that you know?"

"I don't mind if you do."

"All right, I'll tell him, but I wouldn't have, if you'd wanted the confidence kept."

"That's nice to know," Stone said, not believing her.

"What is your background?" she asked.

"Born and bred in Greenwich Village, attended the public schools and NYU—both for college and law school. Spent fourteen years on the NYPD; then I ran into an old law school buddy who runs Woodman & Weld, and he offered me a deal."

"Where do you live in New York?"

"In a town house in Turtle Bay; you know it?"

"Yes, I'm a New Yorker, too."

"Your turn," he said.

"Born and bred on Fifth Avenue, Miss Porter's School, Mount Holyoke, an MBA from Wharton. Married once, for ten years, divorced last year."

"You got the house?"

"This is California; ever hear of community property? He had done well, with my help, so I got more than the house."

"How did Prince find you?"

"Friends introduced us at a restaurant, I had a brief fling with him, and when it was over he offered me the job."

"And, with your background, you don't mind serving iced tea?"

"That's not all I do," she said. "He values my business sense, and I contribute something to almost every deal."

"Sounds like you didn't know about the Centurion thing."

She shot him a glance. "That's right. I didn't, until I heard a snatch of conversation at your meeting this afternoon."

"Why do you suppose he didn't tell you about it?"

"That's a very good question and one I'm going to make it my business to learn the answer to."

"I somehow have the impression that you don't like your boss."

"I like him well enough."

"But you don't trust him."

"Not implicitly. I don't think he's ever lied to me, but sometimes he doesn't tell me things, and I have to figure them out for myself."

"Why wouldn't he tell you about the Centurion offer?"

"Because when I participate in a deal, I get a cut—a small one, but in a deal like that it would be considerable—and I suppose he doesn't want to pay me, not when he thinks he doesn't need me."

"He does seem very confident, doesn't he?" Stone asked.

"If he's confident, it's for a reason."

"Like inside knowledge from the Virginia lawyer?"

"That's just the sort of thing he would do. He bought a house in Virginia a couple of years ago, then flipped it for a nice profit. My guess is, the lawyer probably had something to do with that transaction, and that's how they met."

That was good information, Stone thought. "What's the worst thing you've ever seen Prince do in business?" he asked.

"If you were my attorney, you'd tell me not to answer that," she said.

"Then it must be something pretty bad."

"A lot of people in business have done bad things," she said. "Happens all the time."

The waiter arrived with menus and told them the specials. When he had gone, Stone said, "If you find yourself in a compromised position because of something Prince is doing, feel free to call me," he said, giving her his card. "Knowing too much can sometimes be felonious."

She tucked the card into her bra. "Good point," she said. "I'll keep it in mind."

After a good dinner he took her home and gave her a fairly chaste good-night kiss. She didn't invite him in, and he didn't press the issue.

12

Stone and Dino were having breakfast the following morning when Manolo brought an envelope to the table.

"A fax for you, Mr. Stone."

Stone opened the envelope and took out Arrington's financial statement.

"What's that?" Dino asked.

"It's a list of all of Arrington's assets and liabilities, in detail, and a statement of her net worth."

"So, what's she worth?"

"Sorry, pal, that's a client confidence." Stone began looking through the statement. It was pretty straightforward, even if the numbers were large. She owned her house in Virginia, which she valued at twenty million dollars, the Bel-Air house, valued at fifteen million, her Centurion stock, which she had valued at two billion, but which might end up worth half again as much, a securities account with Chase Private Bank in New York, valued at one point two billion, and cash balances in her various accounts at Chase of just over two million.

Stone's breath was taken away. Even without the Centurion stock, Arrington was a billionaire. He felt a new respect for the intelligence and business acumen of Vance Calder, who had obviously used his earning power as Hollywood's greatest star over nearly half a century very wisely indeed. He also realized that, for him, Arrington's wealth was the key to a new kind of relationship with Woodman & Weld.

Stone had always been the firm's outside man, available to take the cases Woodman & Weld did not want to be seen to be involved with. He had always been well compensated, but given his lifestyle, he had never been able to accumulate much wealth beyond his possessions. Then a few months ago, he had brought a very profitable new client, Strategic Services, to the firm, earning himself a million-dollar bonus for the previous year. Bill Eggers had dangled a partnership before him, but had not mentioned it since. Neither had Stone, but now was the time.

Dino excused himself to go and get dressed, and Stone picked up his phone and dialed Bill Eggers.

"Good morning, Stone."

"Good morning, Bill. Have you a few minutes to talk?"

"Of course, Stone, always for you."

Although they had been friends for more than twenty years, this was a little more cordiality than Stone was accustomed to from Eggers. He seized the moment. "Bill, I'm sure you will recall the generous bonus the firm gave me a few months ago, when I brought Strategic Services into the fold."

"How could I forget it?" Eggers asked.

"And I'm also sure you'll recall the encouragement you gave me regarding a partnership at Woodman & Weld."

Eggers took a couple of beats before replying. "I believe I raised that as . . . a possibility, at some time in the future."

"I believe that time has come, Bill."

Eggers emitted a low chuckle. "I divine that the work you're doing for Arrington Calder has given you new confidence, Stone."

"Let's just say that it raises the . . . possibility of an important new client for Woodman & Weld."

"How important a client?"

"One with a net worth in the range of four billion dollars." Stone heard a sharp intake of breath.

"Would we be representing her in the Centurion deal?"

"*I* would be representing her in that and other business. Whether Woodman & Weld would be involved is now up to you."

There was a thoughtful pause. "You understand that I have a board of management that must approve any new partnership."

"I understand that you run a tight ship, and that the board would certainly respect your wishes."

"I've had the impression that you would not wish the Centurion deal to come to fruition, if you had your way."

"I would hate to see Centurion Studios gutted for the benefit of a rapacious developer and an investor who doesn't need the proceeds of such a sale in order to have any little thing her heart desires."

"The firm would not derive much in the way of revenue from a sale that did not take place," Eggers pointed out.

"There will be many opportunities in the future for the firm to derive revenue from Arrington as a client, continuing into the next generation."

The chuckle came again. "You know, Stone, I met your father several times. Do you recall?"

"Of course. You had many dinners at my parents' home, when we were in law school."

"I retain a very sharp memory of your father's appearance," Eggers said, "and when I met young

Peter Calder, I was struck by his resemblance to your father."

"I have made the same observation," Stone said.

"May I put a blunt question to you without offense, Stone?"

"On this occasion, you may not," Stone replied.

Eggers sighed. "All right," he said.

"All right what?" Stone asked.

"If you bring Arrington into the fold, I will propose to the board of management that you join Woodman & Weld as a full partner, with compensation in line with that paid to other partners, which, of course, is based on the revenues they produce for the firm, and I will make the proposal to the board an enthusiastic one."

"Thank you, Bill, and please be sure that the board understands that the closing of a Centurion deal may very well not be a part of the firm's representation of Arrington."

"I understand."

"Something else," Stone said.

"Yes?"

"All this will hinge on Arrington's successful purchase of Champion Farms. Based on your assessment of the value of the company, she will make a one-time offer of thirty-seven million dollars to Rex Champion, and we must insist that he immediately stop selling his blood stock."

"I will start the process, Stone. When do you want to close? I think an early closing would be an incentive for Rex to accept the offer, given his cash-flow problem."

"Thirty days, but two weeks, if he insists. If Arrington needs cash to close, I'm sure Chase Private Bank would be happy to advance it, given the size of her portfolio."

"I know people there."

"Since you are personally acquainted with Rex Champion, Bill, I think it's appropriate that you handle this offer and the subsequent transaction."

"I will do so," Eggers said. "Do I have authority to proceed?"

"You do," Stone replied, "but until all our other arrangements are concluded, please withhold knowledge of Arrington's net worth to your people." Stone paused for a moment. "One other thing: Arrington's affairs have heretofore been handled by a Charlottesville attorney named Howard Sharp, and it is essential that Rex Champion understand that word of this deal not reach Sharp until it is concluded. When that is done and the Centurion situation has been resolved, Arrington will fire Mr. Sharp."

"Of course," Eggers replied. "Stone, let me say that I am excited by not only the acquisition of Arrington as a client, but with the prospect of your closer ties to Woodman & Weld."

"Thank you, Bill." They said goodbye, and Stone hung up, breathless with the adrenaline this conversation had fired into his system.

13

Stone called Mike Freeman at Strategic Services. "Good morning, Mike."

"And to you, Stone."

"I would like to retain Strategic Services on the account of Woodman & Weld."

"Of course," Mike said. "How can we help?"

"The firm has a client who is contemplating entering into a large transaction involving the purchase of her shares in a movie studio by a man named Terrence Prince, of Los Angeles, who wants to build a hotel and an office/residential development on the studio's land."

"I understand. We used to provide personal security to Mr. Prince, before he got so rich he hired his own people."

"Good, because I want to know everything

about him, where his money comes from and who else's money he's playing with."

"We can investigate and supply that information," Mike said. "Our file on him is by now out of date, but I can tell you that the origins of his wealth are shady."

"Is this about the brother who ran the drug ring in the Amazonian jungle?"

"It is. His brother is said to have backed him to the tune of a hundred million dollars, perhaps as much as two hundred million in cash laundered through a dozen banks in the Caribbean and the Far East. When Terry's brother was killed in the big raid by the Colombian army, the debt evaporated, as did any influence from the brother, so for all intents and purposes, he has been clean since that time."

"How very convenient," Stone said. "You think Terry ratted out his brother?"

"It's a possibility; we'll look into that, too, if you like. What sort of time frame are we talking about?"

"Very short," Stone said, "no more than a few days. This deal has been brewing for several weeks, but I only recently became involved, after that phone call I took at Elaine's."

"We're on it," Mike said. "Anything else?"

"Yes. There are a couple of people who work for Prince I'd like profiles on, too: one is his driver, name unknown, white male, thirtyish, shaved head, bulky build; the other is his executive assistant, Carolyn Blaine, thirty-fiveish, five ten, a hundred and thirty pounds, born New York City, educated at Miss Porter's School, Mount Holyoke, and Wharton for an MBA, divorced last year."

"What are you looking for?"

"With the driver, a criminal record and any violent activity in his past; with the assistant, just whatever you can find."

"I'll get back to you, Stone, on the cell?"

"Yes, I'm still in L.A. and will be for at least a week."

Mike hung up, and so did Stone.

Dino came out of the guesthouse. "Anything you need me for?"

"No, I've set some things in motion, so I'm pretty much just waiting to hear from people."

"Mind if I take the car, then? I'd like to do some sightseeing."

Stone tossed him the keys. "Keep it as long as you like; if I have to go out, I'll take Vance Calder's Bentley."

"Have a nice day," Dino said, then walked toward the front of the house.

Stone relaxed in the sun and was soon asleep. Then he was being lightly shaken by Manolo. Stone opened his eyes. "What is it, Manolo?"

"Mr. Stone, your secretary has been trying to reach you on your cell phone but got no answer. She's on the house line."

"Thank you, Manolo," Stone said, and reached for the phone on the table next to his chaise. "Hello?"

"It's Joan. You were asleep by the pool, weren't you?"

"I've had a busy morning," Stone said. "Lots happening."

"Lots happening here, too. Somebody broke into the offices last night."

Stone sat up. "A burglar?"

"I don't think so; it was too subtle. I called Bob Cantor; he's here now and wants to speak to you." Bob Cantor was a retired cop who often did technical work for Stone.

"Put him on," Stone said. He heard a click. "Bob?"

"Yeah, Stone; somebody gave your place a good going-over last night."

"Anything missing?"

"A lot of information, I suspect. It was a real pro job. They even got into Joan's safe and yours, too."

"You know, Bob, I'm going to have to hire somebody to get in there and install a top-notch security system," he said, archly. Bob had installed his current system.

"You've already got a top-notch system, Stone, or we wouldn't know how far these people got. As it was, if you'd been here, you'd have gotten half a dozen alarms on your phone system, but since neither you nor Joan was in the house, and since you wouldn't let me install a police alert, it didn't matter what they set off."

"All right, all right, Bob. You're right. It's my fault."

"As long as I'm here I want to update some things about the system, and I want you to spring for the high-def cameras, too. That way, if they come back, I'll have a few surprises for them."

"Good idea, go ahead."

Joan came back on the phone. "Any idea who's behind this?" she asked.

"Yes, I have an idea; it's this guy Prince. It's funny, but I've just put Strategic Services onto him, though I didn't tell them to break into his offices."

"That was sweet of you."

"If there's nothing missing, then there's no harm done," Stone said. "Just relax and let Bob do his work; he's going to beef up the system and install some cameras, so don't start running around the office naked, unless you want me to have you on tape."

"I'll try and restrain myself," she said. "Bye-bye."

Stone hung up, and his cell phone vibrated on the table. "Hello?"

"Stone, it's Rick Barron. I'm sorry I didn't get back to you sooner; Glenna and I have been at our place in Santa Barbara for a couple of days."

"Good morning, Rick. I have some news on the death of Jennifer Harris."

"Good."

"I'm sorry to tell you she was murdered, Rick."

"My God! How?"

"Ice pick into the brain from the back of the neck, above the hairline. It was a professional job; the killer took the trouble to seal the wound with spirit gum, so the ME wouldn't notice it, but Sergeant Rivera had already alerted him to be thorough."

"I'm having trouble believing this," Rick said.

"I think it's important that you find out what her will says in regard to her Centurion stock," Stone said. "Can you do that?"

"I know her lawyer," Rick replied. "He might tell me."

"Will you let me know what he says?"

"I will, Stone; I'll call him now." Rick hung up.

Stone thought about what was happening. He wasn't sleepy anymore.

14

Dino came back late in the afternoon. "How was your day?"

"Both busy and idle," Stone replied. "I got a call from Joan and Cantor; somebody broke into my offices last night."

"Connected with what's going on out here?" Dino asked.

"What else?"

"What did they get?"

"A look at whatever they wanted, I guess."

The house phone rang, and Stone answered it. "Hello?"

"Hello, Stone," Charlene Joiner purred. "Would you and Dino like to come to dinner at my house in Malibu this evening? I'm cooking, and I've got a cute date for Dino."

"Hang on." He covered the phone. "I don't suppose you'd like to have dinner with a movie star in Malibu tonight, would you? She's got you a date."

"Who do I have to kill?" Dino asked.

Stone uncovered the phone. "I talked him into it; what time?"

"Seven?"

"Seven it is."

"You remember the way?"

"I do."

"I'll let the guard at the gate know. Bye-bye."

Stone hung up. "If I know Charlene, she's planning to get you laid."

"I can live with that."

They drove out to Malibu in the early evening, missing rush hour, so the Pacific Coast Highway was fast. Stone pulled into a gated area and gave his name to a guard, then was waved through.

"What is this place?" Dino asked.

"This is the Malibu Colony," Stone replied. "The most expensive real estate anywhere on the Pacific Coast, I should think." He drove to Charlene's house and parked out front.

She answered the bell on the intercom. "Come straight through the house and out to the pool," she said, buzzing the door open.

They walked down the center hallway and emerged onto a large rear patio with a pool, over-looking the Pacific. Charlene and another woman were arrayed on chaises, facing the setting sun. They both got up.

"Hey, Stone," Charlene said, giving him a wet kiss. "Hey, Dino. This is my friend Hetty Lang; she's a contract player at Centurion."

Everyone shook hands. Dino appeared to be trying not to salivate.

"Anybody feel like a plunge in the Pacific before the sun goes down?" Charlene asked.

"Sure," Stone said.

"Swimsuits are in the dressing room, over there," she said, pointing.

Stone and Dino found suits the right size.

"I hadn't expected to get wet," Dino said, hanging up his clothes.

They walked back to the pool, and followed as the girls ran off the patio and raced for the ocean. Stone hit the water running and was stunned at how cold it was. Everybody swam out a few yards, then bodysurfed the waves back to the beach.

"Cold, fellas?" Charlene asked.

Dino's teeth were chattering. "A little," he said.

"Well, we don't want shrinkage, do we? You guys hit the showers and fix yourselves a drink. We'll be down in half an hour."

Stone and Dino went back to the dressing room.

"I've never been so cold in my life," Dino said, turning on the hot water.

"It's a cold ocean," Stone said.

"Thanks for the warning."

They showered and dressed, then went into the house.

"There's a bar in here, as I recall," Stone said, turning into the study. He poured Dino a Johnnie Walker Black and himself a Knob Creek, and they sat down in a pair of large chairs.

"Refresh my memory," Dino said. "Wasn't Charlene involved with a president?"

"It was Will Lee," Stone said, "but before he was president and before he was married. They're both from Georgia, and he was representing her fiancé, who was charged with murder. They had a brief fling; then, when the fiancé was convicted, he tried to get it overturned on the grounds that his attorney was sleeping with his girl. It didn't work."

"I've read about that," Dino said. "Didn't he get his death sentence commuted?"

"Yes, and the rumor was Charlene slept with the governor of Georgia to effect the commutation."

"I'd have *pardoned* the bastard, in those circumstances," Dino said.

They sipped their drinks until they heard the girls coming down the stairs, giggling.

"Hey, fellas," Charlene said. "Let's all go into the kitchen."

"Dino, you and Hetty go ahead," Stone said. "I need to talk with Charlene for a minute."

She gave him another kiss. "What's up, lover?"

"Cool down for a minute, sweetheart," Stone said. "I have some news, and it's not good."

She backed up a step. "What is it?"

"Jennifer Harris—the other stockholder Rick was counting on?"

"The one who died?"

"The one who was murdered," Stone said.

Charlene's face fell. "*Murdered?*"

"And by a professional." Stone explained what the medical examiner had found. "I think you should be very careful for a while."

"Why?"

"Because you hold shares committed to Rick, too. I don't think you're going to be safe until this whole thing with Centurion and Terrence Prince is resolved."

"Excuse me a minute," Charlene said. She went to a telephone and dialed a number. "Hello? This is Charlene Joiner; who's this? Hello, Jerry, listen carefully: I want a team at my house, *right now*, and 24/7, until further notice, got that? Good. Yes, I anticipate a threat. Goodbye." She hung up and took Stone's hand. "Let's go cook dinner," she said.

Stone followed her into the kitchen, where Dino had mixed Hetty a drink from another bar, and Charlene turned on the grill. "How do you like your steaks?" she asked.

Stone marveled at how cool she was, given the circumstances.

15

Stone woke up the following morning, sprawled across Charlene's bed, naked. The scent of bacon cooking wafted up from the kitchen. He showered and shaved and went downstairs.

Dino and Hetty were seated at the kitchen table, looking rested and fresh, while Charlene was dishing up scrambled eggs, bacon, and toast. They all sat down, and Stone found a *Los Angeles Times* on the table. A story just above the fold caught his eye: DEATH OF MOVIE HEIRESS WAS MURDER.

Stone held up the paper for the others. "Did you see this?"

"We were talking about it when you were still asleep," Dino said. "I wonder who let the press know?"

"I don't think it was Prince," Stone said. "Somebody who knows a reporter, I guess."

"Maybe Rick Barron?" Dino offered.

"Could be," Stone replied. "Charlene, I think this takes the heat off you, at least a little. The opposition can't afford two murders in the papers."

"I'll stick with my security people for a while," Charlene replied. "Better safe than dead."

Stone's cell phone hummed on his belt. "Excuse me for a moment," he said, getting up and walking out of the kitchen. "Hello?"

"It's Eggers."

"Good morning, Bill."

"It's afternoon here."

"Yeah, I remember."

"I spoke to Rex Champion early this morning, offered him thirty-six million. He ranted for a while, then accepted. I'm sending him a deal memo; the price is contingent on our due diligence turning up nothing untoward and on his putting an immediate stop to selling blood stock."

"That's great news, Bill."

"Closing is a week from today."

"*What?*"

"I know, I know, but Rex is hard up and needs the cash immediately."

"How are we going to raise the cash for Arrington that fast?"

"Look, Stone, I know you're not accustomed to dealing with billionaires, but Woodman & Weld is. When one of our clients needs a loan, he doesn't fill out an application and wait for word from the loan committee. Call Arrington, tell her to instruct Chase to deal with us, and we'll have it wrapped up in a day or two. And send me her financial statement, so I'll know what I'm dealing with."

"You're dealing with a billion two in investments with Chase; that's all you need to know."

"You're right, it is. I need a letter from Arrington appointing us as her attorneys and authorizing us to act for her. Can you get that faxed to me right away?"

"Yes."

"I'll look forward to hearing from her." Eggers hung up.

Stone called Arrington. "Good morning," he said.

"It's afternoon."

"Yes, it is. I have good things to report," he said. "Rex Champion has accepted your offer of thirty-six million dollars for Virginia Champion Farms."

"That's wonderful! It's less than I offered."

"It's what you offered," Stone said. "We thought the extra million was too much."

She laughed. "Thank you for ignoring my orders."

"Improving on your orders. Now, we're closing in a week, and I need some paperwork from you right away. Got a pen and paper?"

"Yes," she said.

"First write a letter to Woodman & Weld saying as follows: 'Dear Sirs: I herewith appoint your firm as my sole legal representatives, under the supervision of your partner, Stone Barrington.'"

"Partner?"

"We've been talking about that for months; your business sealed the deal."

"Well, congratulations!"

"Thank you, ma'am. Please get that typed up on your letterhead, sign it, and fax it." He gave her the number. "Then mail Bill Eggers the original. Then, as soon as you've done that, send the following letter to the person who supervises your accounts at Chase Private Bank. Ready?"

"Ready."

"'I have appointed the firm of Woodman & Weld as my sole legal representatives. You may deal with either Mr. Stone Barrington, the supervising partner on my account, or Mr. William Eggers, the firm's managing partner, on my behalf.'"

"Got it."

"Fax that to both your Chase banker and Bill Eggers and mail Chase the original."

"Will do."

"Time is of the essence," Stone said. "We have to arrange a bridging loan from Chase right away to close the sale of Champion Farms, so that you won't have to sell stocks at a loss."

"I understand."

"As soon as Eggers and Chase receive your faxes, we're in business. I'll have Eggers fax you the deal memo on the sale, which will protect you from undiscovered liabilities."

"Thank you, Stone, I appreciate your getting this done with such dispatch. What's happening with the sale of Centurion?"

"There's been a bad turn of events," Stone said. He told her about the murder of Jennifer Harris.

"Am I in any danger?"

"No. Just don't tell Howard Sharp what we're doing with Champion and don't talk to him about anything else, either. Write him a letter discharging him and instructing him to overnight all your files to me in New York."

"I'll get it done today," she said. "Bye-bye."

Stone returned to breakfast.

"Everything okay?" Dino asked.

"Better than okay," Stone said.

"Did you save Centurion?" Charlene asked.

"Not yet, but that's next on my to-do list."

*   *   *

When Stone and Dino left Charlene's house, there were two men in the front garden and an unmarked van parked out front.

"Good morning, gentlemen," one of the men said. "May I see some ID?"

They both complied.

"Charlene doesn't waste any time, does she?" Dino said as they got into the car.

"Never, on any occasion, about anything," Stone replied.

16

They arrived back at the Bel-Air house. Stone was having a second cup of coffee by the pool when his cell phone rang. "Hello?"

"It's Mike Freeman, Stone."

"Hello, Mike."

"I have some preliminary results on the two background checks you asked us to do, on Prince's chauffeur and executive assistant."

"Shoot."

"The chauffeur's name is Alexei Popov, thirty-one years of age, born Ukraine, emigrated to this country with his parents at age thirteen. He has a juvenile record, now sealed, with charges of vandalism, auto theft and—always a bad sign—cruelty to animals. We couldn't get the details. He was also charged with a murder-for-hire three years ago, before he went to work for Terrence Prince, but the case against him was dismissed in midtrial when the main witness against him vanished."

"Uh-oh," Stone said.

"Exactly. Now, about Carolyn Blaine: she doesn't exist."

"Beg pardon?"

"She owns no property in Los Angeles, has no telephone listing, no registered vehicle, no credit record, and no one by that name has been divorced in L.A. County for the past five years. The educational institutions you named—Miss Porter's School, Mount Holyoke, and Wharton have no record of attendance by anyone of that name."

"Well, well," Stone said. "I wonder if Mr. Prince is aware that his trusted assistant doesn't exist."

"If you like, I can have her followed by someone who might get her fingerprints at some point, and we can run them. That might give us something more to go on."

"Please do," Stone said.

"I'll get back to you." Both men hung up.

"Dino?" Stone said.

Dino looked up from the *New York Times*. "Yeah?"

"Terrence Prince's driver is now a suspect in the death of Jennifer Harris. Can you drop the dime on him with your friend Sergeant Rivera?"

"Sure," Dino replied. "What evidence can I give him to support a charge?"

"No evidence, just an educated guess."

"You want me to tell Rivera that my friend Barrington has a *hunch* that the guy killed Harris?"

"Is he looking at anyone else for the murder?"

"Not that I know of."

"Then he'll have plenty of time on his hands. Name is Alexei Popov, thirty-one, a previous murder-for-hire charge, dismissed, dead witness. He's a driver for Terrence Prince, who has a strong financial motive for wanting Miss Harris dead. Tell him about the Centurion thing."

"Okay," Dino said, picking up the phone.

Stone dug out Carolyn Blaine's card and called her on his cell phone.

"Good morning," she said cheerfully.

"Yes, it is, isn't it?" he replied. "I'm staying at a beautiful house in Bel-Air with a wonderful cook. Would you like to come here for dinner tonight?"

"Just the two of us?"

"There may be another couple; I'm not sure yet."

"What time?"

"Seven?" He gave her the address.

"See you then."

Stone hung up and waited for Dino to finish his conversation with Rivera. "Dino, do you think you might like to have dinner with your new friend Hetty again tonight?"

"Why not?" Dino asked. "Where are we going?"

"We're dining in," Stone said. He picked up the phone and buzzed Manolo.

"Yes, Mr. Stone?"

"We'd like to dine here this evening, Manolo. Will that be all right?"

"I'll tell Carmen," he said. "How many people and at what time?"

"Four; we'll sit down at eight, if that's convenient for her. She can cook whatever she likes."

"And at what time will your guests arrive?"

"Seven—a Ms. Blaine and a Ms. Lang, arriving separately."

"It will be a warm evening; would you like to dine by the pool?"

"That would be perfect," Stone said.

"I'll see to everything."

"Thank you, Manolo." Stone hung up.

"Why don't we kidnap Manolo and Carmen and spirit them back to New York?" Dino asked.

"What a good idea! What did Rivera have to say?"

"I passed everything on and he seemed very interested, until I brought up Prince's name. Then he sort of shied away."

"Mr. Prince's reputation apparently precedes him," Stone said.

"Oh, yeah. He promised he'd look into it, though."

"Do you believe him?"

"I got the impression he'd be looking into it without telling his superiors," Dino said.

17

Carolyn Blaine and Hetty Lang arrived nearly simultaneously, and Manolo brought them out to the pool, where Stone and Dino, freshly scrubbed, awaited them. Manolo took their drinks orders, then returned and served them.

"Thank you, Manolo," Stone said.

"What a lovely place," Carolyn said. "Whose house is it?"

"Vance Calder's," Stone said.

"Gosh, I was his complete fan," Carolyn said. She looked around at the gardens. "There seems to be quite a lot of property."

"Fourteen acres," Stone replied, "and an option to buy another four." He turned to Hetty. "Are you working on a film now, Hetty?"

"Yes, on a thriller that the studio seems to be

very excited about. It should be good for my career."

"An option for four more acres?" Carolyn asked.

Stone ignored her. "How long have you been under contract with Centurion, Hetty?"

"A year and a half," she replied.

"Are you enjoying it?"

"Oh, yes. The other kids say it's just like Metro in the thirties. They teach us everything."

"Stone," Carolyn said, "about this house . . ."

"Ah," Stone said, "it looks like dinner is about to be served."

Manolo was wheeling a cart to the poolside table. "In one minute, Mr. Stone," he said.

"What classes are you taking?" Stone asked, again ignoring Carolyn.

"Acting, dancing, and fencing," Hetty replied.

Carolyn was starting to ask again, but Manolo interrupted her.

"Ladies and gentlemen, dinner is served," he said.

They all rose and took seats at the table. Stone tasted the wine and nodded to Manolo to pour.

Carolyn was looking antsy, and throughout dinner Stone did nothing to relieve that. When they were finished and after-dinner drinks had been served, Dino asked Hetty if she'd like to see the gardens, and the two of them left Stone and Carolyn alone.

"Now," Carolyn said, "about this property and the other four acres . . ."

Stone turned and looked at her. "Who are you?" he asked.

She froze for a moment. "Didn't I give you my card?" she asked.

"Your card and a brief bio," Stone replied. "Why do I have the very strong feeling that, if I investigated, I'd find that everything you told me was a lie?"

Carolyn tried not to look flustered. She took a sip of her brandy and a deep breath.

"That's a very odd thing to say to a dinner guest," she said.

"Forgive my rudeness. Again, who are you?"

"Perhaps you'd be more comfortable if I left," she said.

"I wouldn't be more comfortable," he said, "but you might. If you wish to leave, then, by all means, do so. But if we should meet again, my first question would still be, who are you?"

She stared into her brandy glass. "All right," she said, "I fudged my résumé to get my job. Is that so terrible?"

"You did a great deal more than fudge your résumé," Stone said. "Everything you told me—and, no doubt, Terrence Prince—was a bald-faced lie. You made yourself up out of whole cloth."

"Sometimes in life," she said, "there is a need to just start over from scratch."

"I suppose," Stone replied. "But usually people who start over begin with the same name and credentials, then try to improve on those credentials as time passes."

"All right," she said, "I'm not proud of my past."

"Are you a fugitive from justice?" Stone asked.

"No," she replied. "No one is looking for me."

"So you got away clean?" Stone asked, taking a leap.

"I'm not a criminal," she said with some heat.

"Not in your own eyes, anyway," Stone said. He was flying, now, making it up as he went along.

"What do you mean?"

"Do you know what a sociopath is?" Stone asked. This just might push her over the edge, he thought.

But she sat perfectly still. "A person with no conscience," she replied.

"Correct. A person who thinks only of herself and no one else. A person who could never admit wrongdoing, because she figures that, if she did it, it couldn't be wrong."

"That's a very harsh judgment of someone you hardly know," she said.

"Don't know at all," he responded. "Why don't we start over. Who are you?"

"My name doesn't matter," she said.

"It matters in that was your first opportunity to tell the truth, and you passed on that."

"All right, my name—at birth—was Olga Chernik. I was born in Chicago of Polish parents, I attended the public schools through the eighth grade, and then I ran away from home."

"Where did you go?" Stone asked.

"Eventually, to Las Vegas."

Stone thought he knew where the rest of this was going. "And you came under the aegis of a pimp, who got you hooked on heroin, and thereafter you led a life of degradation. Come on, Carolyn, you can do worse than that."

"*Worse?*" she asked, incredulous.

"That's a standard con; you get caught in a lie, so you make up something so much worse that the mark figures it must be true."

She looked defeated. "Are you going to tell Terrence Prince about this?" she asked.

"I doubt if the occasion will arise for me to speak to him again."

"Aren't you going to close the Centurion deal?"

"If I do, it won't require a personal visit from Mr. Prince; I'll just vote the Calder shares at the stockholders' meeting."

"What does the Virginia Champion Farms deal

have to do with your position on Centurion?" she asked.

"Is that what Prince sent you here to find out? All right, I'll tell you: it has nothing whatever to do with Centurion." That wasn't a lie, but it wasn't entirely the truth, either.

"I'm confused," she replied.

"It's not my job to start you thinking clearly," Stone said. "But when you do, give me a call, and maybe we can do some business. In the meantime, it would behoove you not to speak to Prince about this house and property. There will come a time when it will be more to your advantage." He took a sip of his brandy, then stood up. "Good night," he said.

She stood up, flustered. "Thank you for dinner." She got out as fast as she could.

Stone was very satisfied with the way that went. Of course, he still didn't know who she was, but her fingerprints on her brandy glass might help with that.

Stone sat sipping his brandy for a few quiet moments. Then his cell phone went off. "Hello?"

"It's Mike Freeman."

"Good evening, Mike; you're up late."

"I got a call from my operative who's tracking Carolyn Blaine; he's having trouble getting her fingerprints."

"I have them," Stone said. "Tell him to drive to the house and ring the bell."

"Perfect," Mike replied. "I'm coming out there tomorrow. Perhaps we can get together?"

"I'd like that. Where will you stay?"

"At the Bel-Air Hotel."

"Has it reopened?" The Bel-Air had been closed for more than a year, undergoing a complete renovation.

"The Grand Reopening is tomorrow night—would you like to go?"

"Sure. Come here for a drink first; we're just around the corner."

"Six o'clock all right?"

"That's fine." They both hung up.

18

The following morning Stone joined Dino at poolside for breakfast. "Where's Hetty?" he asked.

"She had an early call at the studio," Dino replied. "How did you and Carolyn get on?"

"Not very well," Stone replied. "She left early."

"It's unlike you to send a lady home early, Stone."

"She's no lady," Stone replied. "Mike Freeman is coming out here today. He's invited us to a reopening party at the Bel-Air Hotel."

"Sounds like fun," Dino said. "Should I ask Hetty?"

"If you like. You might do better at the party, though."

"That's a thought."

Manolo brought them breakfast. "Will you be wanting lunch, Mr. Stone?"

"Probably so, Manolo; I have no plans until six, when a friend is coming for drinks. We'll be out for dinner. How about you, Dino?"

"I may wander the town for a while," Dino replied. "No lunch for me, Manolo."

The man returned to the house.

Stone spent the morning reading the newspapers and doing the crossword; then he swam for a while. He had just finished lunch when his cell rang. "Hello?"

"It's Eggers."

"Good afternoon, Bill."

"I've obtained a one-hundred-million-dollar line of credit for Arrington," he said. "At prime."

"Well done."

"I'm faxing you the paperwork to look over. If you think it's okay, I'll messenger it to Arrington for her signature."

"Thanks, Bill."

"I have other news," Eggers said. "The board of management met this morning and unanimously elected you partner."

"That's very good news indeed, Bill," Stone said with feeling. "Thank you for your support with the board."

"I'll fax you the partnership agreement in a few minutes. Everybody signs the basic agreement;

then we can talk about compensation and other things."

"All right."

"I'll find you some decent office space on our floors in the building."

Stone thought fast; for some reason it hadn't occurred to him that he would be expected to move into the Seagram Building offices of the firm. "Bill, if it's all the same to you, I'd prefer to continue working out of my office in Turtle Bay."

"I guess that would be all right. What about your secretary?"

"I'll stick with Joan. If I need more help, I'll let you know."

"We'll give you an allowance for office space and staff, then, just to even things out with the other partners. I'll base it on the square foot cost for the average partner's space."

"That will be fine."

"There'll be a generous expense account, of course, and I propose a draw against earnings of a hundred thousand a month, adjusted annually."

"That will be satisfactory."

"You can use your own airplane for travel whenever you wish. Let me know what the hourly operating costs are. For other travel, we have an in-house department that will make any necessary arrangements for you."

"What other perks should I be asking for?" Stone asked.

Eggers chuckled. "Well, you already have a car."

"Not really," Stone replied. "I totaled it a month ago, remember?"

"I had forgotten. What would you like to drive?"

"Let me get back to you on that," Stone said. He was currently driving an armored Bentley Flying Spur that Strategic Services had lent him.

"How about club memberships?"

"I don't belong to a club."

"Is there one you'd like? The Metropolitan? The Century? The Racquet Club? We have partners who could propose you for almost anything."

"Let me think about that." Stone had never thought of himself as a clubman.

"We can help with most of the golf clubs in the area, too."

"That's a thought."

"You really ought to get yourself a place in the Hamptons, Stone. The firm has a very favorable mortgage program."

"Thanks, but I'm all right with my place in Connecticut. Maybe at some later time."

"As you wish. I'll get these papers off to you right away."

"Thanks, Bill, and thank you again for your support."

Stone hung up feeling lighter than air. A partnership at Woodman & Weld! He had never thought it possible until recently, and now it had actually happened.

Manolo came and took his dishes away, then came back and presented him with an envelope. "A fax for you, Mr. Stone."

Stone opened the envelope and found the partnership agreement. He read it through quickly, then signed it and set it aside for FedEx pickup. Then he read the note for Arrington's line of credit, which was well drawn and required no changes. As he returned the papers to the envelope, a movement caught his eye. He looked up.

"Arrington!" he said. She was standing there looking gorgeous, as usual. He got up and met her halfway. "I wasn't expecting you; why didn't you let me know?" They hugged and kissed.

"I remembered last night that the Bel-Air is reopening tonight," she said, "so I thought what the hell, good excuse to come out. We left early this morning."

He held a chair for her. "Would you like lunch?"

"I had something on the airplane, which was a charter. There wasn't time to send for the Centurion jet. You know, Stone. Maybe it's time I got my own airplane. What do you think?"

"I think it's a wonderful idea."

"You'll have to advise me on what to get."

"I'll be glad to do that and to get you more expert advice than I'm able to offer."

"Can I afford it?"

"Arrington, you can afford anything your heart desires," Stone replied. "By the way, I have the papers for your line of credit." He opened the envelope and handed them to her.

"I think this is yours," she said, handing back his partnership agreement. "And congratulations again."

"Thank you; you helped make it possible."

She glanced at the first page of the agreement. "A hundred million dollars!"

"You don't have to borrow it all, just enough for the Champion deal and whatever else you want, like the airplane."

"Do you have a pen?" She accepted one and signed the papers where Stone indicated.

Manolo came out with iced tea for both of them, and Stone handed him the partnership and line of credit agreements in the envelope, first writing the address on the outside. "Will you fax these, then FedEx the originals to New York, please, Manolo?"

"Of course, Mr. Stone."

"I've been making some plans, Stone," Arrington said. "Let me tell you about them."

"I'd like to hear them." He sat back and morphed into his listening lawyer mode.

19

Arrington brushed a strand of her blond hair from her forehead and took a long drink of her iced tea. "I haven't told you about this," she said, "and you haven't visited, so you haven't seen it."

"Seen what?"

"My house."

"I recall your saying that you were thinking of building."

"That was years ago. I went a little crazy after Vance's death. I had never had access to huge amounts of money, and Vance was—how shall I put it?—prudent. I looked for a big house in Virginia and didn't find anything I liked, so I decided to build the house to end all houses, and I did. Twenty thousand square feet of it."

"Wow."

"Well, yes. I hired an architect and an interior designer, and I went on a shopping spree all over the South to find just the right pieces to furnish it. The local gentry were peeved, because I was denuding the antiques shops in the county and running the prices up on whatever was left, but eventually, I got it done." She sighed. "Perhaps 'overdone' would be a better word."

"I see."

"No, you don't, and I don't want you looking through old *Architectural Digest*s for the piece they did. So, for weeks now, I've been tagging pieces in the house, and I'm going to throw the biggest auction anybody in Virginia has ever seen. Sotheby's is sending down an auctioneer. And—you won't believe this—I've found a buyer for the house whose tastes are probably better than mine. I won't get all my money out of the place, but I'll get three-quarters of it and be happy to have it."

"Where will you live?" Stone asked.

"At Champion Farms," she said.

"I wasn't aware there was a suitable house on the property."

"There isn't, but there used to be. It was contemporaneous with Thomas Jefferson's Monticello, but it was destroyed by fire in the 1920s. A researcher has been able to find the original plans in the Charlottesville library—no one even knew they were there. So, I'm going to re-create the place on the original spot. It's wildly overgrown, but there are beautiful trees, including a neglected colonnade of old oaks to the house. I'll replace the damaged and fallen trees."

"That sounds wonderful."

"It's going to take all my time for the next two years, and then I'll be looking for another project to keep me busy. I've learned that I'm dangerous when I'm not busy."

Stone laughed. "I can imagine."

"There's something else: I want to talk to you about Peter."

"All right, perhaps it's time you did."

"Peter is fifteen, and he's at Episcopal High School, in Alexandria; it's the best prep school in the South, on a level with the best New England preps. He is very, very bright, and he's a grade ahead. He's also very handsome, and tall for his age." She retrieved a photograph from her purse and handed it to Stone. "For you."

Stone stared at the boy—young man, really—and sighed. "He looks extraordinarily like my father."

"I remember that photograph in your house," she said. "Anyway, the school was reluctant to accept him at first, but then three of the senior faculty had a long lunch with him—I wasn't present—and they were impressed with his maturity and seriousness, so they accepted him as a boarding student in the ninth grade. From what they've said about him so far, he'll probably graduate in three years, maybe even two."

"That's breathtaking," Stone said.

"I'm sure you were bright, too, Stone," she said. "God knows he didn't get it from me."

"Now, now."

Arrington reached into the large handbag resting next to her chair and handed Stone a thick envelope. "This is my will and the trust I set up for Peter. I'd like you and the people at Woodman & Weld to look it over and redraw it. My beneficiaries haven't changed, but I'll be interested to see if you think the trust needs work."

"Of course," Stone said. "We'll do that as a courtesy."

"You'll never make any money that way, Stone."

"We'll do all right."

"You'll see that I've appointed you Peter's trustee. I didn't tell you, because, I suppose, I felt invulnerable, but recently I had a brush with ovarian cancer. They caught it early, but I had to have my ovaries out, and now I'm on hormones. If I get sick again, I'll give you as much notice as I can, but you could, possibly, find yourself being a father to your son."

"That would be an honor," Stone said.

"Considering that you're his father, it's more of a duty," she said. "Maybe he'll find that out one day, but I don't want you to tell him. He's Vance's son to the world, and that will be an advantage to him, if you help him handle it properly."

"I can see how it would be."

"You're going to have to keep it from him how rich he's going to be."

"I expect he may have already figured that out," Stone said, "and if he hasn't, the kids at his school are going to tell him."

"I suppose you're right. Then we'll both have to do what we can to keep his feet firmly planted on the ground."

"One way is not to give him control of his trust until he's older," Stone said, "perhaps at thirty-five."

"That's a very good idea, and one I'm happy to leave in your hands."

"Thank you; I'll try and do right by him."

"I'd like to bring him to New York to see you," she said.

"You'd both be very welcome; I'll look forward to it."

"Now," she said, taking another sip of her iced

tea, "what are we going to do about this Centurion business?"

"You want my recommendation?"

"Yes, please, and I'll tell you up front, I'll follow it. I'm not equipped to deal with this."

"All right. First, I think that you should not sell your shares. In fact, I think you should buy more."

"Why?"

"Because Centurion is giving you a better return on your investment that just about anything could. It's extremely well run and profitable. Right now, you own a third of the shares. I think you should, over the next few years, increase your share to fifty-one percent."

"My goodness!" Arrington said, sounding a little breathless. "I never thought of controlling the studio! Can I afford to buy that many more shares? Terrence Prince has run up the price, hasn't he?"

"If we can get one or two owners on our side, that will kill the sale, and the price will go down. There may even be some who would prefer to sell to you at a lower price than to get into bed with Prince."

"What do you think of him?" she asked.

"I think he's a shark; maybe even a killer."

"Then he'll do just fine in the Virginia hunt country," she said.

"I'd heard that he'd once bought a house there, then flipped it."

"Now he's bought another," Arrington said. "I've sold him mine."

"Prince is your buyer?"

"I think he bought the place as a way to get next to me and get my Centurion shares," she said, laughing. "We closed yesterday."

Stone began to laugh. "That's wonderful."

"You may have the pleasure of telling him I'm not budging, if you like."

"Not yet; we still have to be sure we have a voting majority of the shares on our side."

"I suppose so. Would you like to go to the Bel-Air party with me?"

"I'm already going with Mike Freeman, the CEO of Strategic Services, a client of mine, so you must join us."

"I'd love to. Where's Dino? Surely he's here."

"Out running around town," Stone said. "Mike's coming for drinks at six; Dino will be back by then."

"Well, then," she said, "I think I'll go and have a nap. Care to join me?"

"Maybe later," Stone said. "I want to read your estate documents."

"Oh, all right." She set down her iced tea, picked up her handbag, and walked toward the main house. Just before entering, she looked over her shoulder to be sure he was watching, then gave him a little smile.

20

Arrington excused herself to change for the Bel-Air Hotel party, and Stone changed clothes as well. Uncharacteristically, in L.A., he wore a suit and tie.

Mike Freeman arrived on time, and Stone sat him down by the pool and ordered drinks. "There's someone joining us, if that's all right," Stone said.

"Of course," Mike replied.

"Her name is Arrington Calder, an old friend and now my client."

"Vance Calder's widow?"

"Yes, and this is her house."

"It's extraordinary," Mike said, looking around.

"So is Arrington," Stone said.

She chose that moment to appear, wearing a white silk pajama suit, so Stone didn't have to continue the description. He introduced the two.

Dino trotted past them. "I'll change and be with you shortly," he said, disappearing into the guesthouse.

"Mike," Stone said, "Arrington is thinking of buying herself a jet, and I hope you can advise her, having had some experience yourself along those lines."

"Of course," Mike said. "We often advise clients on jet purchases. What will be your typical mission, Arrington?"

"Mission?"

"What sort of travel will you be doing?"

"Well," she said, "I'm based near Charlottesville, Virginia, and I sometimes travel to L.A., Dallas, Miami, other cities."

"Would you like to fly internationally?"

"Yes, to Europe."

"How about the Far East?"

"I don't go there very often."

"If you don't need to fly regularly nonstop to Tokyo or Hong Kong, you'll save a great deal of money on an airplane by giving up range."

"Then let's save some money."

Mike raised a finger. "You know, a client sent me a brochure on an airplane last week to ask my opinion. I think it's in my briefcase. It's a Gulfstream Three, known as a G-III. It might be just the thing."

"Why didn't your client buy it?" she asked.

"Because of the Far East travel; he decided he needed a longer-range airplane."

"Would this G-III get me to London, nonstop?"

"Yes, and to anywhere else in Europe," Mike said. "It's three years old, but very low time—less than a thousand hours, as I recall. It was owned by an elderly couple, but he died recently, and his widow is not well enough to travel anymore. It has a very nice custom interior, and it's based in Burbank. I can arrange for you to see it, if you like."

"I'd like that very much," Arrington said. "Will you show it to me?"

"Of course," Mike said. "Excuse me for a moment." He got out his cell phone and stepped away. He was back in a few minutes. "May I pick you up at ten tomorrow morning?" he asked Arrington.

"Perfect."

"This is a very good time to buy an airplane," he said, "and a bad time to sell. When those three automobile executives each flew alone to Washington in their private jets to beg for money from the government, that knocked the bottom out of the market for jet airplanes. Since then, the recession has slowed aircraft sales badly, and although things are picking up again, they're not where they were a couple of years ago. Airplanes of the size and quality of the G-III are a particularly good buy."

"I'll bring my checkbook," Arrington said.

"That won't be necessary," Mike replied, chuckling. "Buying an airplane is a bit like buying a house: a title search has to be done and financing arranged. Then the logbooks have to be gone over and a prepurchase inspection completed, and insurance obtained. I can help with all that."

"I expect Arrington will make it a cash purchase," Stone said, "so that should shorten the process."

"This particular G-III has been on a Gulfstream maintenance program since new," Mike said, "so that will help, too."

Dino came out of the guesthouse in his best Armani suit. "Ready when you are," he said.

Manolo had brought around Vance Calder's Bentley Arnage, and Stone drove them to the Bel-Air Hotel, two minutes away.

As they walked across the bridge from the parking lot over the little creek that ran through the property, they saw that the lawns were full of people, drinking champagne and looking happy. From the top of the bridge, Stone spotted Terrence Prince, surrounded by a knot of people.

"There's the purchaser of your Virginia house,"

Stone said to Arrington. "Would you like to meet him?"

"Why not?" Arrington replied.

Stone led his group toward Prince, snagging champagne glasses along the way. Stone and Prince shook hands, and he made the introductions. Carolyn Blaine was among Prince's group.

"I'm very happy to meet you," Prince said to Arrington, shaking her hand. "I have a thousand questions to ask you about your house."

"It's your house now," Arrington replied, "but I'll tell you whatever you want to know, including about the colony of raccoons in the attic and the bat infestation in the cellar."

Prince looked startled, then laughed. "Don't scare me like that," he said. "I understand you're about to take ownership of Virginia Champion Farms."

"That is so," she replied, "and I'm going to build a house there."

"Tell me about it," Prince said, cutting her out of the group like a sheepdog at work.

Mike was talking to someone he knew, and Carolyn drew Stone aside. "So," she said, "when can I tell Prince about the Calder property?"

"Haven't you already?" Stone asked. He looked over her shoulder and spotted an extremely tall man with a beautiful blonde. "Why, there's my friend Ed Eagle, from Santa Fe," Stone said. "Come, let's go meet him." He took Carolyn's arm. "Do you know Ed? He's a famous trial lawyer in these parts."

"No," Carolyn replied, "I've never been to Santa Fe." She pulled away. "Will you excuse me? I need to find the ladies' room; I'll join you in a few minutes." She hurried away.

Stone walked over and greeted Ed and Susannah Eagle. "Good to see you, Ed," Stone said, shaking his hand. "It's been a long time."

"Too long, Stone," Eagle replied. "Have you met Susannah?"

"No," Stone replied. "That's how long it's been. How do you do, Susannah?"

"I'm glad to meet you, Stone; Ed has told me a lot about you."

"Not too much, I hope," Stone said.

"Stone," Eagle said, "who was the blonde you were with until a moment ago? There's something familiar about her."

"Her name is Carolyn Blaine," Stone said. "She's executive assistant to Terry Prince, but you haven't met her. She said she'd never been to Santa Fe."

"Maybe it was out here, then," Eagle said.

"Oh, Ed," his wife interjected, "every pretty girl looks familiar to you."

"She'll be back in a minute," Stone said. "She's just gone to the ladies'. Then we can resolve where you've met."

Stone and the Eagles talked for a few minutes, but Carolyn never returned. He reckoned she'd found someone more interesting to talk to.

21

Stone and the Eagles moved toward the garden restaurant, where a buffet dinner had been set up. He saw Prince and Arrington a few steps ahead of them. Then someone behind him tapped Stone on the shoulder. He turned to find Rick and Glenna Barron. He greeted them warmly.

"Just the man I wanted to see," Stone said.

"What can I do for you, Stone?"

"I'm wondering what, if anything, you've found out about the disposition of Jennifer Harris's shares in Centurion."

"I know her attorney, and I spoke to him, so I know that her will leaves the shares to her estate, instead of a particular beneficiary."

"Does her attorney have the authority to sell them on behalf of the estate?" Stone asked.

"Yes, and I think he would be amenable to the sale, as long as it brought market value. Unfortunately, he knows about the offer from Mr. Prince, so he will want at least what Prince has offered."

"Are you going to buy them?" Stone asked.

"I'm afraid that's a bit of a stretch for me, financially," Rick replied. "I might be able to swing it, but I'd have to sell some other investments, and that would take time we don't have."

Stone looked around, then lowered his voice. "I think it might be possible for Arrington to buy them," he said.

"That would be perfect," Rick replied. "What with Charlene Joiner's shares, that would give us a majority."

"Surely Prince would be bidding for them, too," Stone said.

"And if he got them, he'd have a majority," Rick pointed out.

"I think what we have to do," Stone said, "is canvass all the other share owners and see if we can buy another bloc or two that would give us fifty-one percent."

"Let me talk to some of them and see if they would rather sell to us than to Prince."

"It would be in their interests, wouldn't it, to keep the studio operating as it is now?"

"Certainly, for some of them who want to continue

to make pictures. I'll start on that tomorrow morning and get back to you." Rick looked around. "In fact, I've seen a couple of them here tonight; perhaps I'll get an opportunity to speak to them."

"Good idea," Stone said. "Face-to-face might work best."

They worked their way through the line for dinner, and Stone found a large table. Arrington left Prince and rejoined him.

"What did you think of Mr. Prince?" Stone asked her.

"Oh, he's charming," she said. "I knew he would be. I wouldn't trust him any farther than I could throw him, though."

"What good instincts you have," Stone said, laughing. "I was in line with Rick and Glenna Barron, and he's going to talk with some of the other shareholders about our buying their shares. I think we've got a shot at this, starting with those owned by Jennifer Harris's estate."

"If you say so," Arrington said. "As long as I don't have to sell other securities."

"Something I think you should do," Stone said, "is to take up the option on the four acres adjoining your property here. I think that addition would make your acreage much more valuable."

"Vance got those options just before he died," Arrington said. "There are two parcels of one point eight and two point two acres, both with very nice houses on them. The owners are elderly and would probably like to move into some sort of assisted facilities. The prices are very good, too, given the appreciation of real estate in this neighborhood. I'd have to pay, let's see, about eighteen million for the two."

"When do the options expire?" Stone asked.

"Quite soon, I think; I'm not certain of the date."

"We'll get Woodman & Weld on that tomorrow," Stone said. "We don't want to miss this opportunity."

Dino came and sat down at their table. "I didn't get a chance to tell you earlier," he said, "but I talked to Sergeant Rivera this afternoon, and he's going to arrest Prince's driver tomorrow."

"What for?" Arrington asked.

"For the murder of Jennifer Harris," Dino replied.

"We think Prince had her killed to get hold of her shares," Stone said.

"Prince plays that rough?" Arrington asked.

"We believe so."

"Should I be worried?"

"No, harming you wouldn't help him. Your shares would go into the trust for Peter, and I'll be his trustee. The Woodman & Weld trust department is already working on the documents."

Arrington took a deep breath and let it out. "That's a relief," she said.

"Also, having his driver in jail and maybe talking is going to make Prince more circumspect in his actions," Stone said. "He won't be able to pull that again. In fact, if the driver talks, that could solve all our problems. Prince wouldn't be starting a big new development, if he were looking at a trial and possible conviction."

"If that happens, can we go to the trial?" Arrington asked.

Stone laughed. "I'll see if I can get tickets."

22

Stone and Dino had breakfast with Arrington beside the pool the following morning. Then Mike Freeman collected Arrington and took her off to Burbank Airport to look at the available G-III.

Dino's phone rang. "Bacchetti," he said, then listened. "Have you got a line on him? Well, shit. Thanks for calling; keep me posted, if you will." Dino hung up. "Prince's driver ran; he's nowhere to be found."

"How would he have known he was going to be arrested?" Stone asked.

"Rivera thinks somebody in his office, maybe even his boss, tipped off Prince."

"I heard you ask if he had a line on the driver."

"Nothing. He apparently didn't sleep at his apartment last night, and his car was still there."

"This gets weirder and weirder," Stone said.

Stone's cell phone buzzed. "Hello?"

"Good morning, Stone. It's Rick Barron."

"Good morning, Rick."

"I've got some news on the share-buying front."

"Shoot."

"One of the share owners, an elderly producer named Walt Baird, is willing to sell to us, because he needs money now and doesn't want to wait until Prince does his deal. He'll sell for twenty-five hundred a share. The bad news is, he only owns five thousand shares."

"That's a start. Tell him we'll pay him this week."

"All right, and there's better news, too. Baird tells me a producer named Jim Long is willing to sell his shares, because he needs cash for a lawyer; he's being held in jail without bail in L.A. on an attempted murder charge. He's a close friend of Ed Eagle's ex-wife, Barbara, and he's accused of helping her try to kill Ed. You may recall that he was attacked by a man with a knife outside his home a while back. Long apparently introduced Barbara to the man, who was a dogsbody and sometime pilot for Long."

"I heard about that," Stone said.

"Are you willing to go and see Long in jail and talk to him about buying his shares? He's got fifteen thousand so he could put us over the top. His attorney's name is Harvey Stein." Rick gave him the number.

"Sure, I'll go see him. Arrington is out looking at an airplane at Burbank. When she comes back, I'll brief her about this."

"Good. Let me know how it goes with Long, will you? You can tell him I sent you; we had a cordial relationship when he was on the lot."

"I'll do that." Stone hung up. "Can you get me into the L.A. City Jail?" he asked Dino.

"Sure, just throw a brick through a window, and I'll get Rivera to throw you in there."

Stone called Harvey Stein's number and, after working his way past a couple of secretaries, got him on the line.

"What can I do for you, Mr. Barrington?"

"I'm an attorney with Woodman & Weld in New York," Stone said.

"Yeah, I know the firm; I've heard your name, too."

"I have a client who is interested in buying James Long's shares in Centurion Studios."

"Who's the client?"

"Arrington Calder."

"Vance Calder's widow?"

"That's right."

"I heard about Terry Prince's pending deal."

"Long's friend Rick Barron asked me to talk to Mr. Long. Rick thinks Long might prefer to sell to us rather than to Prince."

"As his attorney, I don't give a shit who he sells to. Either way, I get paid what Long owes me."

"Will you arrange for me to see him in jail?"

"Sure, I'll leave your name there. He's in Metro Jail, at Parker Center." Stein gave him the address. "Visiting hours today are two to four."

"Thanks very much."

"Tell Jim to call me as soon as he can."

"I'll do that." Stone thanked him and hung up. "Long is at Parker Center," he said to Dino.

"That's where Rivera works; I'll go with you and see if he's found Prince's driver."

"Okay." Stone's cell buzzed again. "Hello?"

"Hey, it's Arrington."

"Hi, there."

"I just bought an airplane! Got a great deal, too, Mike says."

"Well, don't fly it away; we've got some paperwork to take care of first."

"I'm on the way home; Mike wants to talk to you, though." She put Freeman on the phone.

"She liked it the minute she saw it," Mike said. "Great interior; it's even got a bed—unusual for a G-III."

"What do I need to get done?"

"You need to get a corporation set up to own the airplane, for liability and tax reasons."

"I can get that done."

"I'll deal with the logbooks, the preflight inspection, and the insurance agent. I'll send Arrington home in my car, and it can come back for me."

"Okay, call me when you know when we'll close."

"Will do." Mike hung up.

Stone called Bill Eggers in New York.

"Afternoon, Stone, what's up?"

"Our client, Arrington, has bought an airplane, a G-III. I need to get the proper corporate setup done right away."

"We've got a tax lawyer here who can do it. He's going to need some information about the airplane."

Stone gave him Mike Freeman's cell number. "Tell him to call Mike; he's with the broker now. They'll get him whatever information he needs."

"Will do. Anything else?"

"Arrington is going to buy some more shares of Centurion, hopefully in the next day or two."

"Is there enough left of her line of credit?"

"We'll have to see about that. She also wants to take up the option she has on two pieces of property adjoining her estate in Bel-Air, so you might speak to Chase about extending her line of credit another one hundred million, just in case."

"Will do. I have some paperwork on the property option; it came to us yesterday, along with her other files from her former attorney. I'll take care of it."

"The option expires soon, so time is of the essence."

"Got it. Bye." Eggers hung up.

"Okay," Stone said to Dino. "Let's have some lunch and then run down to Parker Center and see this guy in jail."

23

Stone signed in at Metro Jail and sat down to wait to be called. The waiting room was jammed, mostly lawyers and women, many with children. Half an hour later Stone was shown to a lawyers' meeting room, apparently a courtesy that Harvey Stein had requested.

James Long was shown into the room by a guard and had his handcuffs removed. He was a tall, slender man in his fifties with graying hair and the start of a beard. He was wearing the standard orange jumpsuit. They shook hands.

"Mr. Barrington? Harvey Stein said you were coming to talk to me. I'm glad to see you; it's good to talk to anybody besides my cellmate."

"I understand," Stone replied. "I hope you're being treated well."

"Not especially," Long said. "I'm in here, not because I've committed a crime, but because they want me to rat out my friend Barbara Eagle. Funny thing is, I don't have any knowledge of what they say she did. All I did was meet her in Mexico and fly her to Yuma, where she left us. In the process, she, of course, met my pilot, and it's that introduction that they're holding me on as an accessory. Somebody murdered him in his home, so he can't back me up."

"I hear Barbara escaped from jail down there," Stone said.

"I didn't know that. She called and asked me to meet her in Acapulco, and I did. We spent a couple of days there, then came back to this country. I don't even know where she went after Yuma. In any case, she's managed to get herself a pardon in Mexico, so she's not wanted for anything. The LAPD has gone nuts over this business, and she's not even in L.A.; she's in San Francisco."

"Has your attorney explained all this to the DA?"

"Of course he has, but they don't want to listen to the truth; they just want a witness against Barbara. Harvey is filing for a writ of habeas corpus to get me out."

"Well, good luck. In the meantime I have some good news. A client of mine is interested in buying your shares in Centurion Studios."

"What is he offering?"

"It's a she, and she's offering twenty-five hundred dollars a share."

"Yeah, I heard about Terry Prince's takeover attempt of the studio. I'll bet he'd give me more than twenty-five hundred."

"Twenty-five hundred is his current offer, and I have some reason to believe that the deal is not going to work out for him, and if that happens, then his current offer disappears, so your shares might be worth quite a lot less."

"Yeah, so you say."

"It's up to you, Mr. Long: you can accept my client's offer or stick with Prince and take a chance of losing a lot of money on your shares. It's up to you."

Long fidgeted in his seat. "Oh, hell, all right; I'd rather be on Rick Barron's side in all this, anyway."

"Rick has asked me to give you his regards and to thank you for selling to us. This way, you'll still have a studio to go back to when you get out of here. If Prince got his hands on the property, it would have made it impossible for Centurion to continue as they have."

"All right, how do we go about this?"

"Where are your share certificates?"

"In my office safe at Centurion."

"Does your attorney have the combination?"

"I'll give it to him when I see him; he's coming tomorrow."

"I'll see that he gets the sales documents to sign, so he can bring them with him. He asked me to tell you to call him as soon as you can."

"I'll try to call him this afternoon, if I can get to the phone. There's always a line."

"I'll have the documents faxed to him from New York first thing tomorrow morning. They're already closed for the day."

"I'm sure that will be fine. When will I get the money?"

"As soon as Harvey sends me the signed documents, I'll have it wired to your bank account. We might be able to manage it tomorrow, certainly the day after."

"Good." Long stood up and rapped on the door. The guard came in and cuffed him. "Nice to meet you," Long said.

"I hope you get your writ," Stone said.

Dino was waiting on the front steps when Stone emerged from the building. "How'd it go?"

"Long has agreed to sell us his shares. With the five thousand from the other guy, Baird, we should have a majority ownership in a day or two."

"I've got some news, too: Alexei what's-his-name, Prince's driver, has turned up dead. Somebody dumped his body at the La Brea Tar Pits, where they found all those prehistoric bones of animals that went down to the water for a drink, got stuck in the tar, and sank. Luckily, they found Alexei's body before it could sink. Want to take a guess on cause of death?"

"Tell me."

"Ice pick to the back of the neck, like Jennifer Harris."

"I guess it would be easy to make that happen if you're being driven by Alexei, sitting behind him."

"Prince has an alibi, of course."

"Of course. Man, I'll be glad when this business is over," Stone said. "And I hope it's over before somebody else gets ice-picked."

"You can hope," Dino said.

Arrington was at the Calder house when they got back, and she was very excited about her airplane.

"It's beautiful, Stone, just exactly what I wanted. It's already got a crew and everything, and they're willing to move east."

"Sounds perfect," Stone said. "Mike is working on getting you an early closing, and a tax attorney at Woodman & Weld is setting up the corporate structure."

"Corporate structure?"

"Jet airplanes are usually owned by corporations,

for liability and tax purposes. You'll own the corporation. And I have other news."

"Good news, I hope?"

"It looks like Rick has found us the shares we need to gain control of Centurion. They should be transferred in the next day or two."

"Well, I'm glad to hear that. I hope Mr. Prince doesn't hear about it before we get it done. I'm not sure how much more of his personal charm I can stand."

"We'll have a lot of paperwork for you to sign tomorrow, on the Centurion thing, Champion Farms, the Bel-Air property options, and the airplane. You should be able to fly out of here in your new airplane in a couple of days, with any luck at all."

"I'm anxious to get back and go to work with the architect on the new house," Arrington said.

"You'll be back by the weekend," Stone said, "unless there's a snag." Please, he thought, no snags.

24

Stone went back to the Calder house and called Rick Barron.

"How did it go?" Rick asked.

"Very well; Long has agreed to sell to us. Woodman & Weld will produce the sale documents and fax them to his attorney tomorrow. We'll wire the funds, and we'll be done."

"That's great news, Stone," Rick said.

"Rick, we've discussed this before, but what instructions have you left for your estate's disposal of your shares?"

"They'll go to our grandchildren."

"Do your grandkids want to be in the movie business?"

"One is a doctor, the other an architect," Rick

said, "but Centurion will produce a nice income for them."

"Do you think they might just as well have cash?"

"They might," Rick admitted. "Are you and Arrington offering to buy my shares?"

"I haven't discussed it with her, but if you would consider selling her your shares, I'll bring it up."

"I would consider that," Rick said. "It's likely that some of the shares would have to be sold, anyway, to pay estate taxes."

"I'll speak to her about it," Stone said, "and get back to you." The two men said goodbye and hung up.

Stone went looking for Arrington in the main house. She wasn't in the living room or the study, so he knocked on her bedroom door.

"Who is it?"

"It's Stone."

"Come in."

Stone walked into the large room and found Arrington sitting at her dressing table, fiddling with her makeup, and dressed in only a bath towel. "Would you like me to come back?"

"Don't be ridiculous," she said. "You've seen me naked often enough."

"And enjoyed the experience," Stone replied, standing behind her and rubbing her shoulders.

She looked at him in the mirror, then dropped the towel, exposing her lovely breasts. "Would you like to enjoy it again?"

Stone's reaction was immediate, and Arrington knew it. She moved her head back until it came in contact with his crotch.

"I think that's an affirmative answer," she said.

"You may be sure of that." He reached down and fondled her nipples.

"You know what that does to me," she said.

"I do, and it seems to be working."

She spun around on her stool, unzipped his fly, and took him into her mouth.

Stone gave a little gasp. "I believe that's a bed over there," he said.

She stopped what she was doing, took his hand, and led him to the bed. "Get out of those clothes," she said.

But Stone was way ahead of her. They fell onto the bed, and she resumed her earlier activity.

"Wait," he said, pulling her into his arms. "I don't want to finish too soon."

"I don't want that either," she said, pulling him on top of her and helping him inside her. "It's been too long," she breathed as she began to move under him.

"You're right," he replied.

She came in less than a minute. "Again," she said. "This time with you."

Stone held it back as long as he could, and her rising orgasm finally set him off. They were both noisy about it.

An hour or so later, Stone disentangled himself from Arrington and used her shower. When he returned, she was back at her dressing table, wearing a slip. "Isn't this where I came in?" he asked, rubbing her shoulders while she brushed her hair.

"It is, and what did you want to talk about?"

"We've got the shares we need to control the studio, in conjunction with Rick Barron. It occurred to me that it might be good for you to buy his shares, too. Rick's in his nineties, and if he leaves them to his grandchildren, we could find ourselves back in the same situation in a few years."

"Can I afford it?"

"I've already asked Bill Eggers to extend your line of credit for another hundred million."

"That's a breathtaking amount of money," she said. "How will I ever pay it back?"

"When the market goes up again, and it will, you'll sell other stocks and repay the loan. Hardly anything in your portfolio would be a better investment than Centurion."

"I'll do whatever you recommend," she said. "You know I trust you."

"Then I recommend that you buy the twenty thousand shares from Long and Baird."

"And that will give us control?"

"With Rick voting his hundred thousand shares and Charlene Joiner voting her fifty thousand, yes."

"What about Jennifer Harris's shares?"

"We don't know yet if her estate will sell them to us, but we don't need them, because we have Long's and Baird's shares."

"Sounds good to me," Arrington said. "By the way, I've arranged for dinner here tonight and invited Mike Freeman, too. I hope that will be all right with you and Dino."

"Of course. Why don't we invite Rick and Glenna and Charlene Joiner, too? We can call it a celebration of both your new airplane and our achieving voting control of Centurion."

"Sounds wonderful. Will you call the Barrons and Ms. Joiner?"

"Of course." Stone got on the phone and issued the invitations.

"They'll be here at six-thirty for drinks," he told Arrington.

"Good. Now go away before you and I get started again. I have to do my hair and makeup."

"You overestimate me," Stone said, retreating.

"No, I don't," she replied.

Stone fled. He went back to the guesthouse, got Bill Eggers's voice mail at Woodman & Weld, and left him a description of the sales documents for the purchase of both Long's and Baird's shares, and instructions to fax Long's to Harvey Stein and Baird's to himself. Now he wouldn't have to rise at six o'clock the next morning to get that done.

Dino woke up from a nap, and Stone told him of the dinner arrangements.

"Good excuse for a party," Dino said.

"Two good excuses," Stone replied. "Don't forget Arrington's new airplane."

25

Stone walked out to the pool a little before six-thirty and found half a dozen bottles of ten-year-old Krug champagne in a copper tub of ice. Arrington appeared from the main house in a gossamer white dress, looking ravishing.

"Why don't you pop one of those corks?" she suggested.

Stone popped the cork and found a pair of her Baccarat champagne flutes. "To the movie business and fast airplanes," he said, and they drank. "Yeasty," he offered.

"Crisp," she said. "Wonderful stuff. It's been in the cellar for years."

Dino appeared and accepted a flute. "Arrington," he said, "you've never looked more beautiful."

She kissed him lightly on the lips. "Dino, you've

just paid the rent on a permanent lease of my guesthouse."

"A bargain," Dino said. "Hey, what is this champagne? It's different from what they sell at Elaine's."

"Elaine sells Dom Pérignon; this is Krug Brut, the good stuff."

"I like the good stuff."

"When are you going to retire, Dino?" Arrington asked.

"Retire from the NYPD? What would I do for fun?" he replied.

Manolo showed Mike Freeman out to the pool, arm in arm with Charlene Joiner. "Miss Joiner and I have just met," he said. "I'm a big fan."

"Isn't he sweet?" Charlene said.

Stone introduced Arrington and Charlene. Each eyed the other up and down as they shook hands.

"Arrington," Mike said, "everything is in hand for your airplane purchase. The insurance has been arranged, and we'll have the prepurchase inspection finished tomorrow. I've faxed the sales agreement to Woodman & Weld for their approval. Everything seems to be in perfect order."

"Perfect order is what I like," Arrington said.

Rick and Glenna Barron arrived and received champagne.

Rick raised his glass. "To a new day at Centurion, with a long life ahead." They all drank.

They were about to sit down for dinner when Manolo came to Stone and whispered, "There's a Mister Harvey Stein on the phone for you. He said it was urgent."

"I'll take it in the guesthouse," Stone said. "Please excuse me for a moment, everybody." He went into the guesthouse living room, picked up the phone, and pressed the lighted button. "Harvey?"

"Stone, I'm sorry to have to call you in the evening, but I've just had a call from Parker Center. Jim Long is on his way to the hospital."

"What's wrong with him?"

"There was some sort of fight among several inmates in the dining hall during the supper hour, and Jim was knifed with a homemade shank."

"How is he?"

"He's lost a lot of blood, and he's about to lose a kidney, but he's hanging on."

"Is he in the prison hospital?"

"The warden has agreed to move him to Cedars-Sinai for the surgery. He's in the ambulance now. I'm meeting him at the hospital."

"You'd better arrange some personal security for him," Stone said.

"Why? Nobody's going to knife him at Cedars-Sinai, and anyway, there'll be a cop outside his door."

"Harvey, does anybody besides you, me, and

Long know that he's agreed to sell us his shares in Centurion?"

"Why no. . . . well, possibly."

"Who?"

"Terry Prince's attorney phoned this afternoon to try and buy the shares. I was out of the office and an associate took the call. It's possible that he might have spoken out of turn. Surely, you don't think that Prince is responsible for this."

"Did you read the piece in the *L.A. Times* about the death of Eddie Harris's daughter, Jennifer?"

"Yes, I saw it. Was she going to sell you her shares?"

"No, but she was going to vote with us."

"Oh, shit. I had no idea."

"Did you talk to Jim today?" Stone asked.

"Yes, he called my cell and gave me the combination to his safe at Centurion. I went over there and picked up the share certificate; that's why I was out of the office."

"Where is the certificate now?"

"At the office, in my safe."

"I don't suppose Jim had an opportunity to sign it."

"No, I was going to see him tomorrow morning."

"Well, Harvey, I think you'd better get a couple of armed guards over there. A cop napping outside the door isn't going to make him safe."

"I'll do that right away."

"And Harvey?"

"Yes?"

"I don't want to sound callous, but the best thing you can do to keep Jim safe is to get him to sign that certificate at the earliest possible moment—tonight, if possible. And let Prince's attorney know about it."

"I see your point; I'll do what I can."

Stone gave him his cell number. "Please call me when you have his signature. The sales documents will be in your fax machine when you get to your office tomorrow morning."

"I'll do that," Stein said.

Stone hung up, then stood and thought for a moment. There was no point in telling the others about this at the moment, he decided. Why ruin the dinner party? He turned to find Dino standing in the doorway.

"Everybody's sitting down. Everything okay?"

"Not exactly," Stone said. "Jim Long got himself shanked in some sort of fight at Metro Jail."

"Dead?"

"Bleeding. He's on his way to Cedars-Sinai to have a kidney removed."

"Any chance he's going to live to make the sale?"

"His lawyer is taking the stock certificate to the

hospital for his signature. He realizes that Long won't be safe until the stock comes to us."

"Well, Charlene has already got security in place, but what about Arrington?"

"I think I'd better talk with Mike Freeman about that," Stone said. "Strategic Services has a Los Angeles office."

"Prince has a long reach, doesn't he?"

"You could say that," Stone replied. "We're at three bodies, two of them dead, and counting."

They rejoined the party, but everyone had already taken seats at the table, so Stone would have to wait until after dinner before speaking to Mike about Arrington's security.

26

The party continued merrily until nearly midnight, very late for L.A., where movie people rose at dawn and headed to their shoots. As everyone began to drift out, Stone took Mike Freeman aside.

"Mike, that phone call I took before dinner was not good news. One of the Centurion shareholders whose stock we need to acquire to keep the studio from being sold was shanked in jail earlier this evening and is having a kidney removed at Cedars-Sinai."

"Is he going to make it?" Mike asked.

"I don't know; he's lost a lot of blood. What I'm concerned about now is Arrington's safety, since she's the largest Centurion stockholder."

"You think this fellow Prince is behind the stabbing?"

"Two other people, one a stockholder and the other her assassin, are already dead. Can your L.A. office arrange some security for Arrington, starting immediately?"

"I'll take care of it right away," Mike said, reaching for his cell phone. "Let's see, we'll need a man inside the front gate, one inside the house, near Arrington's bedroom, and three patrolling the grounds. Is it fenced the whole way around?"

Stone beckoned Manolo, who was clearing the dining table.

"Yes, Mr. Stone?"

"Manolo, does the wrought-iron fence go all the way around the property?"

"Yes, sir, and, it's all on the alarm system."

"I'll need to take a look at the system," Mike said.

"Manolo," Stone said, "Mr. Freeman is going to arrange for security guards to come to the house tonight. Please let them in when they arrive, and right now, show Mr. Freeman the security system."

"Yes, sir, Mr. Stone."

"And not a word to Arrington about this."

"No, sir, Mr. Stone."

Manolo and Mike went into the house together. Stone and Dino sat down and had a nightcap.

"Mike is arranging security for Arrington," Stone said.

"Great. What about security for you?"

"Me?"

"You're the guy who's running the show that's trying to foil Prince's takeover of Centurion."

"I hadn't thought of it that way," Stone said.

"I think we should start carrying," Dino said.

"I think you're right," Stone replied.

Stone was dressing the following morning when his cell buzzed. "Hello?"

"Stone, it's Carolyn Blaine. It's important that I see you as soon as possible."

"Can't we talk over the phone?"

"No, I don't trust the phone."

"All right, come here for breakfast; you know the way."

"I'll be there in half an hour," she said, then hung up.

Stone was the first up. Dino was apparently still asleep, and Arrington was not an early riser. He buzzed Manolo. "Manolo, I'll be having a guest for breakfast, a Ms. Blaine. She should be here in around half an hour."

"Yes, Mr. Stone. The security people arrived around one a.m. and are doing their work."

"Tell the one in the house not to be standing at Mrs. Calder's door when she wakes up. He must be discreet until I've told her about the security."

"Yes, Mr. Stone."

"We'll have some of your eggs Benedict for breakfast, this time with smoked salmon instead of ham."

"Yes, Mr. Stone."

His cell buzzed again. "Hello?"

"It's Eggers."

"Good day, Bill."

"We faxed the sales documents for Mr. Long's Centurion stock to Harvey Stein a couple of hours ago."

"That's good news. How about Baird's documents?"

"Faxed to you; also, the corporate documents and sales agreement for Arrington's airplane. Also, instructions to Chase to allow us to transfer funds from her account on her behalf. Make sure she signs where indicated. As soon as you fax that back to Chase, we can wire the funds for exercising the options on her adjoining property."

"Certainly. You know, Bill, it's great to have the firm behind me like this. I could never have gotten it all done on my own."

"You need the firm now, because you have the clients to support."

"Of course."

"And the extension of Arrington's line of credit has been granted for two hundred million."

"Again, thanks." Stone said goodbye, then hung up.

Stone ran his belt through the loops, then stopped. He took his travel gun, a Colt Government .380, from his case and put it on his belt, then slipped into a linen jacket to cover it.

His cell buzzed again. "Hello?"

"Stone, it's Harvey Stein."

"How is Jim?"

"He was in a coma when I got there—result of loss of blood, and he hasn't come to since the surgery."

"Prognosis?"

"No better than a fifty-fifty chance of recovery. If he crashes now, we'll have to start thinking about unplugging him. I'm his medical surrogate and his executor, so it will be up to me to decide if and when."

"I don't envy you that, Harvey."

"I don't envy me that, either. I'll call when there's news." He hung up.

Carolyn made it in twenty minutes, and Manolo showed her out to the pool, where he had set the table.

"You look flustered," Stone said. "Breakfast will be here shortly; would you like a mimosa?"

"No, thank you, just some orange juice."

Stone poured them each a glass from the pitcher on the table. "Now," he said, "what's up?"

"First of all, Terry Prince found out yesterday that you had been to see James Long in jail, and that he had agreed to sell you his stock."

"Oh? How did he know about that?"

"Terry is very plugged in to the LAPD, and he has taken an interest in Long, since he learned he's a stockholder. His lawyer talked to Long's law firm yesterday."

"I see."

She fidgeted for a moment. "There's more," she said. "Someone knifed Long during the dinner hour last night."

Stone decided to play dumb. "Is he all right?"

"He had surgery last night at Cedars-Sinai; I haven't heard the result yet."

"Why are you telling me all this, Carolyn?"

"You once said to me that if I needed legal advice to come to you."

"That's right, I did, but you don't appear to have done anything wrong—not from what you've told me, anyway."

"It's not that," she said. "Yesterday, quite by accident, I picked up the wrong phone line and heard Terry order Long's murder."

"Did he say that: 'Murder James Long'?"

"Not exactly."

"What did he say, exactly?"

"He said something like, 'It needs to be done tonight; tomorrow could be too late.'"

"He could have been talking about getting a haircut. What made you think he was ordering a murder?"

"Terry called me and told me to bring in the file on a project we're working on. I was with him for a good four hours before we finished. Shortly before I left, he got a phone call, and I answered. It was a man named Carter, whom I knew from other calls; he works at Parker Center. Terry took the call, and I pretended to go through the file while he talked. He said, 'Is it done?' Then he said, 'Did Long have an opportunity to sign any papers today?' I think the answer to the first question was an explanation of what had happened to Long, and the answer to the second question was no. He hung up, and I asked if everything was all right. He said he wasn't sure; a friend was having surgery at Cedars, and he wouldn't know anything until morning.

"I had some dinner with a friend, and when I got home I heard on the news that James Long had been stabbed at the jail and taken to Cedars-Sinai. It was easy to put two and two together."

"And," Stone said, "since you put two and two together only after the fact, you had no reason to call the police yesterday."

"That's right, and I'm not sure that what I could testify to is enough to get Terry tried and convicted."

"I think you're right about that," Stone said.

Manolo brought breakfast, and they began to eat.

"Tell me, Carolyn," Stone said, "do you have any idea what happened to Terry's driver, Alexei?"

"Only what I read in the papers," she said. "Terry brought up the subject, but he seemed to be as mystified as I. The man hadn't come to work the day before, and when I called his apartment there was no reply. No reply to his cell phone, either."

"What about Jennifer Harris? Any ideas about her death?"

"Who?"

"That was in the papers, too. She was the daughter of Eddie Harris, who used to run Centurion, and she had inherited his stock in the studio."

"Now that you mention it, I think I saw something about her in the papers, too, but I didn't connect her with Terry's attempt to get control of Centurion."

They finished breakfast, and Carolyn got up to go. "What should I do?" she asked.

"Nothing, for the moment—just keep an ear to the ground. Although what you've told me isn't enough for an arrest, it could be very useful at trial in conjunction with other evidence that might be found in an investigation."

"Stone," she said, picking up her handbag, "why did you tell me at the Bel-Air Hotel party not to mention to Terry that Mrs. Calder has an option to buy some property adjoining her estate?"

"I can't tell you that right now, but it's better for you that Prince doesn't know. You'll have to trust me on that."

"All right," she said, "I will."

Stone watched her walk back toward the main house, and he wondered why he was not sexually attracted to her. She was quite beautiful, after all.

27

Stone retrieved the Woodman & Weld documents from the fax machine in the house, and when he returned to the patio, Arrington and Dino were having breakfast. He put the envelope on the table and poured himself a second glass of orange juice.

"You're not eating?" Arrington asked.

"I was hungry; I ate earlier."

"What's the big envelope?"

"Many documents for your signature. Signing them will wrap up the property purchase, the airplane purchase, the purchase of Baird's shares, and it will authorize Woodman & Weld and me to transfer funds from your line of credit to pay for all of that."

"You didn't mention the purchase of James Long's shares."

Stone sighed. "There's a problem with that." He told her about the attack on Long.

"You mean Prince can have people killed in prison?"

"It's not as hard as you might imagine, if you have a contact on the inside."

"I'm beginning to feel unsafe," she said.

"You've had round-the-clock security since late last night," Stone said. "Mike Freeman arranged it, and his people are good."

"Oh, then I feel safer."

"With any luck at all you'll have everything wrapped up and will be able to fly back to Virginia tomorrow—the day after, at the most."

"You mean if James Long doesn't die."

"I mean if he signs the papers. If he dies, then we have to deal with his estate."

"Oh, God," she said.

"We have to take these things as they come," Stone said. "Everybody's working very hard to make this work."

"I know you're working hard, Stone, and I'm very impressed by how quickly you've been able to generate all the paperwork for these various trans-actions." She put her fork down. "Okay, give me a pen."

Stone guided her through the documents, then double-checked to be sure she had signed them all. Then he summoned Manolo and gave him instructions on faxing the documents.

"Before the day is out, you'll own Baird's shares, the adjoining properties, and the airplane."

"Things didn't happen this fast when I was dealing with Mr. Sharp, back in Virginia. He would have taken weeks to get all this done."

Manolo came and told Stone he had a call.

"Hello?"

"Stone, it's Rick Barron. Have you heard about Jim Long? The morning news said he's in the hospital."

"Yes. We're still going to make this happen, Rick. We just have to wait for him to be sufficiently conscious to sign the sales documents. They're in his attorney's hands now."

"What else can go wrong?"

"Don't worry. We're going to get there." Stone didn't feel as confident as he sounded, but it was important to keep the man's spirits up. "His attorney will call me when there's news, and I'll let you know immediately. Did you call any of the other shareholders about selling?"

"I stopped when I thought we had enough shares."

"Well, you'd better get back on the phone, just in case we need more shares."

"All right, I'll do that." Rick hung up.

"Anything I can do?" Dino said.

"Yes, you can call your pal Rivera and tell him there's a man at Parker Center called Carter, who is in Terry Prince's pocket and who may have been involved in Jim Long's shanking."

"I can do that," Dino said. He got up and went into the guesthouse.

"Prince is a persistent son of a bitch, isn't he?" Arrington said.

"Yes, he is."

"What are we going to do if he wins the Centurion battle?"

"Worst case, you'll probably get three thousand dollars a share for your stock. That's not too bad a downside."

"But Rick will see his beloved studio die."

"I hope not, but nothing ever remains the same; things keep changing." Stone thought maybe this was the time. "Worse comes to worst, there may be a way to keep Centurion from Prince, even if he wins this fight."

"How can we do that?" Arrington asked.

"As of today, you own—what?—eighteen acres of Bel-Air?"

"Yes, I suppose so."

"Prince has gone into the hotel business, bought several prime properties around the country. That's mostly why he wants Centurion, so he can build another. He tried to buy the Bel-Air Hotel but failed. I think he wanted it very, very badly."

"So?"

"So, if he owned your property here, he could build his own hotel in Bel-Air."

Arrington blinked. "I suppose there is enough land for that," she said. "But how would that stop him from buying Centurion?"

"You could make the sale of your land conditional on his agreeing not to acquire Centurion. I suspect that, although the Centurion deal might make better business sense, his ego would prefer having his own hotel in Bel-Air."

"You know," Arrington said, "I might like to have my own hotel in Bel-Air. That would be quite a project, wouldn't it?"

"Stop having that dream for the moment," Stone said. "Let's see how this works out."

"If you say so," she said.

28

Stone gave his car to the parking attendant at the Bel-Air and walked across the bridge to the hotel. The swans were back in the little stream, as if they had never left. Maybe they hadn't, he reflected.

Stone presented himself to the headwaiter and was shown to a large, semicircular booth at the rear of the garden restaurant, where Terry Prince was already seated.

"Forgive me for not getting up," Prince said, offering his hand as Stone slid behind the table. "Would you like a drink?"

"Some iced tea," Stone said. He reckoned he should keep his wits about him today.

Prince ordered a mimosa for himself and iced tea for Stone. "I hope you're having a pleasant stay in our city," he said.

"Very much so," Stone replied.

"You mentioned the absence of my driver."

"I read about it in the *L.A. Times.*"

"Ah, yes; I didn't see that myself."

"Then you don't know that Alexei was killed in the same fashion as Jennifer Harris?"

"Really? I did read about Ms. Harris, as I suppose you did."

"Actually, I saw the police report," Stone replied. "The puncture wound was filled with spirit gum, so that it might go unnoticed. It didn't, though."

"That sounds bizarre," Prince said.

"The mark of a practiced professional, I'd say."

"Do you have some expertise in professional murders?" Prince asked.

"I was a New York City homicide detective for many years, before I began practicing law."

"Ah, that wasn't mentioned in the announcement."

"Announcement?" Stone asked.

"You haven't seen this morning's *New York Times?*"

"No."

"There was an announcement of your joining Woodman & Weld as a partner."

"I see. Actually, I've been of counsel to the firm for rather a long time."

"Well, I congratulate you on achieving partner level in such a prestigious firm."

"Thank you."

Menus arrived, and they ordered. Stone could not resist the taco soup, a favorite of his.

"Most of my business interests are on the West Coast," Prince said, "but I'm considering some projects in New York, among them a new hotel."

"Sounds interesting," Stone said.

"I think it will be," Prince replied. "Might you have an interest in representing me for my New York projects?"

"I'm afraid I would have a conflict that would prevent me from doing so," Stone said.

"You're referring to your representation of Mrs. Calder?"

"I am."

"How did you become involved with her?"

Stone paused. Did Prince's use of "involved" have a double meaning? "We've been friends for a number of years."

"I understand she's broken ties with Howard Sharp, in Charlottesville," Prince said.

"I'm not surprised you know about that," Stone said, "having bought her house there."

"Yes, that was Mr. Sharp's last representation of her," Prince said. "I thought he did a good job."

"That means the way he did his job somehow reacted to your benefit, I suppose."

Prince laughed heartily. "You're very perceptive, Stone."

"Let's just say I think she will be happier with Woodman & Weld," Stone replied.

Lunch arrived and they began to eat.

"Stone," Prince said, pausing to take a sip of his tea. "I'm sorry we seem to be working at cross-purposes in the Centurion transaction."

"It's not a transaction yet," Stone said.

"Touché. In the Centurion offer, shall we say."

"Yes."

"I wonder if you might not soften your position in that deal if you were personally participating in it, instead of just representing Mrs. Calder."

"What are you suggesting, Terry?"

"I would not be so crass as to make you an offer," Prince said smoothly. "But if you could somehow bring the deal to a swift conclusion, you might be free to represent my New York interests all the sooner, might you not?"

"As long as you were not involved in a business deal adversarial to Mrs. Calder's interests, that would be ethically possible."

"Well, then, do you think we might move forward on the Centurion deal?"

Stone put down his fork. "I take it that Jim Long is still alive," Stone said, "and I'm beginning to think that he might even have regained consciousness."

Prince said nothing, only shrugged.

Stone's cell vibrated on his belt. "Will you excuse me a moment?" he said, sliding from behind the table and walking into the garden. "Hello?"

"Stone, it's Harvey Stein. Jim Long is awake, but not talking yet. His doctors seem very relieved, and they may let me see him before the day is out."

"That's good news, Harvey. Will you keep me posted?"

"Of course."

Stone hung up and returned to the table. "Wonder of wonders," he said, "Jim Long is awake."

"I'm very happy for him," Prince said. "You must have good sources."

"Not as good as yours," Stone said. "After all, you heard first."

"Only a short time ago."

"Still, you had time to talk with me, before I found out."

"Information is a valuable commodity," Prince said.

Stone signaled for a waiter to remove his plate. "You must have a very large payroll, Terry," he said.

"Large enough for my purposes."

"I understand the police are concerned about connections among the stabbings of Harris, Alexei, and Long. But then, you already knew that, didn't you?"

"I assure you, I have no connection to any of those events."

"No? Even though two of them are Centurion shareholders who take our side in the deal? And the other is suspected of killing Ms. Harris?"

"Again, I have no connection with any of that."

"I think the police are going to become even more interested, should an attempt be made on anyone else associated with Centurion," Stone said. "And let me tell you this: if anyone else associated with my client should have some . . . accident, I am going to take a *personal* interest in the case—over and above the police investigation."

Stone placed a hundred-dollar bill on the table and got up. "Good day," he said, and walked away.

29

Stone drove back to the house in a fury. He found Dino on his way out.

"What are you so pissed off about?" Dino asked.

"Does it show?"

"Oh, yeah."

"I just had lunch with Prince, and I regret having done so."

"Wasn't he nice?"

"He tried to bribe me to throw the Centurion deal his way."

"What did he offer you?"

"Nothing specific, just the promise of a lot of business in New York."

"Anything else?"

"He blithely denied any connection to the stabbings of Jennifer Harris and Jim Long. Long is awake, by the way, and it looks like he'll make it."

"If Prince doesn't get to him again."

"His lawyer has security on the job. Where are you going?"

"I'm going to check in with Rivera, to see if there's anything new on the recent mayhem."

"Did you tell him about this guy, Carter, at Parker Center?"

"Yeah, he's looking into it," Dino said, then added, "Arrington's around somewhere."

"I'll find her."

Stone gave Dino the car keys and watched him go. He walked through the house and emerged to find Arrington sunning herself, topless, by the pool. He walked over and kissed her on each nipple.

"That was nice," she said, smiling.

"It certainly was."

"Where have you been?"

"Having lunch with Mr. Prince."

"Did you enjoy yourself?"

"No." Stone told her the details.

"He really is slimy, isn't he?"

"I hope there's something terribly wrong with the house you sold him," Stone said.

She laughed. "I told him there were bats in the

cellar and raccoons in the attic, but he didn't believe me."

"Are there?"

"As a matter of fact, yes. It will be a nice surprise for him. I put it on the disclosure form, too, but I'll bet he didn't bother to read it."

"He implied that Howard Sharp somehow slanted things in his favor during the proceedings."

"Then he deserves the raccoons and bats."

"I think you're well rid of Mr. Sharp," Stone said.

"Well, I'm certainly a lot happier with you and Woodman & Weld," she said. "I'm very impressed at how smoothly you're all handling things. I would never have dreamed of asking Chase for a two-hundred-million-dollar loan."

"The rich are different from you and me," Stone said. "Well, from me, anyway."

"I never paid much attention to what I have," Arrington said, "as long as the check arrived every month, and there was enough to pay for the house and furnishings. That reminds me: the auction of all my furnishings is this weekend, so I hope to be able to fly home tomorrow."

"I'll speak to Mike and see that everything is ready for you."

"Thank you, sweetheart. When I'm in the new house I want you to come and visit. It would be nice if you got to know your son a little, too. I think you'll like him."

"I'm sure I will," Stone replied, though the thought of dealing with a child frightened him. "I hope I'll know what to say to him."

"Oh, he's easy to talk to; easy to listen to as well."

"I'll take your word for it."

Stone's phone buzzed, and he answered it.

"Hi, it's Mike."

"Just talking about you," Stone said.

"I hope that's good. I just wanted you to know that all the paperwork on the airplane will be finalized by the end of business today. The prepurchase inspection went very well indeed, only a few small things to be corrected. It's in beautiful shape."

"Can she fly out tomorrow morning for Virginia?"

"She can indeed. Our New York office has arranged temporary housing for her crew, while they look for something more permanent, and she now has hangar space at Charlottesville Airport."

"You've done a fantastic job for her, Mike. Please send your bill to me in New York, and I'll see that it's taken care of."

"There won't be a bill; it was mostly a few phone calls."

"You've done a lot more than that," Stone said. "I owe you."

"I have to run," Mike said. "I'll tell the crew to be ready for a nine a.m. departure tomorrow."

"Perfect." Stone hung up and gave Arrington the news.

"Oh, I'm so happy about this," she said. "I hated borrowing the Centurion jet, and I was appalled at what air charters cost."

"You'll be queen of the air," Stone said. "Start making a list of places you'd like to go."

"A happy thought."

Stone's phone rang again. "Hello?"

"It's Eggers."

"Hello, Bill."

"We've received all of Arrington's documents, properly signed, and dispersed the funds required in each case. She now owns the airplane, the Baird shares, and the property adjacent to hers. The previous owners have ninety days to vacate, as per the original option."

"Great news; I'll tell her."

"I had a call from Terrence Prince earlier today," Eggers said. "He made noise about big New York projects to come and suggested he might like us to represent him."

"I've just had lunch with him, Bill, and you can forget about that."

"Oh? I thought it an attractive idea."

"That's what he wanted you to think. He was

trying to soften me up on the Centurion deal with empty promises. You watch—there won't be any New York projects."

"I did tell him that representing him was out, until the Centurion situation is resolved."

"So did I."

"What do you think his next move will be?"

Stone paused and looked over at Arrington. "Arrington is taking her new airplane home tomorrow morning."

"Ah, you're getting her out of harm's way, then?"

"Of course."

"Stone, you might watch your own back, too."

"Dino's doing that for me," Stone said. They hung up.

"Is Bill all right?" Arrington asked.

"Never better," Stone said. He told her about the substance of the conversation with Eggers.

"All good news."

"Let's have a farewell dinner tonight; I'll take you out."

"I'd love that," she said.

30

Stone started to book a table at Spago Beverly Hills, but then thought better of it. He's already had dinner there once this trip, and with Carolyn Blaine, Prince's assistant. Instead, he booked a table at Vincenzo, an Italian restaurant he'd heard good things about.

As he pulled out of the Calder driveway, he noticed a car parked up the street—unusual, because people didn't usually park on the street in Bel-Air; they had plenty of room inside their gates. As he drove away he saw the car move out, too, staying well behind him, headlights off in the dusk. He noticed that his own headlights, on the auto setting, had come on of their own volition.

They chatted idly as they drove, with Stone keeping an eye on the car in the rearview mirror, and a few minutes later Stone pulled up in front of the restaurant. The parking valet opened his door for him, and Stone came up with a fifty-dollar bill. "I'd appreciate it if you'd keep my car parked on the street, right under that lamp ahead. There are some valuable items aboard, and I'd hate to have the car broken into."

"Of course, sir," the young man said, and from inside the restaurant, Stone watched as the car was pulled forward a few yards and parked under the streetlamp.

They were given a good table, in spite of not being regulars, and Stone was able to see his car.

"What's so valuable in your rental car?" Arrington asked.

"Nothing, really. I just don't want to make it easy for anyone to tamper with it."

"You're still concerned about my safety?" she asked.

"You're perfectly safe," he said, then slapped his forehead. "A car followed us here, and I was concerned about it. I forgot that Mike Freeman still has his security people watching you. That's who's in the car."

She laughed. "Spooked by your own people?"

"I'm afraid so."

They had a drink and ordered dinner. "You know, Stone," Arrington said, "when I last saw you, in Maine, I pretty much said that we shouldn't see each other anymore."

"I remember."

"I was hasty, I'm afraid. Of course, you're not going to come and live in Virginia, and I'm not going to live in New York anymore, but there's no reason why we can't get together now and then."

"I'm glad you think so," he replied.

"I was serious when I said that I want you to get to know Peter. If something happened to me and you became his guardian, I'd like him to already know you."

"Nothing's going to happen to you."

"Now, be realistic. I can get sick and die just like anybody else, or I could walk in front of a passing car. I'm not ill, and I'm careful, but you know what I mean."

"I know what you mean," he replied. "Why don't you bring Peter to New York for a few days, when he's on his holidays? You can both stay with me."

"Then I'd have to sneak into your bedroom every night, wouldn't I?"

"One of us would have to do the same thing in Virginia, but it would be good if he knew that we had more than a passing friendship."

"I'll give that some thought," she said.

They dined well and returned to the house, the

car still tailing them. They were greeted inside the house by Mike's inside man, who took Stone aside when Arrington had gone to her room.

"I don't want to trouble you, Mr. Barrington," the man said, "but we had a little incident after you left for dinner."

"Is something wrong?"

"I'm not sure; we had an alert from the security system, which showed a possible breach of the perimeter fence. We checked it out and found nothing."

"Why don't we take a walk around the perimeter?" Stone said.

The man spoke into a microphone dangling from his sleeve into the palm of his hand, and another man appeared. "All right, let's go," he said, producing a small flashlight and borrowing another from his colleague for Stone.

They walked down the driveway to the front gate, where another operative stepped from the shadows and checked them out.

"By the way," Stone said, "thanks for the following car when we went to dinner. At first I thought someone was up to no good."

The man stopped in the driveway. "Following car? We don't have anyone in a car, just inside the fence, as Mr. Freeman directed."

"Follow me," Stone said, "and don't wave your

flashlight around." He made his way along the wrought-iron fence to a point opposite where the car had been parked earlier, then peeked through the shrubbery. "There's the car," he said, "but we can't get at him through this fence, and I don't have a way to open the front gate. Let's just give him a scare, and maybe we can get his license plate number. Get ready with your flashlight."

"All right," the man said, stepping forward.

The two of them parted the hedge, and on Stone's signal, hit the car with both of their flashlights. A startled, wide-eyed man turned toward the light, then started his car and drove away at high speed. "Fortyish, graying hair, sideburns," Stone said.

"Did you get the plate number?" the security man asked.

"No, the license plate light was out—deliberately, I'm sure."

"Plain vanilla sedan," the man said. "I didn't even get a make."

"Maybe we've scared him off for the night," Stone said. "Come on, let's walk the rest of the perimeter."

They trudged on, lighting their way with the flashlights. As they were passing a point behind the guesthouse, the security man said, "Wait." He pointed his flashlight at the top of the fence and spotlighted something hanging on one of the sharp spires that rose from the wrought iron barrier. "There." He parted the hedge, pulled himself up on a crossbar, and retrieved the object. "Piece of blue cloth," the man said, turning his light on it.

"Cotton," Stone said. "Maybe from a shirttail." Then, from behind them a shot fractured the silence. "Come on!" Stone said, drawing the pistol from his belt.

They both ran, flat out, toward the house. Stone opened the rear door and started to run down the central hallway. Then they saw a man crumpled on the floor. The other security man stepped from the living room into the hallway, weapon drawn.

"I hit him," he said, keeping his gun on the inert figure.

The first security man bent down, turned the man over, and kicked away a silenced, small-caliber pistol. He felt for a pulse at the neck. "Nothing," he said. "He's dead."

The man was midthirties, dark hair, dressed in a tail-out dark shirt, jeans, and sneakers. The bullet had exited his chest near the heart.

Stone bent and found where his shirttail was torn, then went through the man's pockets. "Nothing," he said, "absolutely nothing—not a cent, not a wallet, nothing."

"Get the fingerprint scanner from my car," one

security man said to the other. "We'll get his prints before the cops get here. Then you can call nine-one-one."

Arrington came out of a door across the hall and stopped.

"Oh, my God," she said.

Stone led her back to her bedroom. "Everything's all right," he said. "You're perfectly safe."

"I wasn't for a while, though, was I?" she asked.

Stone didn't answer, just hugged her.

31

Stone was standing in the driveway when the police cars—three of them, one unmarked—pulled up and stopped. He flashed his badge: "NYPD, retired," he said. "Please turn off the flashing lights; let's not disturb the neighbors any more than necessary."

Dino came walking up the driveway, followed by another man. He introduced Sergeant Rivera to Stone, and Stone introduced them to the lead detective.

"We've got a man down in the central hall of the house," he said to the detective. "One gunshot wound to the back, exiting the chest, DOA. We have security people here to prevent such a thing, but we found where he came over the rear fence, leaving this." He handed the scrap of blue cloth to the detective. "You'll see where it came from his shirt. We kicked his gun to one side when we turned him over to see how badly he was hurt, but nobody has touched it since."

"Motive?" the detective asked.

"Uncertain," Stone said. "Maybe robbery, maybe something to do with a business deal. This is the home of the late Vance Calder; his widow is in the house, but she saw nothing."

The detective nodded. "I'll need to talk to her."

Stone went and brought Arrington out and introduced them. Then he sat and listened as she was interviewed. When they were done, he took her to her room. "You get some sleep," he said, kissing her.

Somebody from the medical examiner's office showed up, followed by two EMTs in an ambulance. They began to do their work.

Eventually, the ME joined Stone and the detective. "Deceased, probably instantly; gunshot wound, through-and-through, fresh corpse, been dead less than an hour."

"I'll need the gun that fired the shot," the detective said, and Mike's security man handed it over, along with his gun permit and a business card. The detective made some notes, then returned the permit to him. "Remain available," the detective said, and the man nodded.

Mike Freeman turned up shortly. "I'm sorry I was so long; I was having dinner in Malibu," he said.

Stone silently wondered where in Malibu.

"With Charlene," Mike said.

Stone nodded and brought him up-to-date. "Your people did well," he said, "but I didn't. I took Arrington to dinner, and a car followed us, but I thought it was your people. Turned out, I was wrong."

Photographs of the corpse and the scene were taken. Then the police cleared the scene and took down the yellow tape. Manolo turned up with a mop and a pail and cleaned up the blood, as if he did the same every night.

"It's time everybody went to bed," Stone said, shooing everybody out of the house but the security people and Dino. Then he went to Arrington's room and knocked softly on the door.

"Come in," she said, and when he had stepped inside. "Close the door and come to bed; I don't want to sleep alone."

Stone undressed and climbed in next to her. "I told Manolo breakfast at seven; Mike's people will deliver you to Burbank airport whenever you want to leave."

She snuggled close to him. "That's the nice thing about a private jet," she said. "Departure time is whenever you feel like it." She reached down and fondled him, and they had an active half hour before falling asleep.

She woke Stone at six-thirty, already half-dressed. "I'll finish packing and join you for breakfast," she said.

Stone went back to the guesthouse, showered, and changed, then joined Dino at the poolside table.

"You two sleep okay?" Dino asked.

"Yes, considering."

"Are you still rattled? You were last night."

"I'm still angry," Stone said.

"It was Prince, you think? He wants Arrington dead?"

"No, he wants *me* dead," Stone replied. "I've purposely made myself the main impediment to his deal, so he wants me out of the way. Me dead wouldn't cause much of a fuss; Arrington dead would make world-wide headlines."

"I buy that," Dino said. "Still, it seems reckless."

"I think he's beyond caring about that, just obsessed with the deal. What's the news from your pal Rivera?"

"He pulled in this guy Carter, at Parker Center, and scared the shit out of him. No arrest, but the department fired him."

"I'm sure that Prince will see that he receives a nice pension contribution," Stone said.

"Or just kill him, like Alexei," Dino pointed out.

Arrington joined them, looking fresh and rested, and Manolo served them breakfast.

"Didn't take you long to pack," Stone said.

"There isn't much to pack when you're traveling from your house to your house," she said.

"True."

"How long will it take me to get to Virginia?" she asked.

Stone thought about it. "Not more than four hours," he said. "Something you should think about when you get home is buying a hangar."

"Good idea," she said. "Why rent?"

"I'll research it for you, if you like, see what the market is like, what's available."

"Thank you, I'd like that."

They finished breakfast, and Stone walked her to the Bentley. Manolo would drive her, accompanied by two unmarked security cars. "Have a good flight," he said.

"I'm sure I will," she replied. "I'm looking forward to it." She kissed him, got into the Bentley, and was driven away.

Stone was back at the table when Mike Freeman called.

"Hello?"

"Hi, did she get away?"

"She just left."

"I'm on my way to Burbank; I'll fly to Virginia with Arrington, and have our CJ4 meet me there and take me to New York. I had my aviation department check out the hangar situation at Charlottesville," he said.

"I was going to do that myself," Stone replied.

"There's a nice corporate hangar available—office, crew quarters, etc. They want half a million."

"I'll recommend it to her," Stone said.

"I'll call the crew and tell them to take the airplane there when they land. I'll do the deal, if you like, subject to Arrington's approval, and your people can send the check."

"Go ahead." Stone hung up, and Mike called back in ten minutes.

"I got it for four-fifty," he said. "I told them to send the paperwork to Bill Eggers. I'll show it to her when we land and get her approval."

"You make life so easy, Mike."

"It's what I do. Talk to you later." He hung up.

Stone called Arrington in the car and explained the deal to her.

"I approve," she said.

"Just what I always like to hear a client say. Call me when you've actually seen it. Mike's going to fly to Virginia with you and show you the hangar when you land. Let me know what you think."

"Will do."

Stone went back to the remains of his breakfast.

"So," Dino said, "what's next?"

"I think it's time to take the game to Prince," Stone said. "I'm tired of playing catch-up."

32

Stone called Carolyn Blaine. "Are you available for lunch?"

"I don't think we should be seen in public," she said.

"Then come here."

"One o'clock? I want to be sure Terry has left the office before I do."

"That will be fine."

Stone hung up.

"What do you want with that dame?" Dino asked.

"To get to Terry Prince; she'll know how best to do it."

Stone received Carolyn by the pool, and Manolo offered them a lobster salad for lunch.

"I hear Jim Long is in and out of consciousness," she said. "What do you hear?"

"I haven't heard," Stone replied. "I'll hear when there's a change."

"What did you think of your lunch with Terry?" she asked.

"He confirmed all my worst suspicions about him."

"Which are?"

"Do I have to tell you?"

"I'm reluctant to say anything to you that might be quoted later."

"Am I the only attorney from whom you've sought advice?"

"Yes, you are, but I'm very nervous. If your worst suspicions of Terry are valid, then it's very dangerous for me to talk to you, let alone see you."

"I trust you've erased me from your cell phone."

"I have," she said, "and I'd appreciate it if you'd do the same with your phone."

"Are you worried that Terry might somehow gain access to my phone?"

"You never know," she said, digging into her salad.

Stone poured them a glass of Sauvignon blanc. "Let me ask your advice," he said. "Suppose you were in opposition to Terry; how would you vex him?"

"Vex him? That's rather an archaic form, isn't it?"

"How would you get under his skin? Upset him?"

"I'd outbid him for something he wanted."

"That's too expensive a way to vex him."

"Then I'd find something else he wanted."

Stone smiled. "That's a nice thought."

"Do you have something in mind?"

"Maybe it's time to let him know what you know about this property."

"All I know is that there's some acreage."

"There are eighteen acres," Stone replied. "Arrington recently took up her option on two adjoining plots."

"Eighteen of the most expensive residential acres in the United States? That might interest Terry," she said, "but I don't think he would enjoy subdividing it and selling the lots."

"How about living in this house? Or building his own?"

"He's well-stocked with houses," Carolyn said. "He has five, scattered here and there, and two of them are in Beverly Hills and Malibu."

"How about creating his own Bel-Air hotel on the property of America's all-time biggest movie star?"

She put down her fork. "Now *that* would turn his head."

"Would it turn his head away from the Centurion deal?"

"He can afford to do both."

"But he can't do both," Stone said. "If he wants this property, he'd have to end his attempted takeover of Centurion and agree never to try again."

Carolyn took a sip of her wine and looked thoughtful. "I think you've got it," she said. "The one thing in Los Angeles, maybe in the world, that he would most like to have. He was very, very upset when his offer for the Bel-Air Hotel was rejected."

"I suppose I could call and offer him the property," Stone said, "but it might work better if you somehow learned of its availability—not through me—and let him know. I'm sure you could collect a very nice commission on that sale, especially since it wouldn't involve a broker."

Carolyn had stopped eating and drinking; she was just staring into the middle distance. "My God!" she said finally. "How would I have learned about it, except through you?"

"Arrington took up the option on the adjoining acreage just a few days ago," Stone said. "Transactions of that sort are part of the public record, aren't they?"

"Yes, they are," Carolyn said. "And I have a contact in that city office who could very well have let me know about this one."

"Well," Stone said. "There you are."

Carolyn stood up, dropping her napkin on the patio. "I have to go," she said, then practically ran from the house.

"I think that worked," Stone said aloud to himself.

33

Dino returned to the house late in the afternoon. "I've got news," he said.

"Tell me," Stone replied.

"Terry Prince's guy at Parker Center? The one who probably set up Jim Long's shanking?"

"I remember."

"He's disappeared."

"What a shock!" Stone replied, laughing. "What's your best guess: was he paid off and sent away or does he now reside in the La Brea Tar Pits?"

"My friend Rivera would like to know," Dino said.

"My money's on La Brea, or some other equally suitable resting place."

Manolo paged Stone on the house phone, and he picked it up. "Yes?"

"Mrs. Calder is on line one for you," Manolo said.

Stone punched the button. "Hello, there; safe and sound in Charlottesville, I hope."

"Safe and sound at home," she replied.

"How was your flight?"

"Absolutely wonderful! And Mike Freeman was very good company. His company airplane met him in Charlottesville and flew him to New York, but not before he showed me my new hangar. It's wonderful! I could almost live there myself."

"I'll get New York to wire the funds, then," Stone said.

"The crew are living there, until we can find something more permanent for them in town."

"When's your auction?"

"Tomorrow morning. The auctioneers have been working here the whole time I've been away. It's very odd to have a tag on every object in your house."

"When do you move out?"

"Tomorrow morning, early. They're packing my things now. I've taken a very nice furnished house down the road for eighteen months. Phone numbers will be the same."

"How much do you hope to raise in the auction?"

"As much as I spent, I fervently hope!"

"Good luck with that."

"Any news from James Long?"

"No, and frankly, that worries me."

"What will you do if he doesn't recover?"

"Regroup."

"What does that mean?"

"Well, I have an idea for how to redirect Mr. Prince's attention."

"And how would you do that?"

"Get him interested in buying your Bel-Air property for a hotel."

"But that's *my* plan!"

"I didn't say sell it to him, just get him interested. That should buy us some time to get the Centurion shares nailed down."

"Well, I'm certainly not selling to him; you remember that."

"Don't worry."

"I have to go now and finish packing."

"Bye-bye." He hung up. "Arrington is very happy now; she likes her new airplane."

"Who wouldn't?" Dino asked.

Stone's cell phone vibrated. "Hello?"

"Hey, babe, it's Charlene."

Stone felt the usual stirring in his loins at the sound of her voice. "Hey, Charlene."

"Would you and Dino like to go to a Malibu dinner party with Hetty and me this evening?"

"Dino I and would be delighted."

"Then come get us at six-thirty."

"Will do."

"Bye."

"You and I would be delighted to do what?" Dino asked.

"We're taking Charlene and Hetty to a dinner party in Malibu tonight, picking them up at six-thirty."

"I'll pack my toothbrush," Dino said.

They drove out to Malibu in Vance Calder's Bentley Arnage, which Stone thought might get them a better parking spot from the valets at the party. He was right.

The dinner party was a mile up the beach toward L.A. from Charlene's house in the Colony. "Whose party is this?" Stone asked her.

"His name is Jack Schmeltzer; he's an independent producer, and he has a production deal at Centurion. He's produced a couple of my pictures, and I still like him. That's saying a lot."

The house was a Bauhaus wonderland, glass and very little apparent steel. Once inside, they had a spectacular view of the Pacific with the sun low in the sky, and the dinner crowd, at least forty people by Stone's estimate, was pretty spectacular, too. The women were all gorgeous, and the men all looked very rich. Stone was glad he'd brought the Bentley.

They had just placed an order with a waiter for drinks when Stone peered through the glass living room wall out onto the deck. There he saw Terry Prince leaning on the rail, holding court with half a dozen people close around him.

"Shall we go out and say hello?" Dino asked.

"Let's let him come to us," Stone said.

"Why do you think he will?"

"I sent him a message, sort of. Believe me, he is overwhelmingly curious."

"What sort of message?"

"It's complicated; I'll tell you about it later. I wouldn't want to be overheard in this crowd."

Their host, Jack Schmeltzer, appeared, kissed Charlene and Hetty on their cheeks, and introduced himself to Stone and Dino.

"Thanks for letting us come to your home, Jack," Stone said.

"I'm very glad to have you," Schmeltzer said. "I've heard a lot about you the past couple of days. How's Jim Long doing?"

"In and out of it, last I heard," Stone said. "I'm hoping for the best."

"I hear he's willing to sell you his shares," Schmeltzer said.

"The rumor is true."

"And I hear that would give you control of Centurion."

"It would give my client control," Stone said.

Schmeltzer looked toward the front door. "I have more guests arriving," he said. "Perhaps we could find a moment to talk privately after dinner?"

"Of course," Stone said.

Schmeltzer wandered off to greet his guests, and Stone looked out at the deck. Terry Prince had disappeared.

"Good evening," someone said from behind him.

Stone turned to find Prince standing there. He wondered how he had managed to sneak up on him.

"Can we talk?" Prince asked.

34

Prince took Stone's arm and propelled him to a corner of the room behind the grand piano, the player of which was apparently on break. Stone noticed that four other men wearing studiedly casual outfits moved with them. Prince had security, from all appearances, and Stone wondered why.

Stone extricated his arm from Prince's grip. "What can I do for you?" he asked.

"First of all," Prince said, "I want to apologize for the tenor of our conversation when we last met. It was not my purpose to establish an adversarial relationship with you or your client, and things, somehow, went awry. I hope we can establish a more cordial atmosphere for discussions from here on in."

"I hope so, too," Stone replied. "Now, what discussions?"

Prince looked around as if he were worried that someone might overhear them. "I understand that Arrington Calder has bought two pieces of property adjoining her Bel-Air estate. This is a matter of public record."

"Then I have no problem confirming it," Stone said.

"May I ask, then, what do those acquisitions bring her total acreage to?"

"I believe it's eighteen acres," Stone said.

"And this is quite near the Bel-Air Country Club?"

"Some of the property is directly across the street."

"May I ask," Prince said again, "how she and her late husband came to own such a large chunk of Bel-Air?"

"In much the same way that Vance Calder came to own such a large chunk of Centurion: a little at a time, as he was able to afford it. Vance enjoyed his privacy, and he liked having his neighbors, whoever they might be, at some remove."

"It astonishes me," Prince said, "that this piece of property could exist in Bel-Air without my having known about it until now."

"Neither I nor my client has concealed this from you."

"I would like you to know, and I would be

grateful if you would communicate this to Mrs. Calder, that I would be very interested in buying the whole property from her."

"For what purpose?" Stone asked.

"You may recall that I am in the hotel business," Prince replied.

"You want to build a new hotel in the heart of Bel-Air?"

"That is correct."

"In spite of the nearby competition from the well-established Bel-Air Hotel, which has just undergone a major refurbishment?"

"I am competitive by nature," Prince said, "and I am perfectly capable of creating a hotel experience that would outshine that of the present hotel."

"Would this have anything to do with your inability to buy the Bel-Air Hotel?" Stone asked.

"As I said, I am competitive by nature."

"Well," Stone said, "that is a very interesting idea. What makes you think you could get planning permission to build a hotel on that site?"

"I have already explored that possibility with the relevant authorities, and I am assured that they would regard a low-rise, discretely designed and landscaped hotel a welcome addition to the community. They were particularly pleased that I offered to put all parking underground."

"Well, that's all very optimistic of you, Mr. Prince."

"Call me Terry, please."

"Terry, what sort of offer did you have in mind for the property?"

"Something on the order of a hundred and fifty million dollars," Prince replied.

Stone shook his head. "I don't think I could recommend such a price to my client."

"What did you have in mind?" Prince asked.

"Well, I haven't had the opportunity to research the land values, but I should think something north of two hundred million dollars would be a good starting point for negotiations."

Prince blinked. "And you haven't researched the land values?"

"No, but I know what Mrs. Calder paid for her two recent acquisitions, which were based on the property values of four years ago, when her late husband took the options."

"Would she sell at the right price?"

"I don't know, really, but I do know that she enjoys visiting her property in Bel-Air, and since she has no need of the money, I'm uncertain what her reaction would be."

"All right, then," Prince said, "let's see if we can move this along. Please convey to your client that I will pay her two hundred million dollars for her property, *and* I will build her a house of her own design on the property that she may occupy for her lifetime, with full hotel services provided."

"Provided at no cost to her?" Stone asked.

Prince bit his lip. "All right, all services provided at no cost to her."

"Well," Stone said, shrugging, "next time I speak to her, I'll mention your interest and see what she has to say."

Prince looked irritated. "I would appreciate it if you would make it your business to convey my offer to her at the earliest possible moment, certainly no later than close of business on Monday. And please tell her that I wish my offer kept in the strictest confidence until such time as I wish to announce the acquisition permanently."

"I don't think you want to press her," Stone said. "Mrs. Calder is a woman who does not respond well to pressure."

"Of course not," Prince said.

"I should also tell you that I believe strongly that your pursuit of Centurion Studios would be a serious impediment to her consideration of your offer."

"*What?*"

"Both Mrs. Calder and her late husband have had a great affection for their association with Centurion, and she would be extremely reluctant to do business with someone who threatened the existence of the studio as it now is presently constituted."

"My offer does not involve Centurion in any way. These are two separate transactions."

"Mrs. Calder won't see it that way," Stone said. "Shall we just forget this conversation?"

"Please convey my offer to her as it now stands," Prince said. "And call me when you've spoken to her."

Stone shrugged. "If you wish," he said, "but I'm not optimistic about this."

"Perhaps she can learn to be optimistic about two hundred million dollars and a free house."

"Speaking of houses," Stone said, "when are you planning to move into your new Virginia residence?"

"I was planning to move in immediately," Prince said, "but I now understand that there is a problem in the house with raccoons and bats."

"I believe she stated that on the disclosure form," Stone said, "and she told me she also mentioned it to you personally."

"I did not think she was serious," Prince said frostily. "Good day."

And he marched out of the house, followed by his armed retinue.

35

The pianist returned to his work, and Stone moved out of the corner and back into the thick of the party.

Jack Schmeltzer, his host, reappeared. "Why don't we step out onto the deck for a moment?" he said to Stone.

"Of course," Stone replied. They moved through the French doors and onto the now-empty expanse of teak overlooking the Pacific.

"I know, of course," Schmeltzer said, "of the controversy over the sale of part of the Centurion property."

"I suppose word has gotten around," Stone said.

"I invited Terrence Prince here this evening to

get a close look at him. We don't move in the same circles."

"I'm not sure what circles Mr. Prince moves in," Stone said, "though I did notice that he brought more than himself to your dinner party."

"Yes, he told me they are all ex-Secret Service agents."

"Did he mention why he felt he needed that sort of security?"

"I asked him that," Schmeltzer replied, "but he was evasive. Quite frankly, from what I've been hearing, there are people around who need protection from Prince. Are the rumors true?"

"I'm not entirely certain which rumors you're referring to," Stone said. "Can you be more specific?"

"The rumors about Jennifer Harris and Jim Long."

"Ah, yes. I've heard those particular rumors, too," Stone said. "I'm inclined to give them a certain degree of credibility."

"You know," Schmeltzer said, "I knew Vance Calder pretty well; I produced three pictures with him, and I liked him a lot. If Vance were still alive, I would be on his side of this deal."

"How do you feel about his widow?" Stone asked.

"I've met her once, and she was charming, but I don't really know her."

"I see."

"I'll tell you this, though: having now seen Mr. Prince up close, I like Arrington Calder more than him."

"Are you a shareholder, Jack?"

"I own fifteen thousand shares."

"Are you interested in selling them?"

Schmeltzer gazed out to sea. "What do you hear from Jim Long?" he asked.

"I hear he's in and out of consciousness but not well enough to make a business decision."

"And you need his shares for a majority?"

"That's correct."

"Do you know the reason for this dinner party, Stone?"

"No, I'm afraid not."

"I opened a picture last weekend, *Window Shade*."

"I hope it's doing well."

"It brought in sixty-five million dollars domestic for the weekend. It's the biggest hit of my career, and I think it's going to have legs both in this country and around the world."

"I congratulate you."

"I made that picture at Centurion for a third less than it would have cost to produce at a major, and it's going to make me rich beyond my fondest dreams."

"I congratulate you again."

"The fact is, when I agreed to sell my shares to Prince, I did it because I needed the money to make my next film. Now I don't need the money."

"And?"

"I won't sell Arrington my shares, but I'll vote with her and Rick Barron against the sale." Schmeltzer offered his hand. "You have my word on it."

Stone took his hand and shook it warmly. "Thank you, Jack. That means that Centurion is going to be the studio you've always known, both for your next picture and the one after that, and for a long time to come."

Schmeltzer smiled. "Let's go get some dinner."

They walked back into the living room where a line was forming for a huge buffet at one end. Stone found Charlene. "Hungry?" he asked.

"Always. How did you and Jack get along?"

"Famously," Stone replied.

"Is he on board?"

"I believe he is." Stone looked at her. "Did you have anything to do with his change of heart?"

"Well," she said, "this afternoon I fucked his brains out."

Stone burst out laughing.

Dino and Hetty joined them in the buffet line. "What's so funny?" he asked.

"Tell you later," Stone replied.

"You look awfully relaxed," Dino said.

"I think I'm more relaxed than at any time since we arrived in this town," Stone replied.

Dino looked at Hetty. "I'm planning to get more relaxed myself."

The four of them sat at Charlene's breakfast table the following morning.

"Feeling relaxed, Dino?" Stone asked.

"You bet your ass," Dino replied, and the women laughed.

Stone's cell phone buzzed, and he stepped out of the room to take the call. "Hello?"

"Stone, it's Harvey Stein; Jim Long is conscious, and his doctor says he's going to make a complete recovery."

"That's good news, Harvey. Thanks for letting me know."

"I'm going to wait a day or two before asking him to sign the documents and transfer the shares. I want to be sure that he's right on top of things before such a big move."

"That's fine with me, Harvey; we're not so much under the gun now."

"Why is that?"

"We've rounded up another fifteen thousand shares to vote with us."

"Do you still want to buy Jim's shares?"

"Yes, we do."

"Well, that's a relief; he certainly needs the money."

"Has anything developed on the case against him?"

"I'm going to use his condition to try and get him bail, so he can recuperate at home. And once the prosecutor hears he's in the money again and can fight back, I think I can get the case dropped. They're really after Barbara Eagle."

"I understand, and I wish you luck. Let me know when Jim has completed the sale, and I'll get the funds wired."

"Thanks, Stone." They both hung up.

Stone called Rick Barron and gave him the news about Jack Schmeltzer's decision to vote his shares against the sale.

"What a relief!" Rick said. "This has been a real roller-coaster ride; what else can happen?"

"Don't ask," Stone replied.

36

Stone was driving back to the Calder house when his phone buzzed again. He stopped at a traffic light. "Hello?"

"It's Carolyn Blaine; where are you right now?"

"At Pacific Coast Highway and Sunset," he said.

"Can you meet me at a coffee shop in fifteen minutes?"

"Where?"

She gave him the address. "It's near my office."

"I'm on my way." He hung up and turned left on Sunset.

"Who was that?" Dino asked.

"Carolyn Blaine."

"What did she want?"

"She wants me to meet her in fifteen minutes. She's nervous about talking on the phone."

Stone drove to the address in Westwood and parked the car. "I'll leave the a/c on for you," he said to Dino, then got out and walked into the coffee shop. Carolyn was already at a table.

Stone sat down, and they both ordered coffee. "What's up?"

"I should ask you that," she said. "Terry has gotten very edgy and prickly, too."

"Why?"

"For some reason, you really get to him. Every time he sees you he comes back fuming. It's creepy."

"Well, I'm sorry if I've made life more difficult for you."

"What did you talk about last night at Jack Schmeltzer's?"

"Terry took me aside and talked to me about Arrington Calder's property in Bel-Air. Thanks for passing that information."

"You're welcome; what did he say?"

"He offered two hundred million bucks and to build a house for her on the grounds."

"He'll go higher," she said.

"How high?"

"Two-twenty-five, maybe two-fifty mil."

"Wow."

"It's a unique piece of property," she said. "There's nothing else like it in the United States. He likes a lot that it's across the street from the

Bel-Air Country Club. He's a member there, and he thinks he could do some sort of deal with them to let his hotel guests play there."

"He seems to be moving very fast."

"Oh, yes; he's already got his architects doing site plans."

"Yes, he told me about his idea for putting all the parking underground."

"It's a good use of the space; he can put buildings or tennis courts over the garage area. Have you heard anything from Jim Long?"

"I heard this morning that he's conscious and will make a full recovery."

"When Terry hears that he's going to go absolutely nuts."

"You think he might make another attempt on Long's life?"

"In the state he's in, he's capable of anything. Did you come to any sort of agreement on the Centurion deal?"

"No. In fact, I told him that Arrington would not consider selling him the Bel-Air property without a binding agreement for him to withdraw from the Centurion deal first."

Carolyn looked astonished. "And he agreed to that?"

"No, just the opposite, but I think he'll come around."

"I wouldn't count on it," she said.

"What is it that I don't know?"

"I've learned that the money behind the Centurion deal is from some business associates of his late brother, the drug king."

"South American interests?"

"Colombian and Mexican. They're very excited about the Centurion property, and they fronted all the planning money."

"How are they likely to feel about the Bel-Air deal?"

"Oh, Terry would never let them in on that. That will be his personal triumph, his pet project. If those people ever thought that he would kill the Centurion deal in order to buy the Bel-Air property, they would be incensed, and they're not the sort of people you'd want angry with you."

"That's very interesting," Stone said.

"It's Long's shares that will give you a majority of the votes, isn't it?"

"It is," Stone said. He wasn't about to tell her about Jack Schmeltzer's shares.

"How did you get on with Jack Schmeltzer?" she asked.

"I shook his hand; he was very cordial."

"Did the Centurion deal come up in your conversations?"

"No. Why do you ask?"

"Well, he's one of the shareholders that Terry has in his pocket."

"I didn't know that," Stone said.

"You didn't know Schmeltzer before last night?"

"No, someone else invited me to his party. I'd never heard of him before that."

"Are you really serious about selling Terry the Bel-Air property?"

"If the price is right, and I think building Arrington a house would be a very good carrot."

She looked at her watch and set down her coffee cup. "I've got to get back," she said. "He'll be out of his meeting soon, and I want to be back in my office by then."

"Carolyn, if you get the impression that Prince is going to make a move against Jim Long, please get in touch. He's got personal security now, but he may want to beef it up."

"Well, I can give you my opinion on that," she said. "If Long goes back to jail, he's a dead man."

"Thanks, I'll pass that along."

She shook Stone's hand and left.

Stone paid the bill and went back to the car, where Dino had a jazz station on the Bentley's radio.

"So?"

"She says Prince is getting crazy," Stone replied. "She says the money behind the Centurion deal is

drug-related, and if the deal falls through, his partners will . . . well, they'll be very angry."

"Interesting," Dino said.

"I told Prince that there would be no deal on
the Bel-Air property unless he dropped his bid for
Centurion."

"Well," Dino chuckled, "he can't do that, can
he? Not without making the wrong people mad."

"Seems that way," Stone said.

"You're going to nail him to the wall, aren't
you?" Dino asked.

"Only if I get the chance," Stone replied.

37

Stone was back at the Calder house when Rick Barron called.

"Stone, the Centurion shareholders' meeting is set for early next week to take a vote on Prince's final offer."

"Has he come up with a final offer yet?"

"No, and he's playing his cards very close to his vest."

"We have a couple of new cards, too."

"Tell me."

"Jim Long is recovering; I think we'll own his shares before the meeting."

"And if we don't?"

"We have fifteen thousand new shares that will vote our way."

"From whom?"

"I promised I wouldn't say. He doesn't want it known until he actually votes. Frankly, I don't blame him, what with the way that others have been dealt with."

"Neither do I," Rick said. "Do you feel confident he will actually vote with us?"

"He gave me his word, and I had a very strong impression that he meant it."

"God, I hope I get through this without having a stroke," Rick said.

"Just relax, Rick; it's going to be all right."

"I hope you're right, Stone. Talk to you later." They both hung up.

Manolo came out to the patio and handed Stone a brown envelope. "This was delivered by messenger a moment ago."

Stone opened the envelope and found a formal offer for the Bel-Air property for two hundred fifty million and the new house. There was no mention of the Centurion deal. Stone called Arrington.

"Hello?"

"You out of your house?"

"I am; I'm in the rental."

"We got an offer from Prince for your Bel-Air property a moment ago: two hundred fifty million and a house for you, built to your specs."

"Wow!" she said. "I never thought he'd go that high."

"It's a rich offer, no doubt."

"But?"

"But there's no mention of the Centurion deal. I told him you wouldn't consider an offer that didn't include that."

"What do you think he will do?"

"I've learned that the Centurion deal money is coming from some very sleazy people who would go nuts if he backed out of it."

"So he's—what's the expression?"

"Between a rock and a hard place."

"Exactly. What do you want to do?"

"I want to ignore the offer."

"And how do you think he will react?"

"He'll be very upset. The Centurion shareholders' meeting is scheduled for early next week, to vote on his final offer, and we now have the votes to kill the deal."

"Does he know that?"

"No. He's going to get a rude shock when the votes are tallied."

"Do you think he'll still want the Bel-Air property if the Centurion deal doesn't happen for him?"

"I think he will, but I don't know what the consequences of the failed deal might be."

"What should I do?"

"Nothing. I won't even respond to the offer on Bel-Air. Let him stew in his own juices."

"If he calls me directly, what should I tell him?"

"Refuse to discuss it; refer him to me."

"Whatever you say, Stone."

"Those are words I don't hear nearly often enough."

She laughed. "Bye." She hung up.

Stone put the offer back in its envelope and tossed it on the table. It might make a nice souvenir, he thought. He picked up the phone and buzzed Manolo.

"Yes, Mr. Stone?"

"Manolo, if a Mr. Prince phones me, I'm not available, and you don't know when I will be."

"Yes, Mr. Stone." He hung up.

Dino came out of the guesthouse in fresh clothes. "Lunch?"

"Don't mind if I do," Stone said. He called Manolo and ordered for them. Stone showed Dino the offer.

"Wow!" Dino said.

"That's what Arrington said."

"Is she going to take it?"

"Nope. We're not even going to respond."

"I think you'd better start traveling with a bodyguard," Dino said.

"But Dino, I have you; what more security do I need?"

"I hope you're right, pal."

Stone's cell phone buzzed. He checked the caller ID before answering. "Hello?"

"It's Harvey Stein; I have good news."

"I can always use good news," Stone said.

"I saw the judge this morning, and I've gotten Jim released on bail. His doctor says we can take him home tomorrow morning."

"That is good news, Harvey."

"There's more. He signed the sales documents and the stock certificates just a moment ago."

"That's great news, Harvey; messenger them to me at the Calder house, and I'll get the funds wired"—he looked at his watch—"just as soon as I receive them."

"I'll bring them myself," Stein said. "Is now a good time?"

"It is," Stone said.

"I'll be there in half an hour."

They hung up. "Long has signed," Stone said, "and he got bail."

"Congratulations," Dino said.

"Harvey Stein is bringing over the completed documents. Then I'll call Bill Eggers and get the money wired."

Lunch arrived, and they had just finished eating when Manolo escorted Harvey Stein out to the patio. Stone shook his hand and introduced Dino.

"Here you are," Harvey said, handing him the

documents. "Take a look and see if they're properly executed."

Stone went through the papers. "Perfect," he said. "Just a moment." He called Eggers and told him to wire the funds to Long's account, then hung up. "Long's account will have the funds within the hour," he said to Stein.

"What do you think Terry Prince's reaction will be when he hears?" Stein asked.

"Well, if our experience holds, he's already heard about it, and we're both still alive. Now that we own the shares, he has no reason for another attempt on Jim's life, unless he just enjoys revenge."

"I'm not taking any chances," Harvey said. "I've doubled the security at Jim's house."

"Good move," Stone said. His cell phone went off, and he checked it. "That's Terry Prince," he said.

"What are you going to say to him?" Stein asked.

"I'm not going to say anything to him," Stone said, putting away his cell phone.

38

Stone stretched out on his bed after lunch and switched on the TV for something to lull him to sleep. The first image he saw was a car in flames, but what really caught his attention was the glass and steel house in the background.

A voiceover came on. "Early this morning the Malibu Fire Department answered a call to the beach home of film producer Jack Schmeltzer, whose new film, *Window Shade*, opened last weekend to record grosses." A two-shot followed: a reporter and a fireman.

"Somebody apparently soaked a rag in gasoline, stuffed it into the fuel cap, and basically turned the car into a giant Molotov cocktail," the fireman said. "It's a pity; it was a classic 1950s Mercedes convertible."

"Mr. Schmeltzer was unavailable for comment," the reporter said.

Stone rewound the DVR to the beginning of the report and called Dino. "Come in here; there's something I want you to see."

Dino came into the room and took a chair. "Shoot." He watched the news report, an expression of disbelief on his face. "It's Prince at work," he said. "At least he didn't kill anybody this time. How is this going to affect your share count?"

"I don't know," Stone replied. "I guess it hinges on how scared Jack Schmeltzer is. I hope he's just mad."

"I would be," Dino said.

"So would I, but I don't know Schmeltzer."

Stone's phone rang. "Hello?"

"Hey, it's Charlene; have you heard what happened at Jack Schmeltzer's house?"

"I just saw it on TV."

"Have you spoken to Jack?"

"I don't even have his phone number," Stone said.

"I don't have his home number, either," she said, "but you can reach him at Centurion."

"I'll call him," Stone said. "Talk to you later." He hung up, called the studio, and asked for Schmeltzer. A secretary put him on hold.

"Hello, Stone?"

"Yes, Jack; I just saw the TV news report."

"Can you believe that son of a bitch?"

"No, I can't."

"I'd sue him, if I could prove he did it. That car just went through a ground-up, eight-month restoration, a hundred and forty grand's worth."

"Don't do anything, Jack; just stick it to him at the stockholders' meeting. That's the best revenge."

"You're right. I'd like to punch him in the nose, but you're right: that's the way to get him."

"Don't mention this to anyone; if you run into Prince, behave as if nothing has happened. Be cordial, make him think you're still in his corner."

"How'd he find out I'm voting with you?"

"I don't know. His assistant asked if we talked, but I said we'd just met at your dinner party and didn't really talk. I was careful not to let on."

"Charlene wouldn't have talked, would she?"

"Of course not."

"I guess Prince just saw us both in the same room and made an assumption."

"That's probably it."

"Well, I'm going to take a deep breath and start looking for another Mercedes."

"That's the spirit." The two men said goodbye and hung up.

"He took it well," Stone said.

His cell phone rang, and Prince's name appeared on the screen. Stone ignored it.

"I'm going to go have a drink with Rivera and catch up. You want to come?" Dino asked.

"Sure," Stone said. "I've got nothing better to do." Stone changed and met Dino on the patio.

"Which car you want to take?"

"I don't want to take the Bentley for a drink with a cop," Stone said. "He might think ill of us."

"Good point."

Stone handed Dino the keys to the Mercedes. "Will you move our car so that I can put the Bentley into the garage?"

"Sure."

The two of them walked through the house and out to the garage. Dino got into the Mercedes, started it, and backed into a parking spot.

Stone opened the garage door, then got into the Bentley, and pulled it inside.

Dino was standing outside when Stone closed the garage door; the Mercedes was idling, waiting. "I forgot my piece," he said. "You got yours?"

Stone slapped his belt. "Right here."

As if Stone had pressed a button, the Mercedes exploded.

39

Stone and Dino were blown a good six feet backward until they came to rest, hard, against the garage door and bounced back into the driveway. A hedge lining the parking spot that Dino had backed into took much of the debris from the car, but they were both peppered with shattered glass. The car burned furiously.

Dino got up and brushed himself off. "I guess we'd better take the Bentley," he said.

Stone got up, too. "I don't know how I'm going to explain this to the rental company," he said.

Manolo came running from the house. "What happened?" he cried.

"We had a malfunction with the car," Stone explained. "You'd better call nine-one-one and ask for the police and the fire department."

"I'll deal with that," Dino said, reaching for his cell phone. "Rivera is going to have to come over here and have that drink."

Stone nodded. He called the rental car company at Santa Monica Airport and told them he was going to need a new car. "Any color but black," he said. He gave her the address to deliver the new car.

"Where is the old car?" the woman asked.

"It's here, but not drivable. I think you'd better call your insurer and get them to send somebody out here to look at it."

"Did you wreck it?" she asked.

"Somebody did."

"Is it totaled?"

"That would be my estimate," Stone said, "but the insurance adjustor should make that call."

"We'll have a car out there inside of an hour," the woman said, then hung up.

Manolo had gone into the house and came back with a broom and dustpan.

"No, no," Stone said, "leave the pieces where they are. Do you have a fire extinguisher?"

Manolo went back into the house and came back with a small extinguisher.

"Never mind," Stone said. "Let the fire department deal with it."

*   *   *

An hour later the fire department had left, and so had the patrol car. A team from the crime lab were putting the pieces of the Mercedes on a flatbed truck. Stone, Dino, and Rivera sat at the patio table sipping iced tea, while Rivera took notes.

"So you think Prince did this. You want to add anything else?" Rivera asked.

"There's nothing else to say," Stone replied.

"Why do you think Prince did this?"

"He's the only person in L.A. who might benefit from my demise." Stone explained about the upcoming stockholders' meeting at Centurion.

"And you think he destroyed this guy Schmeltzer's car, too?"

"Yes, but I don't think he expected Schmeltzer to be in it at the time."

"Well, he sure must have expected you to be in this one," Rivera said.

"Dino, remind me to always have you start the car," Stone said.

Rivera closed his notebook. "It's not too early for a drink, is it?"

"Why didn't I think of that?" Dino asked.

Stone placed the order with Manolo, and they sat, sipping. "So, what's the latest on Carter, from Parker Center?" Stone asked.

"We think he's in Mexico," Rivera replied. "His

mother is from some little town in Sonora, and he still has family there."

"You going to go after him?"

"Not yet; we have to find a way to prove that he directed some inmate or other to off James Long before we'll have a charge that can stick. Just leaving off his job isn't enough."

"You know," Stone said, "I'm no longer sure that Terry Prince is directing this little campaign of mayhem." He told Rivera about Prince's backers from the drug trade. "Doesn't this sound a whole lot more like them?"

"Very good point," Rivera said. "It's doubtful that a real estate developer would have the kind of direct connections to do these things, except maybe the shanking of Long. After all, we've been told that Prince spoke to Carter."

"Wouldn't hold up in court," Dino said.

"Stone," Rivera said, "do you have any names of the drug people Prince is dealing with?"

"No, I was just told they're out of Colombia and Mexico."

"Do you think you could get some names? That might be a big help."

"I'll see what I can do," Stone said. "Excuse me." He stepped away from the table and called Carolyn Blaine. "Is this a bad time to talk?" he asked her.

"Let me call you right back."

Two minutes later his phone buzzed. "I'm here," Stone said.

"I bought one of those throwaway cell phones," she said. "Now the number is in your cell phone."

"Right."

"Always call me on this phone, not the regular one."

"Carolyn, you said that the drug people backing Prince are from Colombia and Mexico; do you have any names?"

"The Mexican is named Ricardo Montino," she said. "He's based in Tijuana, I think. I don't have a name in Colombia. Why do you ask?"

"Well, this morning, somebody torched the car of Jack Schmeltzer. Remember, you asked about him?"

"Yes, but I didn't pass anything on to Terry."

"And this afternoon, my rented Mercedes exploded a moment after it was started."

"Oh, my God. Were you hurt?"

"No, Dino started the car, then got out; that's when it blew. The police are picking up the pieces now."

"This stuff is too crazy for Terry to be doing it," she said. "It's got to be the Mexican."

"That's why I was asking for a name."

"I wish I could tell you more."

"Just keep an ear to the ground and let me know what you hear."

"All right. Are you going to accept Terry's offer for the Bel-Air property?"

"I've told him the conditions, and he hasn't met them. I don't have anything more to say to him."

"He's very, very nervous," she said. "I've never seen him like this. Normally, he's the coolest guy in town."

"Before this is over, he's going to get a lot more nervous," Stone said. He hung up and went back to give Rivera the name of Ricardo Montino.

40

A woman from the rental car company showed up with a brand, spanking new Mercedes E500. "We had one with the big engine," she said.

"Thanks very much."

"You look like the type who would enjoy the extra power."

"Do I?"

"Oh, yeah. By the way, we're charging your American Express Card sixty-three thousand dollars for the black Mercedes." She handed him a written notice to that effect.

"Hey, wait a minute," Stone said. "That's what the insurance is for."

She produced another document. "Here's the original rental form you signed. See where you initialed in the three circles?"

Stone was stunned. "Yes," he admitted.

"See where it says 'declined'?"

"Yes."

"That means you declined the insurance. Too late to change it, I'm afraid."

"I always decline it, too," Dino said. "Maybe I'd better start accepting."

She put a hand on Stone's shoulder. "Take it easy. American Express will pay for it, if you don't already have car insurance."

"I have car insurance."

"They'll pick it up, less your deductible."

Stone heaved a sigh of relief. "Joan would have killed me."

"Who's Joan?" the woman asked.

"My secretary; she runs my life."

"I run my husband's life," she said, "but I'll bet I don't get paid as well as your secretary." She stuffed the documents in her briefcase. "Have a nice day," she said, "and try not to blow up any more cars. We're running out, and it will make your insurance company unhappy." She left.

"How much is your deductible?" Dino asked.

"Five grand, I think."

"You'd better bill that to Arrington."

"You're right."

Rivera stood up and tucked his notebook into

his pocket. "I'm outa here," he said. "I've got bad guys to chase."

"I hope you catch up with them," Stone said, watching him go.

"Where were we going when the car exploded?" Dino asked.

Stone thought about it. "To have drinks with Rivera."

"Oh, then we got that taken care of, didn't we? What do you want to do now?"

"I think we'd better do *something*," Stone said, "or I'll start dwelling on what would have happened if I had started the car. Or if you hadn't gotten out of it in time."

"I see your point," Dino said. "Let's get out of here."

Stone got into the new Mercedes.

Dino stood over by the garage, where a man in white overalls was already painting the door. "You start this one," he yelled. "I'll wait over here."

Stone took a deep breath and started the car. It didn't explode.

They drove down into Beverly Hills and took a run down Rodeo Drive. Finally, Stone pulled into the alley behind the Ralph Lauren store and gave the car to the valet parker, along with a twenty. "Please park this where you can see it, lock it, and if anybody messes with it, call the police."

"Yes, sir," the young man said, looking at him oddly but pocketing the twenty.

"If it doesn't explode when I come back, there's another twenty in it for you," Stone said. He led the way into the store.

"What are you looking for?" Dino asked.

"I don't know; it's therapeutic shopping. I always go shopping after somebody tries to kill me."

"Does it help?"

"It doesn't hurt." Stone stopped at a counter and picked out a couple of neckties.

"Nobody wears neckties out here," Dino pointed out.

"They must sell them to somebody," Stone said. "Maybe New Yorkers." He wandered into the shoe department and found a pair of chocolate-brown alligator loafers he liked. Then he turned over the shoe and saw the price tag.

A sales assistant approached. "Would you like to try those on?" he asked.

Stone gave him his card. "I wear a 10D; call me when they go on sale." He wandered on.

"Have you forgotten that you're now a partner at Woodman & Weld?"

Stone went back and tried on the shoes. "I'll

take them," he said, handing the young man his credit card.

"Feel better now?" Dino asked.

"Much," Stone replied, accepting a bag containing the shoes.

"What else you looking for?" Dino asked.

"I don't know."

"It's chilly at night out here; how about a sweater?"

"Good idea." Stone found the correct department and picked out a gold cashmere V-neck. "I'll buy you one," Stone said. "After all, you nearly got killed, too."

Dino picked out a red sweater. "You're right," he said. "I feel better, too."

They wandered on through the store.

"You know," Dino said, "we've never been shopping together. Do you think they think we're gay?"

"They don't think we're gay," Stone said, "because they know I could do better than you."

Dino burst out laughing.

They went back to the rear of the store and Stone gave the valet his parking ticket. The car was parked just across the alley, and the valet ran to get it.

Dino pulled Stone behind a large SUV. "Just in case," he said. The valet started the car and pulled it around for them. It didn't explode.

"You know," Dino said as he drove away. "I've always found that valet thing a nuisance, but not anymore."

"You have a point," Stone said. "It's the next best thing to having your own garage." They stopped for a traffic light.

Dino switched off the ignition, extracted the key, and looked at it. "Whaddya know?" he said. "Watch this." He pressed a button on the key, and the engine started.

"I guess they have a big call for that in L.A.," Stone said.

41

Back at the house Stone's cell buzzed. "Hello?"

"Stone? It's Ed Eagle."

"Hey, Ed, how are you?"

"Just fine. Susannah and I are back in town, at the Bel-Air Hotel; would you and Dino like to join us for dinner over here?"

"Sure, love to."

"Seven, in the bar?"

"That's fine, Ed; see you then." Stone hung up. "Ed Eagle is in town and invited us to dinner."

"Fine by me. I don't know the guy very well."

"He's a top defense lawyer in the West; married to Susannah Wilde, actress?"

"Her, I know," Dino said.

"You'll like them."

"I'm prepared to."

*   *   *

They had a drink before dinner in the Bel-Air bar.

"I heard a rumor that Terry Prince is going to build a new hotel in Bel-Air on your client's property," Eagle said.

"In his dreams," Stone replied. He told Ed about the hang-up on the Centurion deal.

"Would she really sell?"

"I haven't had a firm answer from her, but it's possible, I think."

"You think such a hotel could compete with this one?"

"I've no idea," Stone said, "but Terry Prince thinks so, and he's willing to bet a ton of money on his judgment."

"His own money?"

"That, I don't know, but his assistant, Carolyn Blaine, thinks it is."

"Is that the blonde I saw here at the Bel-Air reopening party?"

"Yes. I was going to introduce her to you, but she vanished."

"I thought she looked familiar," Eagle said. "Now I remember why."

"Why?"

"She reminds me a little of a woman who lived in Santa Fe for a while. She worked for a client of mine named Hanks, a pro golfer."

"Sure, I know who he is. He's doing very well on the tour this year, isn't he?"

"He is. But last year, this young woman embezzled something like seven hundred thousand dollars from his bank accounts, then vanished."

Stone's eyebrows went up. "And you think Carolyn is that woman?"

"I'm not sure," Eagle said, "but there's something about her. The one in Santa Fe wasn't a blonde."

"That's very interesting, Ed, because I ran a background check on her, and Carolyn Blaine doesn't exist. I even got her fingerprints and ran those, but nothing came up. She's a blank sheet of paper."

"That *is* very interesting," Eagle said.

"What was her name?"

"I can't for the life of me remember, but it wouldn't matter, anyway, because that name was probably an alias, too."

"Is anybody looking for her?"

"We made all the proper complaints to the authorities, but she seems to have covered her tracks completely. The stolen funds were wired to offshore accounts, but they were unable to trace her through those. I think she may even have been involved in some way with my ex-wife, Barbara."

"Whatever happened to Barbara?" Stone asked.

Eagle and Susannah exchanged a meaningful glance. "Well," he said, "she made another attempt on my life last year, and it nearly worked. I was hospitalized for a spell."

"Do you know where she is now?"

"Yes, I do; she's in San Francisco, remarried, and a hot number on the social circuit there."

"But shouldn't she be in prison? Wasn't she convicted of something?"

"She got off on a charge of trying to kill me in L.A., but she was wanted in Mexico for attempted murder, and I and a couple of PIs tricked her into crossing the border and got her arrested there. She was doing time in a Mexican prison when she escaped and made her way back to this country. You won't believe what happened next."

"Try me."

"Her most recent husband, a very rich man, died in a car crash on a freeway north of Palo Alto, and he left a will limiting her to a monthly stipend and the use of an apartment in San Francisco. Some lawyer heard something in a country club locker room to the effect that her husband's attorney had forged the part of the will cutting her out, and he managed to get it overturned, so she inherited everything, more than a billion dollars. She used some of her money to buy herself a pardon in Mexico, and now she's as free as a bird."

"I don't believe it!" Stone said.

"I said you wouldn't."

"And there's nothing you can do about the attempt on your life?"

"The only witness against her, the contract hit man she hired, was murdered—we think she did that, too." Eagle looked at Susannah again. "I was so angry I flew to San Francisco to deal with her myself, but at the last minute, Susannah talked me out of it."

"He just needed time to cool off," Susannah said.

"If not for Susannah, I would probably be in prison myself by now," Eagle said.

"You're no good to me in prison," Susannah said.

"That was her argument, and I couldn't contest it."

"You're a wise woman, Susannah," Stone said.

"I know," she replied.

They went in to dinner.

Later, as they were waiting for the valets to bring around Stone's car, Stone said, "Ed, I'm going to see what else, if anything, I can find out about Carolyn Blaine, or whoever she is."

"I'd like it if you'd keep in touch about that," Eagle replied. "She has a lot to answer for, and my client is out a lot of money."

"I don't want to blow her out of the water just yet, as she's being very useful to me in dealing with Terry Prince."

"I understand," Eagle said. "Something else: she may be responsible for the murder of my client's wife."

Stone's eyebrows went up. "A murderer, too?"

"My client was initially charged, but evidence was found that the last person his wife was in bed with was a woman, not a man. Your Ms. Blaine may be a lesbian, or at least bisexual."

"Maybe that explains why I'm not attracted to her," Stone said. "God knows, she's beautiful."

"Well, Stone," Eagle said, "it's nice to know there's a woman somewhere you're not attracted to."

"It's a first," Dino said.

Stone's car came, he and Eagle shook hands, and he and Dino drove home.

42

The following day, Saturday, Stone and Dino, with nothing else to do, drove out to Malibu for lunch. They found a nice little Italian restaurant in the shopping area and shared a bottle of wine.

After lunch they left the restaurant and began to wander among the neat rows of boutiques.

"Sighting at four o'clock," Dino said.

Stone swiveled to four o'clock and his eyes came to rest upon Carolyn Blaine, window-shopping about thirty yards away. It was the first time he had seen her casually dressed, in shorts and a Polo shirt. He was about to approach her when another very attractive older woman got there first, and after a brief greeting they embraced in a way that got Stone's attention.

"That," Dino said, "was done the way it's usually done with a man."

"I noticed that, too," Stone said.

The two women began walking among the shops, their hands occasionally touching in an affectionate way. At one moment, the older woman's hand came in firm contact with Carolyn's ass and remained there for a long moment, finishing with a squeeze.

"The plot thickens," Dino said.

Hanging well back, the two continued to follow the women until they came to a parked Rolls-Royce, its engine idling. A driver in a suit leapt out and opened the rear door for them. Then, apparently having been instructed to go away, he did so.

Stone grabbed a tiny table at a little open-air bar and ordered them a beer. "This is very interesting," he said.

Dino took his notebook from his pocket and wrote something down.

"You're going to run the plate, aren't you?" Stone asked.

"You bet your ass."

"I wish I'd thought of that."

"Have you noticed that the car moves a little now and then?" Dino asked.

"Yes, I noticed that. And the windows are too darkened to see through."

"It must take quite a lot of action to get a Rolls to move around."

Stone laughed. "Go ahead, run the plate."

Dino called his office in New York, and in a minute or so he handed Stone his notebook with a name and address.

Stone looked at it. "Means nothing to me," he said.

"San Francisco," Dino said.

"I don't know anybody in San Francisco," Stone said. "Do you?"

"Nah, not a soul."

They nursed their beers for a few more minutes, then suddenly the rear door of the Rolls opened and Carolyn got out, adjusting her clothing and hair. She called to the driver, who was standing nearby, and he went back to the car, got in, and drove away. Carolyn resumed wandering among the shops.

"I'll be back in a minute or two," Stone said. He got up and walked to where she was gazing into a shop window. "Good afternoon," he said.

She turned, looking surprised. "Oh, hello, Stone. What brings you out here?"

"Lunch and some downtime," he replied.

"All ready for the stockholders' meeting Tuesday morning?"

"I don't really have any preparations to make,"

Stone said. "I've just been enjoying my time in L.A."

"What have you been doing?"

"Lying around, mostly. Had dinner last night with some friends from Santa Fe who are in town." He caught just a tiny flicker of concern in her face. "Nice town, Santa Fe. Have you spent any time there?"

"Once, half a dozen years ago; a weekend with somebody I shouldn't have gone there with."

Stone laughed. "Yes, we've all had weekends like that, haven't we?"

"Have you talked to Mrs. Calder about the offer on the Bel-Air property?"

"No, I haven't received a revised offer that meets her requirements," he said.

"Is this still about Centurion?"

"Yes."

"Well, we'll have that out of the way on Tuesday, one way or another."

"One way or another," Stone said. "If the Bel-Air deal should go through, would you be involved?"

"I would head up the project for Terry," she said. "I think it would be a lot of fun, designing and building a new, top-of-the-line hotel."

"I expect it would," Stone said. "It would be a disappointment for you, wouldn't it, if Terry got his hands onto the Centurion property."

"Not necessarily," she said. "Terry can be very persuasive."

"I'm afraid his charms are lost on me," Stone said. "Well, if you'll excuse me, I've left Dino over there somewhere with a beer."

"See you Tuesday," she said.

Stone went back to the bar and sat down. "Something's wrong," he said.

"What do you mean, wrong?"

"She's been nervous as a cat the last couple of times I've talked with her, and she constantly talked about how wired Terry Prince was, but now, suddenly, she's perfectly calm, and apparently looking forward to the Centurion stockholders' meeting on Tuesday."

"Maybe," Dino said, "having sex in the backseat of a Rolls-Royce has a calming effect."

Stone sat, sipping his tepid beer, trying to think of something to do.

43

When Stone and Dino got back to the house there was an envelope on the poolside table addressed to Stone and marked, "By Messenger." The return address was Terry Prince's office.

Stone sat down and opened it. "Looks like a new offer on the Bel-Air property," he said.

"The guy doesn't give up easily, does he?"

A slip of paper fell from the envelope, and Stone picked it up. "And a check for twenty-five million dollars, too!" Stone scanned the agreement. "The last offer was from Prince's company," he said. "This one's from him personally, and the twenty-five-million-dollar deposit is nonrefundable. The check is drawn on his personal account."

"What does that mean?" Dino asked.

"I suppose it means that he wants to do the

project without investors. At least, at the beginning. That's not how deals of this size are done; there's always a corporation, even if it's wholly owned."

"Are you sure this guy is entirely sane?" Dino asked.

Stone shook his head. "No, I'm not entirely sure he's entirely sane. I think maybe he's just trying to impress Arrington." Stone picked up the phone and called Virginia.

"Hello?"

"Hi there. It's Stone."

"Funny, I was about to call you."

"Then you first."

"I think I'll come out there for the Centurion shareholders' meeting on Tuesday."

"That would be great, but you don't have to; I already have your proxy."

"I think I might enjoy voting my shares personally," she said.

"I think you just want to fly somewhere in your new airplane."

She giggled. "Well, there is that. Okay, your turn."

"We got a new offer from Prince today," he said. "It's the same amount, but it's from Prince personally, not from his company, and there was included a check for twenty-five million dollars as a nonrefundable deposit. You have until five p.m. on Tuesday to accept."

"I've never seen a check for twenty-five million dollars," she said.

"Neither had I, until today."

"Well, don't lose it," she said.

"When will you be out here?"

"How about dinner tomorrow night, you and Dino?"

"I think I can talk Dino into that; you're on. Call me from the plane and give me an ETA, and I'll meet you at the airport."

"How sweet of you; I'll do that. See you then."

"Bye." Stone hung up.

"What do you think you can talk me into?" Dino asked.

"Dinner tomorrow night with Arrington."

"You talked me into it."

"She's coming for the stockholders' meeting; wants to vote her own shares."

"Okay by me."

"Me, too," Stone said.

"Stone, why don't you marry the girl?"

"We talked about it a while back, in Dark Harbor; decided it wouldn't work."

"Why not?"

"I don't want to live in Virginia, and she doesn't want to live in New York."

"Oh. Somehow I could see you living the life of a Virginia gentleman, riding to the hounds and all that."

"I haven't been on a horse since I was twelve, at summer camp," Stone said, "and if I started a hunt on horseback, the horse would very likely finish without me."

"How about being a gentleman farmer?"

"Not the slightest interest," Stone said. "Isn't that what grocery stores are for?"

"When was the last time you were in a grocery store?" Dino asked.

"I don't remember. Joan and my housekeeper Helene do all the shopping."

"Have you heard from Joan?"

"We've talked most days."

"Is she happy about your partnership?"

"Yes, since she found out she doesn't have to work in the Seagram Building. She likes it at my house."

"How is the partnership going to change your life?"

Stone sighed. "I don't know, really. I suppose I'll have to attend more meetings, but I'm going to keep life as much like it is now as I can."

"Everything changes."

"Not everything; you're still a lieutenant, when you could be a captain, or maybe even chief of detectives."

"I don't want that to change," Dino said. "I've got it really good as it is; I pretty much work for myself, don't have to take daily orders from anybody else. The commissioner likes me, the chief likes me, and the chief of detectives likes me. If I let them promote me, I'd be somebody's rival, and the politics would start."

"You're right; you've got a sweet deal, and it would be a shame to screw that up."

"You want to know what I'm doing right this minute?" Dino asked.

"You're sitting on your ass," Stone said.

"No, I'm liaising with my counterparts at the LAPD, comparing procedures and programs."

"You could have fooled me," Stone said.

"Didn't you wonder what all that stuff with Rivera was about?"

"I thought you were just keeping your hand in."

"Well, that, too."

Stone's cell rang. "Hello?"

"Stone, it's Mike Freeman."

"How are you, Mike?"

"Very well, thanks."

"Thank you again for doing the airplane and hangar deals for Arrington. She's very appreciative."

"You're both very welcome," Mike said. "I enjoyed doing it."

"What's happening in New York?"

"It's weirdly quiet," Mike said. "Things are just rolling along; the company seems to be taking care of itself. None of our security clients has been shot or had his car blown up."

"Oh, that reminds me," Stone said. He told him about the exploding Mercedes.

"Well, shit," Mike said. "I should have kept some people at the house. I thought that, after Arrington left, there wouldn't be any further problems."

"So did I," Stone said.

"I'll have people there in an hour."

"You don't have to do that," Stone said. "Dino and I can handle it."

"You didn't handle it too well the last time, did you? And anyway, you're our corporate counsel and a member of our board, and you have to be protected."

"If you insist."

"I do insist! I'm glad I called to see how things were, since things are so terrible in L.A. I'm going to come out there and personally see that you don't die before Tuesday."

"You're just bored and looking for an excuse to get out of New York."

"You could be right," Mike said. "Between now

and Tuesday, we're all going to watch your ass. I'll be there tomorrow. Dinner?"

"You can join Arrington, Dino, and me."

"I've got an airplane to catch," Mike said, then hung up.

44

Stone managed to sleep late on Sunday morning. He had eggs Benedict in bed and read both the *New York Times* and *Los Angeles Times*. It was nearly noon when the bedside phone rang.

"Stone? It's Rick Barron."

"Good morning, Rick. How is everything?"

"I'm not sure," Rick replied.

"What's making you unsure?"

"Something's wrong with Jim Long."

"Rick, he's suffered a knife wound and lost a kidney; of course something's wrong with him."

"No, I mean about his shares in Centurion."

"Rick, you can rest easy about those shares; they're bought and paid for, and I have the stock certificate."

"Yes, I know that, but I just had a call from the

attorney for Jennifer Harris's estate, and he told me he's had an offer for her shares."

"So Prince is still trying to get them."

"No, the offer is not from Prince; he wouldn't tell me who it was, but he did tell me it was for four thousand dollars a share."

"Four thousand!"

"That's what he said. He's waiting for an answer from her trustees, and he wanted to give us a chance to match the offer."

"Then that means that Prince is going to show up on Tuesday and make that offer to all the stockholders."

"Stone, I told you, the offer isn't from Prince."

"Who else could it be?"

"I don't have the slightest idea, and I'm very worried about it."

"It doesn't matter, Rick; we have enough shares on our side to get along without Jennifer Harris's."

"There's something else, Stone."

Stone felt a trickle of apprehension run through his bowels. "What else, Rick."

"The attorney intimated that Jim Long's shares might be in play as well."

"That's not possible, and Long knows it," Stone said. "At least, his attorney, Harvey Stein, does."

"I hope you're right, but I just have the feeling that everything is about to go wrong."

"Then there's the shareholder who promised to vote with us."

"Yes, you wouldn't tell me his name. Maybe you'd better call him and have a chat."

"I can't; it's Sunday, and I don't have his home number."

"Is his office number at Centurion?"

"Well, yes."

"Then I probably have his home number in my book."

"But if I ask you for that, I'd be violating his confidence, and I can't call him and ask him for his permission."

"Stone, there's nothing wrong with your asking me for somebody's home number."

"Tell you what, Rick, can you give me the home numbers of Jim Long, Charlene Joiner, and Jack Schmeltzer? This has nothing to do with what we were talking about."

"Sure, Stone." Rick read out the three numbers, and Stone dutifully wrote them down.

"Do you want me to call anybody for you?" Rick asked.

"No, please, don't. I want to talk to the shareholder and to Harvey Stein. Then I'll get back to you."

"I'm at the studio," Rick said, "on stage four."

"What are you doing at the studio on a Sunday morning?"

"I'm arranging a little reception for our shareholders," Rick said. "You'll see on Tuesday. I've got to run." He hung up.

Stone called Jack Schmeltzer's home and got an answering machine. "Hello, Jack. It's Stone Barrington. I'd be grateful if you'd give me a call at the first opportunity." He left his cell number. Then he called Harvey Stein's cell, got voice mail, and left the same message. He hung up. He didn't know what else to do.

Stone and Dino had a late lunch on the patio, and late in the afternoon the house phone rang.

"Hello?"

"It's Arrington. We'll be landing at Santa Monica in an hour," she said. "We're parking at Atlantic Aviation."

"I'll see you there," Stone said. "Oh, by the way, Mike Freeman is going to join us for dinner."

"He called me. I've already added him to our table."

"Great, see you in an hour." Stone hung up. He told Dino about the call from Rick Barron earlier in the day.

"That sounds ominous," Dino said.

"Yes, it does. I've called both Schmeltzer and Harvey Stein, and neither of them has gotten back to me."

"It's Sunday afternoon," Dino said. "They're probably on the golf course."

"Why didn't I think of that?" Stone said. "You're probably right; they'll call back this evening."

Stone got Vance Calder's Bentley Arnage out of the garage, and they drove to Santa Monica Airport and got buzzed through the security gate and onto the ramp.

"Here comes a G-III," Dino said, pointing.

Stone looked up to see the beautiful plane turning from the taxiway into the Atlantic Aviation ramp. "That is she," he said. He waited until the airplane was chocked, then drove out and parked near the door. The airstair dropped into place, and Arrington walked down the steps, looking fresh as a teenager.

Stone hugged and kissed her, and she gave Dino a kiss, too. "How was your flight?" Stone asked.

"Heavenly," she replied. "It's like having your own railroad car, except it moves at five hundred knots. I actually had a shower, so I wouldn't have to change at home."

Stone opened the trunk of the car so that the crew could load her luggage; then he turned to see another G-III taxiing onto the ramp. "There's the Strategic Services airplane," he said. "I'd thought Mike would go into Burbank."

"We coordinated," Arrington said. "I was actually able to telephone him from my airplane to his. Isn't that extraordinary?"

"It is," Stone agreed. He watched a black SUV pull up to Mike's airplane and saw Mike get out.

"Why don't we go straight to the restaurant?" Arrington said. "It's Michael's, in Santa Monica. Mike's car can take his luggage to the Bel-Air."

"Good idea," Stone said, and in little more than a moment they were all in the Arnage, and shortly after that they were settled in a garden table at Michael's.

Arrington was facing the door. "Well, that's awkward, isn't it?" she said, nodding toward the restaurant door.

Stone turned and saw Terry Prince, Carolyn Blaine, and two other people enter the garden.

"Yes, it is," Stone said. "Ignore them."

45

Drinks and menus arrived, but Stone was preoccupied with Prince and his dinner guests. "Dino," he said, nodding toward their table, "isn't that the woman we saw out in Malibu, the one with the Rolls-Royce?"

"I thought we were ignoring them," Dino said.

"What was her name?"

Dino produced his notebook. "The car was registered to an E. K. Grosvenor, of San Francisco. The name meant nothing to you."

"It still doesn't," Stone said, but he had an oddly unsettling feeling about the woman.

"Oh, come on, Stone," Arrington said, "order something. I'm hungry."

Everyone ordered. As they were waiting for their food, Terry Prince got up and walked over to their table. "Good evening, Mrs. Calder, Stone, everybody."

Replies were muttered.

Prince turned to Arrington. "Have you had an opportunity to consider my offer yet?"

"I've just arrived," she said. "I haven't seen it."

"You'll get an answer Tuesday," Stone said, "after the Centurion business is settled."

"Very well," Prince said. "Enjoy your dinner." He turned and ambled back to his table.

Stone reflected that Prince was looking a lot more relaxed than the last time he had seen him. Carolyn, too, he recalled. What were they so relaxed about? Then his mind made one of those off-the-wall connections, put two and two together and got eight. The thought didn't make him feel any better. Dinner arrived, and he turned his attention to his sweetbreads with a sauce of morel mushrooms.

Mike spoke up. "Arrington, how are you enjoying your new airplane?"

"It's just wonderful, Mike, and I thank you again for helping me choose it."

"I thought you would like it."

"Mike," she asked, "what, exactly does your company do?"

"Strategic Services supplies security and investigative services to governments, corporations, and individuals worldwide," Mike replied. "We also have several manufacturing divisions, including those for armored vehicles, body armor, and electronics associated with our work."

"Is it fun?" she asked.

Mike laughed. "Sometimes."

"Mike," Stone said, "Woodman & Weld would like to buy me a car. Is the one you loaned me for sale?"

Mike took a card from his pocket, wrote something on the back of it, and handed it to Stone.

It was a number: 100K. "That seems low," Stone said. "Are you sure?"

"It's about what it would bring on the wholesale market or at auction."

"Consider the deal done," Stone said. He was thrilled but tried not to show it.

"Is it one of your armored models?" Arrington asked Mike.

"Yes."

"Good. Stone needs it."

Everybody laughed.

It was still early when they got home, and Stone called Ed Eagle at the Bel-Air.

"Hello?"

"Ed, it's Stone. I'm glad to catch you in."

"Hey, Stone, I'm glad you called. I remembered

the name of the woman, the embezzler: her name was Dolly Parks. As I said before, that may not mean anything, since she would certainly have changed it when she left town."

"Thanks, Ed. It was another name I called you about. You said your ex-wife, Barbara, was living in San Francisco and had remarried. Do you know her new name?"

"Well, she changed it from Barbara to Eleanor when she married Walter Keeler."

"Walter Keeler, the avionics guy?"

"One and the same. He was the one killed in the auto accident."

"And she has a new husband now?"

"Yes, a car salesman, an Englishman. When she married him, she bought the dealership and gave it to him."

"What kind of dealership?"

"Rolls, Bentley, Aston Martin, that sort of thing."

"And his name?"

"Grosvenor; he changed the dealership name to his. I don't know his first name."

"So E. K. Grosvenor could mean Eleanor Keeler Grosvenor?"

"Yes."

"What does she look like?"

"Fairly tall, slim, always fashionably dressed; quite beautiful."

"And she knew this Dolly Parks?"

"Yes. I had a pair of PIs following her, and they made that connection."

"Ed, she's in L.A."

"Why do you say that?"

"Dino and I saw her with Carolyn Blaine out in Malibu yesterday, and she was being driven in a Rolls. Dino ran her tag, and E. K. Grosvenor of San Francisco came up."

"I hope she's not staying at the Bel-Air," Eagle said. "It would be awkward to run into her, not to mention dangerous. Do you have any idea what she's doing here?"

"Well, she had dinner with Terry Prince this evening; we were at the same restaurant."

"You think she's mixed up in the Centurion deal?"

"How much did you say she was worth?"

"When she got Walter Keeler's will set aside, she came into his entire fortune. Word on the legal grapevine was that it came to one point six billion."

"*Billion?*"

"Right, and, apart from some real estate and an airplane, it was all in liquid assets."

"And since she was a surviving spouse, tax-free?"

"I assume so."

Stone silently thought about that.

"Stone, are you still there?"

"Sorry, Ed, I was just thinking."

"You think she's in the Centurion deal?"

"It makes sense," Stone said. "Terry Prince is seeming a lot more confident the past few days."

"That's interesting, because Jim Long, the producer, is Barbara's closest friend, maybe her only one. In fact, she could be staying at his house."

"And if she is, she would know about the attack on him in jail."

"I suppose so."

"Then why would she be doing business with the man who arranged the attack?"

"Good question. He probably doesn't know how dangerous she is. Is there anything I can do to help? Do you want me to let the authorities in Santa Fe know that this Carolyn Blaine could be Dolly Parks?"

"No," Stone said, "not yet, anyway. I have to think this thing through. Thanks for your help, Ed." The two men said good night and hung up.

Stone tried to make sense of the association of Barbara Eleanor Keeler Grosvenor and Terry Prince, but he got nowhere.

46

Stone had hardly hung up the phone when Arrington padded into his room, shucked off her robe, revealing all, and slithered into bed next to him.

"I was waiting for you to come to me," she said.

"I'm sorry, I had to make a phone call."

"That's all right," she said, "I'm here now." She felt under the covers for him.

"Right where you should be," Stone said.

"Do you have to get up early in the morning?" she asked.

"Not that I know of."

"Good, because I'm going to keep you busy."

And she did.

* * *

Stone woke up early in spite of himself. He tried to sneak out of bed to the bathroom, but she snagged his wrist.

"Oh, no, you don't," she said, pressing herself against him. "Do you remember when we started every morning this way?"

"I certainly do," he said, kissing her. That had been back when she was practically living with him in New York, before she had met Vance Calder and he had stolen her away to Bel-Air.

She rolled over and sat on top of him, taking him inside her. "There," she said, "I've got you pinned."

"You surely have," he said, "and I'm enjoying the experience." They both enjoyed it for a few minutes until they shared an orgasm.

Stone and Arrington were having breakfast on the terrace.

"We need to talk about Prince's offer for your property here," he said, handing her the contract and the twenty-five-million-dollar check.

"Why, it's a personal check!" she said, looking at it. "I didn't know anybody wrote personal checks in that amount."

"He wanted to impress you," Stone said.

"Well, I'm impressed. What's your advice on this sale?"

"First, let me ask you a couple of questions."

"Shoot."

"Are you really ready to sell the property? Would it make you sad to see it go?"

"Yes, to your first question; no, to your second. My life isn't here anymore. I would still enjoy visiting, but having a house in his new hotel would make me feel at home when I'm back here."

"All right, let me make a suggestion."

"Again, shoot."

"Sign the contract, and let me decide tomorrow afternoon whether to tear it up or go through with the sale, depending on circumstances."

"I trust you that much," she said. "After all, if the sale doesn't go through, I can still build my own hotel on the property."

"Woodman & Weld could partner you with the right hotel group on that. You'd need professional management, anyway. You don't actually want to *run* a hotel, do you?"

"Oh, God, no! I just want to be able to complain about the service and get instant results."

"I think we can guarantee that," Stone said, laughing.

"What if I end up in business with Prince?" she asked. "Am I going to like that?"

"You'll never have to see him or speak to him," Stone said. "I'll take care of that. Also, I've been on his hotel company's Web site, looking at his properties, and they're all top-notch. I've stayed at two or three of them, and they were all beautifully run."

"Okay. You decide tomorrow."

Stone handed her the document and a pen, and she signed it. "He's put in an early closing date of this Friday, noon, and if he misses that, his twenty-five million are yours."

Dino came out of the guesthouse and joined them. "Witness this, will you?" Stone said, passing him the document and the pen.

Dino signed the document with a flourish. "There you are."

"What does your day hold?" Stone asked him, slipping the document and the check into his briefcase.

"Rivera and I are working on something," Dino said.

"What are you working on?"

"It's a secret for the time being," Dino said smugly. "You'll know when you need to know."

"You're very mysterious, Dino," Arrington said.

"Yes, I am," Dino replied, smiling.

Stone's cell phone rang. "Hello?"

"Stone, it's Harvey Stein. I'm sorry, but I was down at Palm Springs for the weekend, and I didn't get your message until this morning."

"Thanks for calling back, Harvey. I've heard

some rumblings about Jim Long's trying to back out of our stock sale."

"Well, it's too late for him to do that, isn't it? Mrs. Calder owns the stock now. What's done is done."

"Harvey, you know Barbara Eagle, don't you?"

"I've met her a couple of times; she and Jim are close."

"She's back in town, and last night she had dinner with Terry Prince. You know anything about that?"

"Not a thing," Stein replied.

"Did you speak with Jim over the weekend?"

"Yes, I called him yesterday from Palm Springs, just to see how he was doing, and he sounded much like his old self."

"Did he mention Barbara?"

"No, he didn't."

"I'd heard that she might be staying with him while she's in town."

"That would be news to me," Stein said.

"Are you coming to the shareholders' meeting tomorrow?"

"Since I no longer represent a shareholder, no."

"Well, if I don't speak to you again, Harvey, thanks for all your help in getting this sale closed."

"My pleasure," Stein replied. They both hung up.

Stone called Rick Barron. "Rick, I just spoke to

Harvey Stein, and he says there's no problem, that Jim Long's shares now belong to Arrington."

"Well, that's a relief," Rick said. "We're perilously close to the fifty-one percent level, and his stock just puts us over the top."

"Then we're okay." Stone heard noises in the background. "Are you still in the editing suite?"

"Yes, it will be tonight before we finish scoring and tomorrow morning before we have a print."

"I can't wait to see it, whatever it is," Stone said.

"I think you'll find it entertaining," Rick said. "Gotta run."

They hung up. "Everybody's mysterious today," he said to Arrington. "First Dino, now Rick Barron. He's working on some sort of presentation for the meeting tomorrow."

"I think I know what it is," Arrington replied, "but I'm not going to tell you."

47

It occurred to Stone that he had not heard from Jack Schmeltzer, and he wondered why. He called the producer's office at Centurion, reached his secretary, and gave his name.

"I'm sorry, Mr. Barrington," the woman said, "but Jack is in a meeting and will be for the entire day. I would expect the earliest he might be able to get back to you would be, perhaps, tomorrow morning."

"Thank you," Stone said, and hung up. What had been a feeling of mere uneasiness now grew into a solid knot of anxiety in his stomach. Was Schmeltzer going to renege? They were little more than twenty-four hours from the shareholders' meeting, and Stone had by now expected to be fully confident of success. Unwillingly he allowed himself to think of the consequences if Rick Barron did not prevail at the meeting. Stone had been operating on a steady wave of mostly good news for the past week, especially his elevation to partner at Woodman & Weld, but now what had seemed within grasp—the rescue of a fine, old name in filmmaking—seemed to be slipping away. The fabric of their plan was unraveling.

Arrington had repaired to her rooms to do whatever women did in the morning, and Dino had gone off to do whatever it was he was doing with Rivera, and Stone was uncomfortably alone. His cell phone rang, and he picked it up, not recognizing the number displayed on the screen. "Hello?"

"Mr. Barrington?" a well-modulated female voice said.

"Yes?"

"My name is Eleanor Grosvenor."

Stone was taken aback. "Yes?"

"Do you know who I am?" she asked.

"Yes, Mrs. Grosvenor," he replied. This was the woman who had married his friend Ed Eagle, then attempted to steal his accumulated wealth and had, after that, repeatedly tried to murder him, a woman who had escaped from a Los Angeles courtroom, not realizing that she was about to be acquitted; who had escaped from a Mexican prison and somehow wangled a pardon for that and other crimes; who now was one of the richest women in the United States. Stone felt at once overmatched. "You are the former Barbara Eagle, are you not?"

"I am," she replied, "and since you know that, I hope you will not hold against me whatever you may have heard."

"Mrs. Grosvenor, so much of what I have heard about you strains credulity, and I hope I may be forgiven for not having had time to formulate an informed opinion."

She laughed, a pleasing sound. "You must know that we dined in the same garden last evening, but I would not wish you to be overly concerned about my presence there."

"I have not been able to decide whether I should be concerned or merely baffled."

She laughed again. "You and I may soon be doing business," she said, "and while I don't want to go into that on this occasion, I do want you to know that what I have heard of you is favorable, and I don't want you to be alarmed about my presence in town at this moment."

"I'm afraid I don't understand what any of that means," Stone replied. Had she really gained a favorable impression of him by dining with Terry Prince? That seemed unlikely in the extreme.

"I'm sorry to be mysterious, but you will

know more soon. Now I must go. Goodbye."
She hung up.

Stone sat with the phone still in his hand, wondering what had just happened. He called Ed Eagle.

"Hello, Stone."

"Ed, I've just had the most extraordinary phone call from your ex-wife."

"*What?*"

"She called me just a moment ago."

"For God's sake, why?"

"I have no idea; I hardly understood anything she said, except that she seemed to want to be reassuring."

"Reassuring about what?"

"I'm not sure. I think she may be mixed up with Terry Prince in the Centurion deal."

"Believe me," Eagle said, "if she is, then you should not take that as reassuring."

"But if she is in bed with Prince, why would she call and say that she has a good opinion of me?"

"Stone, I would normally say that anyone of whom Barbara has a good opinion is not worth knowing or is, at the very least, someone to steer clear of."

"She must understand that if she's in bed with Prince, I'm her opponent."

"Being Barbara's opponent is a dangerous position

to hold," Eagle said. "I warn you to proceed with extreme caution, should you find yourself dealing with her."

"That seems like sound advice, coming from someone who should know."

"You are correct," Eagle said. "If she should communicate with you again, I urge you to call me for advice, and whatever you do, don't make her angry. She is thin-skinned, and there are people whose conduct she has taken amiss who are now no longer with us. I count myself very nearly among that lot."

"I'll keep that in mind," Stone said.

"I have to run, Stone. Watch yourself." Eagle hung up.

Stone sat there, more baffled than before.

The shadows lengthened, and Stone still sat there alone. Arrington was, apparently, having a long afternoon nap, and Dino had not reappeared. Then Manolo came striding onto the patio, followed by Rick Barron.

"Excuse me, Mr. Stone," the butler said, "Mr. Barron for you."

Stone stood and shook Rick's hand and took the opportunity to examine him closely. He looked very tense. "Please sit down, Rick," he said, wondering if it were a good idea to offer a man of his age a drink at this time of day.

"May I have a large scotch?" Rick asked.

Problem solved, Stone nodded to Manolo, who went in search of whisky and returned shortly with a glass.

Rick took a deep draught of the scotch. "I just had a call from the attorney for Jennifer Harris's estate," he said. "The trustees ordered him to accept the offer for her stock without waiting for further bids. We've lost it."

"Shit!" Stone said. "Manolo, please bring me a large Knob Creek on the rocks."

Rick sighed. "By my count, we now have forty-eight percent of the votes."

"That's my count, too," Stone said, taking a gulp of his bourbon.

48

Stone and Rick sat, each staring silently into the middle distance. The only sound was the occasional clink of ice cubes as they imbibed.

"Hello, Rick!" Arrington said cheerfully, as she swept onto the patio in a silk pajama suit. Then she stopped in her tracks. "Did somebody die?"

"Not yet," Stone said. He explained what had occurred.

"Only forty-eight percent?" she asked, taking a seat. "Manolo, bring me a large rum and tonic! No, make it a dark and stormy."

"What's a dark and stormy?" Rick asked.

"It's Gosling's Black Seal—a black Bermudan rum—and ginger beer."

"Oh," Rick said. He turned to Manolo and

swung a finger between himself and Stone. "Re-fills," he said.

"What are we going to do?" Arrington asked.

"Good question," Stone said, staring into his empty glass, which was immediately replaced by Manolo.

"That means you have no answer, doesn't it?" she asked.

"Pretty much," Stone said, sipping his new bourbon.

"That's about the size of it," Rick said, sipping his own new drink.

"Well, it isn't the end of the world," Arrington pointed out.

"It's the end of *my* world," Rick said.

"Oh, Rick, I'm so very sorry," she said. "That was unfeeling of me."

"Have we forgotten to talk to anyone with shares?" Stone asked.

Rick shook his head. "I've spoken with every single shareholder personally," he said, "some of them three or four times."

"There's still Jack Schmeltzer," Stone said. "Oh, you didn't hear that, Rick."

"I didn't," Rick replied. "Have you heard anything from Jack?"

"I've left messages at his home and office, but he hasn't returned my calls," Stone said. "His secretary said he would be in meetings all day and wouldn't be able to get back to me before tomorrow morning."

"I've used that excuse myself," Rick said, "more than a few times, when I didn't want to talk to someone."

"Why wouldn't he want to talk to you?" Arrington asked Stone.

"I think Terry Prince has gotten to him, and he's embarrassed," Stone replied. "Maybe I should call Charlene Joiner and ask her to fuck him again."

"*What?*" Arrington and Rick said simultaneously.

"It was Charlene who talked him around to voting with us," Stone said, "after an afternoon in bed."

"I didn't know people did that sort of thing anymore," Arrington said.

"At least as much as ever," Stone replied, "maybe more."

Stone's cell rang, and he picked it up. "Hello?"

"Stone, it's Harvey Stein." He didn't sound happy.

"Yes, Harvey?"

"I don't quite know how to tell you this, but there's a problem with the transfer of Jim Long's shares in Centurion."

Stone felt sick. "What kind of a problem, Harvey?"

"It appears that the stock may not have been entirely Jim's to sell."

Stone put the phone on speaker and set it on the table. "Rick Barron and Arrington Calder are here. Tell us."

"It appears that a friend of Jim's holds a lien on his shares. A Mrs. Charles Grosvenor lent him some money a while back, and he signed a note using the shares as collateral. She neglected to ask for the stock certificate."

"Who the hell is Mrs. Charles Grosvenor?" Rick asked.

"I'll explain that later," Stone said. "Harvey, do you know if Mrs. Grosvenor may have bought some shares from the estate of Jennifer Harris?"

"I'm not sure," Stein replied.

"Have you spoken with Mrs. Grosvenor?"

"Briefly. I'm afraid I'll have to refund Mrs. Calder's money and ask for the share certificate back," Stein said. "Mrs. Grosvenor wants it before tomorrow's shareholders' meeting."

"Harvey," Stone said, "have you read the actual note Jim signed?"

"Yes, and I consider it airtight. Jim is very apologetic; he thought he would have Mrs. Grosvenor's support in selling the shares. I don't know why he didn't tell me about the note."

"I'm sure you understand, Harvey, that I'm

going to need to see the note before I can surrender the stock certificate."

"Of course."

"I don't think this is your fault, Harvey," Stone said.

"I have already taken the liberty of wiring the funds back to Woodman & Weld," Stein said. "May I send someone to pick up the share certificate now? I'll send along a copy of the note."

"Yes," Stone said. He punched the phone off.

"Who is Mrs. Charles Grosvenor?" Arrington asked again.

"From all reliable accounts," Stone said, "a crazy person."

"How crazy?"

"A homicidal maniac," Stone said. He began to explain the woman's history.

When he had finished Rick said, "I've lived a long life and met all sorts of people, but that is the wildest story I have ever heard."

"Rick," Arrington said, "is Glenna at home?"

"No, she's in Santa Barbara; she'll be back tomorrow morning."

"Then you're having dinner here with us," she said.

"Thank you, Arrington, that's very kind."

Stone's cell phone rang; the caller ID said Woodman & Weld.

"Hello?"

"Stone, it's Bill Eggers."

"Hey, Bill."

"Our bank just called; we've received a wire transfer of the funds we sent Harvey Stein a few days ago. What's going on?"

"Turns out Jim Long didn't have the right to sell his shares; they were entailed."

"Oh. How is that going to affect your gaining control of Centurion?"

"I don't know; nobody knows anything at the moment. The shareholders' meeting is tomorrow; any suggestions?"

"Yeah, use these funds to buy more shares."

"None are for sale."

"Then, unless you've got more than fifty percent without Long's shares, to put it in legal terms, you're fucked."

"Well said, Bill."

"Good luck to you."

"Thanks so much." Stone hung up. "Woodman & Weld got the funds paid for Long's shares back, so if the note is in order, we'll have to surrender the share certificate."

"Swell," Rick said.

49

Dino returned in time for dinner, and they all sat down. "How did your day go, Dino?" Stone asked.

"Nothing I can talk about," Dino replied. He didn't look any happier than anyone else.

Manolo came to the table to say that a messenger had arrived from Harvey Stein. Stone got up, retrieved Jim Long's stock certificate from his briefcase, and went into the house to find Carolyn Blaine, clutching an envelope, waiting for him.

"Since when are you Harvey Stein's messenger?" Stone asked her.

She handed him the envelope. "I can't talk about that," she said, avoiding his gaze. "The note is inside. Did you receive the funds Harvey wired back?"

"Yes," Stone replied, opening the envelope and

removing the photocopy of the note. He read it and found it in perfect order. "I suppose I could insist on seeing the original note before giving you the certificate," he said.

"It wouldn't matter," Carolyn replied. "Jim's attorney would just object to your voting his shares at the meeting, and you'd be back to square one."

Stone knew that was true. He handed her the stock certificate and wondered if now would be a good time to tell "Carolyn Blaine" that he knew she was Dolly Parks—a large-scale thief and embezzler and possible murderer. He decided not, that a better time might come, though he couldn't imagine when that would be, unless it was as the cuffs were being clapped on her beautiful wrists. "Good night," he said, then turned and went back to the dinner table.

"I hope you found some flaw in the note Jim signed," Rick said.

"I'm afraid not," Stone replied. "I couldn't have written it better myself."

As the dinner dishes were being taken away Stone's phone buzzed. "Hello?"

"Stone, it's Ed Eagle. Would you like to come over to the Bel-Air and have a drink with me?"

Stone looked at his watch; only a little past nine. "Sure, Ed, be there in five minutes." He hung up.

"Arrington, Rick, will you excuse me? A friend has asked me to come over to the Bel-Air for a drink, and I'd like to talk to him."

"Of course," Arrington said.

"I've got to be getting home anyway," Rick replied. "I'll walk you out."

"Dino, you want to join us for a drink?"

"Sure, why not."

Stone and Dino walked out to the car, accompanied by Rick. Stone opened the car door for him, relieved that a driver waited. "Good night, Rick."

"I'll see you tomorrow at two, stage four," Rick said, then was driven away.

Stone and Dino drove the mile to the Bel-Air, abandoned the car to the valet, and walked up to the bar. Ed Eagle sat at a table with Mike Freeman.

"Well, this is a surprise," Stone said. "I didn't know you two knew each other."

"We met only once, a while back, on business," Ed replied, "but I found him at the bar tonight, so we had dinner together."

Stone and Dino ordered brandy. "Well, Ed, it seems certain now that your ex-wife has inserted herself into the Centurion deal." He explained what had happened with the Jennifer Harris and Jim Long shares.

"How the hell did that happen?" Ed asked.

"I can only guess: you told me that she and the woman who now calls herself Carolyn Blaine had known each other in Santa Fe. I think Carolyn must have introduced her to Terry Prince. Maybe his Latin friends are getting cold feet, and he needed a new source of money."

"I guess that makes a kind of weird sense," Ed replied.

"Tell me," Stone said, "in Barbara's tangled felonious history, is there something she could still be nailed for?"

"Well, let's see," Ed said. "She got off for trying to kill me; she got pardoned in Mexico; and she didn't get charged with trying to kill me the second time, because somebody got to the hit man before the cops could. Besides his murder, there are two others that I'm sure she arranged, but again, nobody is alive to testify against her, so she is, for all practical purposes, beyond the reach of the law. I wish my clients were as lucky."

"I don't think I've ever felt so helpless," Stone said. "I had it all together, and now it's gone. Centurion is going to become a shell of a studio and will probably get snapped up by some conglomerate that knows nothing about making movies."

"At least Arrington will come out unscathed in the deal," Ed said.

"Yes, but the studio that produced all the films

that made Vance Calder rich, then Arrington, will be gone."

"Companies come and go," Mike said. "It's the American way. Used to be a successful business could endure for a century or more; now they last about as long as restaurants."

"I'm glad Vance Calder isn't alive to see this," Stone said. "He did as much as anyone alive to ensure the success of Centurion. Did you know that he made more than seventy films there, not one of them for another studio?"

"I didn't know that," Ed said. "It's a remarkable record."

"He also made nearly every one of them for a minimal fee and a percentage of the gross. Every time one of his movies is shown anywhere, Vance—or rather, Arrington—gets a nice check."

"I guess that in a few years, young Peter will be a very rich fellow," Mike said.

"Yes, and I'm now his trustee, so it will be up to me to help him hold it together—what's left of it."

"Good luck dealing with all that," Ed said. "It's more than enough to destroy any young man with too much, too soon."

"I'm going to try to write the trust documents— with Woodman & Weld's help—in such a way that he'll be eased into it gradually."

"I hope, for your sake, Stone," Ed said, "that

nothing happens to Arrington for a long time. You could end up running what's left of Centurion for Peter."

"Perish the thought," Stone said.

"I wish I had something to offer that would help you tomorrow," Ed said.

"So do I," Mike echoed.

"At this point," Stone said, "nobody can do anything. We'll just have to let avarice take its course."

Driving back to the Calder house, Dino said, "I don't think I've ever seen you so sad."

"I don't think I've ever been so sad," Stone said.

50

Stone slept fitfully, when he slept at all. He had a recurring dream of Terry Prince on a bulldozer, razing the soundstages at Centurion. He finally got out of bed, shaved, showered, dressed, and walked out to the patio.

It was too early for Manolo to be about, but Dino had made a pot of coffee in the guesthouse kitchenette, and he held up a cup for Stone. "Feeling any better?" he asked as Stone took a seat.

"No," Stone said, "not at all."

"I wish there were something I could do to help," Dino said; then he brightened. "Actually, there is something I can do."

"What?"

"You've got Arrington's signature on the agreement to sell this property to Prince, haven't you? And his check for twenty-five million dollars?"

"Yes."

"Here's my advice: cash the check, get it cleared as quickly as possible, and give Prince the agreement as soon as you see him."

"Why are you giving me that advice?" Stone asked.

Dino shrugged. "Suffice it to say that it's my best advice, and I don't think you would regret taking it." Stone started to respond, but Dino held up a hand. "That's all I have to say on the subject."

"All right, I won't press you. I'll call Eggers when New York opens for business and get it done."

Dino smiled happily. "This is going to be a good day," he said. "I can feel it coming."

"I wish I could share your optimism," Stone said.

"What's the song say? 'Don't worry. Be happy!'"

"That's mindless optimism," Stone said.

"No, it's not. I told you, I have a feeling."

"You get these feelings all the time, do you?"

"No, just once in a while, but they're always right."

"How about the Centurion business? You have a feeling about that?"

"Nope, just about the day in general. I think we should have a celebratory dinner."

"Even if you don't know what we'll be celebrating?"

"I didn't say I didn't know *anything*," Dino said. "I just don't know how the Centurion thing is going to play out."

"You're making me crazy," Stone said. "I've never seen you like this. Did you take some weird kind of sleeping pill that hasn't worn off yet?"

"Nope, I never need sleeping pills. I sleep like a Labrador retriever."

"Why do you say that? You don't have a Labrador retriever."

"No, but I met one, once, and I was impressed with the way he slept."

Stone's cell buzzed, and he picked it up. "Hello?"

"Good morning, it's Eggers. This is your big day, isn't it?"

"That's what Dino says, but I'm not too sure. Things haven't gone well here the past couple of days."

"So why is Dino so up?"

"Who knows? He says he has a feeling."

"He's Italian; I wouldn't discount it."

"Why did you call, Bill?"

"Just to wish you luck at your stockholders' meeting today."

"Well, I was going to call you at nine, New York time, so I'm glad you called."

"What can I do for you, Stone?"

"I have a check from Terry Prince made out to Arrington in the amount of twenty-five million dollars. How can I cash it before he changes his mind?"

"Jesus, what's it for?"

"It's a nonrefundable deposit on the sale of her Bel-Air property to him."

"What bank is it drawn on?"

Stone got out the check and looked at it. "Wells Fargo," he said.

"What branch?"

"It's on Wilshire, near Prince's offices."

"Here's what you do: you be at the branch when it opens and ask for the manager. You show him the sales contract—has Prince signed it?"

"Yes, it came already signed."

"Has Arrington signed it?"

"Yes."

"Get her to endorse the check, too. Then you tell the manager you want the funds wired to our trust account immediately. Got a pen?"

Stone got out his pen and jotter pad. "Ready."

Eggers dictated the account number. "He'll feel better about wiring it to our account, instead of a private account. Tell him to make the wire to my attention."

"What, so you won't get it mixed up with all the other wires for twenty-five million dollars?"

"Yeah. I'll have somebody call you when the funds are in our account, and we'll transfer the money to Arrington's account at Chase this morning."

"Okay, I'll follow your instructions."

"Good. By the way, I sent you a little gift package; you'll get it by FedEx, early delivery."

"Is it a fruit basket, Bill?"

"Not exactly, but you could look at it that way."

"Chocolates?"

"Again, not exactly."

"Well, I just can't wait! I'm on pins and needles!"

"Oh, shut up. I have to go to work, now; they get up early at Boeing." He hung up.

Stone turned to Dino. "I have to be at Prince's bank, on Wilshire, when it opens."

"You do that," Dino said.

Arrington came out to the patio in pajamas and a dressing gown, glowing, in spite of no makeup. "Good morning, all," she said. "I think this is going to be a wonderful day!"

"Talk to Dino," Stone said, handing her Prince's check. "In the meantime I need you to endorse this check."

"Of course," she said, signing it with a flourish.

Manolo appeared to take their breakfast order, and he was holding a FedEx box. "This just came for you, Mr. Stone," he said, handing it to him.

Stone looked at the waybill. "It's a gift from Bill Eggers," he said. He ripped open the box and shook another, more elegant box from it. He opened the box and removed some tissue paper. Underneath was a stack of Woodman & Weld stationery and envelopes and a smaller box. Stone shook that open, and it was filled with cards. He held one up and read it: it proclaimed him a partner of Woodman & Weld. He handed one each to Arrington and Dino. "My card," he said; then he looked at the letterhead and found his name among those of the partners listed there.

"Congratulations!" Arrington and Dino said simultaneously.

Stone glowed.

51

Stone left the house at eight-thirty and drove down to Wilshire. He was right, the Wells Fargo branch was near Prince's building: it was *in* his building. He parked in the underground garage and took the escalator to the ground floor. He was ten minutes early, so he strolled over to the building's directory and looked at the list of occupants. There were two: Wells Fargo Bank and Prince Properties. Management occupied the two top floors, and all the others seemed to be Prince subsidiaries, since they all had his name in their titles.

A man came to the bank door from the inside and unlocked two dead bolts in the glass doors. Open for business. Stone walked inside and approached the first desk, where a middle-aged woman in a business suit sat. "Good morning," he said.

"Good morning, how may I help you?"

Stone handed her one of his new cards. "I'd like to speak to the manager, please. It's a matter of some urgency."

"One moment, Mr. Barrington," she said, reading his name from the card. She got up, walked a few yards to a mahogany door, rapped on it, and then went inside.

Stone looked around. Seemed to be a normal banking day. People made deposits; people cashed checks; people filled out loan applications.

The woman returned. "Mr. Woolich will see you," she said. "Right through that door." She pointed.

Stone followed her finger to the mahogany door, knocked twice, and entered. A plump, balding man in his fifties sat behind a mahogany desk. He rose and offered his hand.

"Good morning, Mr. Barrington. Please be seated."

Stone sat himself in a leather armchair.

"How may I be of service?" Woolich asked.

"I'd like to cash a check," Stone replied. He handed it to Woolich.

Woolich took a look at it, apparently thought he'd read it incorrectly, then took another look at it. He gulped. "You wish to *cash* this check?"

Stone handed him a copy of the sales agreement. "Pursuant to this agreement with Mr. Prince."

Woolich read the document carefully. "Well, this certainly seems to be in order, Mr. Barrington, but we don't have that much cash in the branch's vault, and I'm not sure we have that much in the city of Los Angeles."

"Forgive me," Stone said. "I didn't make myself clear. I wish to wire the funds to the trust account of the law firm of Woodman & Weld, in New York." He handed Woolich another of his cards upon which he had written the account number.

"I'm relieved to hear it," Woolich said. "I had visions of having to hire an armored car."

Stone chuckled appreciatively.

"Would you excuse me for a moment," Woolich said.

"Of course; as long as you leave the check with me. I wouldn't want it out of my sight."

"Of course," Woolich said, handing back the check. "I just want to be sure that the account holder has sufficient funds to pay the check." He chuckled at his own joke, then left the room.

Stone saw a light go on on Woolich's phone, and after a moment, the light began to blink.

Woolich returned. "Mr. Prince would like to speak with you," he said. He indicated that Stone should come around the desk. "Just press the flashing button," he said.

Stone pressed the button. "Good morning, Terry," he said.

"Good morning, Stone. May I take this request for a wire transfer as an indication that your client has accepted my offer?"

"You may."

"Do you have the signed contract with you?"

"I do."

"I'll send someone down for it immediately. Then I'll speak with Mr. Woolich again." He hung up.

Stone resumed his seat, and Woolich resumed his.

"Lovely day," the banker said.

"Every day out here seems to be a lovely day."

"Ah, well, sunny California," Woolich replied.

There was a knock at the door, and Carolyn Blaine walked in. "Good morning, Stone," she said.

"Good morning," Stone replied, handing her one copy of the sales agreement. "Duly witnessed by a member of the New York Police Department."

She looked at it, checked the signatures, and smiled broadly. "Congratulations!" she said.

"And to you. I'm sure that running the project will be a lot of fun for you."

"Oh, yes." She produced a cell phone and pressed a speed-dial number. "All is in order," she said. She listened, then handed the phone to Woolich.

"Yes, Mr. Prince? As you wish." He handed the phone back to Carolyn. "Thank you, Ms. Blaine." He sat down again, and Carolyn left the room.

"Please send the wire to the attention of William Eggers, Managing Partner."

"Of course." Woolich turned to his computer, pulled up a form and began to type, entering the numbers Stone had given him. "Here goes," he said, pressing the SEND key with a flourish. "Done." He pressed a couple more keys and the printer beside his desk spat out a sheet of paper. Woolich signed it, then handed it to Stone. "The transfer is confirmed; the funds are in your trust account."

Stone read the confirmation, then stood up. "Mr. Woolich, it has been a pleasure doing business with you," he said. The two men shook hands, and Stone left the bank, whistling a merry tune.

Stone arrived at the house and found Arrington, in a bathing suit now, lying on a chaise beside the pool. He walked over, kissed her, and handed her the wire transfer receipt. "You are officially twenty-five million dollars richer," he said.

"How nice," she replied. She patted the chaise next to her. "Sit for a moment."

Stone did so.

"Rick Barron called ten minutes ago. He said that Jack Schmeltzer called him this morning and told him that he would be voting with Prince this afternoon."

That knocked the wind out of Stone. "That's bad news," he said. "What with Mrs. Grosvenor buying the Jennifer Harris shares and taking charge of Jim Long's, we are, to put it as gracefully as I can manage, fucked."

"That seems so," Arrington said, "but Rick, bless his heart, seems to remain just slightly optimistic."

"Did he say why?"

"No. He just said he will see us at the meeting at two o'clock on stage four."

"Well," Stone said, sighing, "let's hope that Rick's and Dino's optimism is not misplaced."

52

Stone was tying a necktie in anticipation of the shareholders' meeting when the phone in his room rang. "Hello?"

"Stone, it's Ed Eagle."

"Afternoon, Ed."

"I have some interesting news regarding Dolly Parks/Carolyn Blaine."

"Tell me."

"I've had a phone call from the Santa Fe Police Department, from the detective in charge of the investigation into the murder of the wife of my client, Tip Hanks."

"Something new?"

"Something old, actually. During the investigation a lipstick smear was found on a pillowcase in Mrs. Hanks's bedroom. It wasn't thought to be possible to extract a DNA sample from it at the time, but newer technology has prevailed, and the police have a fully constituted sample. All that remains now is to have Ms. Blaine tested for it."

"That's good news, Ed."

"A problem, though; since there is no existing evidence that Ms. Blaine is Ms. Parks, there is no probable cause for the police to request a warrant requiring her to give a sample for testing."

"That is a problem, isn't it?"

"It is, unless you can help."

"What would you like me to do?"

"Do you think there is some way you might be able to get a sample of her DNA?"

"What, exactly, did you have in mind, Ed?"

"I don't know; get her into the sack and get a swab, I guess."

"Aren't you forgetting that Ms. Blaine, if she is Ms. Parks, is a lesbian?"

"More likely bisexual," Eagle said, "in that she slept with Mr. Hanks as well as Mrs. Hanks."

"I don't know what to tell you, Ed; she hasn't shown the slightest interest in sex with me, and to tell you the truth, I have no interest in sex with her."

"Force yourself," Eagle said.

Stone laughed. "There's got to be another way."

"All right, find another way."

"Ed, all I can tell you is that, should I have an opportunity to snag some small part of her precious bodily fluids, I will do so."

"I guess I can't ask any more than that," Eagle said.

"You have already done so."

"My apologies."

"No apology necessary," Stone said.

"Your shareholders' meeting is today, isn't it?"

"It is, but I'm afraid our side has come up short in the quest to deny Mr. Prince his opportunity to raze much of the studio, in favor of a hotel."

"I'm sorry to hear that."

"On the bright side, I did bank twenty-five million dollars of his money this morning—a down payment on his purchase of Arrington Calder's Bel-Air property."

"So, it's a clean sweep for Mr. Prince, is it?"

"Looks like it. I had hoped to see him laid low, but a quarter of a billion dollars for the Bel-Air property is a nice consolation prize."

"We should all be so consoled."

"Yes, we should. Gotta run, Ed."

"Keep in touch; I'm relying on you."

"Oh, the pressure!" Stone said, and hung up.

The phone rang again almost immediately. "Hello?"

"It's Eggers."

"Good day, Bill; where are you?"

"Still in Seattle. I wanted you to know I've been informed that we received Mr. Prince's twenty-five million dollars into our trust account this morning. It has already been transferred to Arrington's Chase accounts. Perhaps she should give her banker some instructions on how to invest it; you don't want to lose a day's interest on that kind of balance."

"Good point, Bill."

"And don't forget to pay the taxes."

"Will do."

"When is your meeting?"

"At two, L.A. time."

"Good luck."

"I'm afraid we're all out of that, but thanks."

"You don't have the votes?"

"Only forty-eight percent, or thereabouts."

"That's sad."

"Yes, it is. Gotta run, Bill; thanks for the call."

Arrington and Dino were chatting on the patio when Stone got there.

"Hi," Arrington said. "Mike Freeman is joining us for lunch."

"Good," Stone replied. Mike arrived a moment later, and they sat down to eat.

Everyone was uncharacteristically quiet.

"Such a nice day," Dino said.

"Ever the conversationalist, Dino," Stone replied.

"I thought somebody ought to say something."

Things got quiet again.

"Arrington," Mike said, "would you mind if I come to the shareholders' meeting with you?"

"I'd be delighted to have you, Mike. Why are you interested?"

Mike looked a little sheepish. "Well, I've never seen the inside of a movie studio," he said.

Everybody laughed, and the conversation improved after that.

53

Manolo got out the Bentley, and the four of them piled in, Stone driving.

"I have the terrible feeling that we are about to witness bad history," Arrington said. "Like standing on an Oahu hilltop and watching Pearl Harbor get bombed."

"I have exactly the same feeling," Stone said. "Dino, are you still all up about this?"

"My bones tell me it's going to be a good day," Dino said.

"Well, if it turns out not to be, we're going to stand you against a wall and shoot you."

Everybody laughed a nervous laugh.

They drove down into Beverly Hills and on toward the Centurion lot. They passed an empty bus going the other way with a banner stretching from

one end to the other, saying SAVE CENTURION STU-
DIOS FROM THE PHILISTINES!!!

"It seems we have support from somebody,"
Stone said. "I wonder who?"

"Movie lovers," Dino replied.

As they approached the main gate to the studio,
they saw police cars with lights flashing, and a couple of hundred people were gathered, many carrying homemade signs exhorting shareholders to
vote with the studio. There were two television
vans parked near the gate with satellite dishes
pointed skyward, and reporters and cameras at-
tached to them by long cables.

"I hadn't expected this," Arrington said from
the front passenger seat.

"Neither had I," Stone said.

"How the hell did they even know about this
meeting?" Dino asked.

"I suppose it must have been in the papers,"
Mike said, "but I swear, this looks like something
put together by a publicist or a political campaign
manager."

A young woman with big hair rapped on Arrington's window with a microphone, shouting
her name.

Arrington pressed the button and the window
slid down. The previous silence was replaced by dis-
orderly chanting. "Yes?" she said to the reporter.

"Mrs. Calder," the reporter said, "how would your husband feel about this meeting today, if he were here?"

"He would be totally opposed to voting for the sale, as am I, and I will be voting all the shares he accumulated over his lifetime *against* the sale." She raised the window.

Stone finally got the car to the guard at the gate. "Mrs. Calder's car," he said, and was rewarded with a security pass placed on the dashboard. He drove on. "That was a very good statement to the press, Arrington," he said. "Have you been rehearsing?"

"Rick asked me to have something ready to say," she replied. "I'm glad you liked it."

"The studio should hire you as its spokesperson," he said. "Which way is stage four?"

"Straight ahead, then right, then left," Arrington said. "I used to pick up Vance after work when he was shooting there."

Stone followed directions until he saw a large sign proclaiming the stage number. Perhaps a better identifier of the stage was the large group of golf carts parked along the road between the stages, indicating that most of the people attending the meeting worked on the lot. There were only two cars parked on the road, the Rolls belonging to Mrs. Charles Grosvenor and the Bentley

Mulsanne of Terrence Prince. Stone parked near them.

"Let's not go in right away," Arrington said. "I'm sure they've reserved seats for us, so let's make an entrance."

"Fine by me," Stone said. "Dino, Mike, you want to make an entrance?"

"Sure," Mike replied.

"Damn straight," Dino said. He seemed to be enjoying himself.

More golf carts arrived and were parked carelessly along the road.

"I wonder how they find their own carts when they come back?" Arrington asked. "They're all identical."

"Then it doesn't matter which one they take, does it?" Stone pointed out.

"I guess not."

Others arrived on foot and made their way through the large door, which was propped open. There was an unlighted red bulb above the door with a sign saying DO NOT ENTER WHEN RED LIGHT IS LIT.

"It's oddly quiet," Mike said.

"Soundstages are soundproof," Arrington explained. "After that door is closed, a freight train could pass, and you wouldn't hear it from inside." She sighed. "Vance's funeral was held on this

stage," she said. "The studio didn't have an audi-
torium big enough."

Stone remembered the elaborate service in a ca-
thedral set on the stage, complete with stained-glass
windows and a boys' choir. He also remembered
that, because of a packing malfunction, he had
been wearing a suit owned by the corpse. "How
many shareholders are there?" he asked.

"I'm not sure," Arrington replied. "Forty or
fifty, I think."

"Then why are they holding the meeting in a
building big enough for a Busby Berkeley dance
number?"

"I don't know," she said. "Rick must have his
reasons."

No one had arrived for a minute or two. "Are
you ready for your entrance?" he asked, checking
his watch. It was ten minutes past two.

"Why not?" Arrington replied.

Dino jumped out and held the door for her.
They formed a very short column of twos and entered the soundstage.

Stone had expected to see the audience at once,
but instead, a broad, carpeted path led toward the
interior, and on either side were larger-than-life
blowups of stills from Centurion Studios over the
past decades. It was impossible to walk quickly by

them; they continually stopped and commented on this photo or that.

There were several with Centurion's biggest pre-Vance star, Clete Barrow, who had died at Dunkirk, in World War II, and a dozen or more were of Vance Calder, in various costumes: business suit, western gear, on horseback, driving a vintage racing car, and one in the rigging of a pirate ship, with a sword in his teeth. They made their way slowly down the path, turned a couple of corners, and emerged into a dimly lit, cavernous space.

Suddenly, a spotlight came on and found Arrington, and from the darkness beyond, a roar of shouting and applause welcomed her. She stopped and waved, as if she had just walked onto a stage. It struck Stone that the noise was being made by more than forty or fifty people, but when the lights came up a bit, that was as many as he saw.

Stone, Mike, and Dino followed in Arrington's wake as she proceeded down the center aisle, where Rick Barron awaited to seat her party in the fourth row.

Stone spotted Jim Long, in a wheelchair, seated next to Mrs. Charles Grosvenor, in the first row to the left. Seated across the aisle from them was Terry Prince, his back to Stone.

Rick walked up a couple of steps to a raised platform and took a seat in an arced row of a dozen people, presumably the Centurion board of directors.

Lined up across the edge of the platform were larger replicas of the Oscar, several dozen of them.

Stone was impressed.

54

Stone expected Rick Barron to call the meeting to order, but that did not happen. Instead, the lights went down, and in the darkness a screen must have been lowered, because suddenly a large, wide-screen image of the Centurion main gates, filmed from above, appeared, and the music of a full symphony orchestra welled up.

The camera was in either a blimp or a stabilized helicopter, and it rose and began to move slowly over the studio grounds, past the administration building and over the soundstages. Various standing stages, like the New York street and the small town square with its courthouse passed beneath. Then the camera moved over the lake, where an eighteenth-century sailing vessel was anchored.

In the distance could be seen the main street of

a western town, with its Boot Hill at one end. From the opposite end of the street a man on horseback was at full gallop in the direction of the camera, which descended to ground level to meet him. As he approached the camera he reined in the horse, which skidded to a halt in a small cloud of dust, as its rider jumped gracefully to the ground. The man was Vance Calder.

Tall in his heeled boots, wearing a buckskin shirt with fringed sleeves and the Stetson he had worn in many Westerns, Vance looked wonderfully handsome, Stone thought.

Vance slapped his horse on its ass, and it galloped off-screen, while he walked to the side of the street, outside the saloon, swept off his hat and tossed it a few feet to where it landed on one end of the hitching post. He leaned against the rail and contemplated the camera for a moment, allowing the audience to take in his lean figure, his graying hair, and his deeply tanned, finely cut face. He smiled, revealing a beautiful set of teeth.

"Hello," Vance said, in his beautifully modulated baritone. "I believe we've met before."

The audience of film people went nuts, and it was as if the dead man on the screen had anticipated this, because he paused until the noise subsided, before continuing. "Welcome to my home for the past half-century," he said, waving an arm around him. He pushed off the rail and began to move with the camera up the street, past the sheriff's office, the general store, and the undertaker's parlor, continuing to speak as he strolled.

"I've made seventy-five films at Centurion, from Westerns . . . to comedies . . . to romances . . . to war films . . . to police procedurals and just about every other kind of picture . . ."

And as Vance strolled and talked, something magical happened. Without his so much as pausing for a breath, the actor's image dissolved as he continued to speak, through a series of shots of him in different costumes, on different sets around the lot. It was completely seamless, something that could only have been accomplished by a ghost—or a superb film editor.

Finally he reached the town square, and dressed in a brass-buttoned blue blazer and gray flannel trousers, and an open-necked white silk shirt with a colorful scarf tied at the neck, he took a seat on a park bench in front of the courthouse, crossed his legs, and continued.

"Centurion has survived, intact, over all these decades, because of the management of people who wanted more than to rake in big grosses, who wanted to make fine motion pictures, films that will still move audiences a hundred years hence, and beyond. The more than seven hundred films made on this lot since the late thirties have won more than a hundred and fifty Oscars, for everything from costumes, makeup, and production design to scoring, producing, directing, and acting. Six of those came to me—not just because I did a good job, but because from their inception, each of those pictures had invested in it the brains and creativity and skill of a group of extraordinary people, working together to craft some of the best entertainment this industry has ever seen.

"The board of directors, of which I am glad to be a member, has always followed a policy of offering ownership of the studio to a wide variety of the people who work here, in the belief that this practice will maintain the structure of our business in such a way that will allow the excellence of the work done here to continue for decades into the future.

"Technical advances will come along, and Centurion will embrace them, but it is the talent and creativity and hard work of the people who make our films that will always be at the heart of the work we produce, and that will enable us to keep this studio in the forefront of the motion picture business.

"You are all part of that, and I am very proud to be one of you." Vance paused, then stood and said, "I'll see you in the movies." Then as the music swelled again, he turned and strolled off down the street, until, with a little wave, he disappeared around a corner.

The audience were on their feet again, applauding and shouting, many of them in tears.

Slowly, the lights came up, first on the row of Oscars, then on the people seated at the table onstage.

Rick Barron adjusted the microphone in front of him and spoke. "Now we will vote on a motion to sell forty percent of our property to Prince Enterprises."

55

Stone turned and looked at Arrington. She was still staring at where the screen had been, and tears were running down her cheeks. He gave her his linen handkerchief.

"That was wonderful!" she said, trying not to sob.

"And showing it was brilliant," Stone replied.

Rick began calling names of shareholders: "Gladys Hemmings, Wardrobe," he said. "Fifty shares."

"I vote with Centurion!" a woman shouted from the rear, and applause broke out again.

"Harry Bland, Maintenance, sixty-five shares."

"You've got my vote, Rick," a man shouted.

"Martin Manulis, Production, twenty thousand shares."

A man in the front row stood. "I vote with Centurion!" he shouted.

The roll call continued, and fifteen or twenty names had been called before someone voted his ten thousand shares with Prince. A low rumble of disapproval began.

Stone had his notebook out and was keeping score. The studio was ahead about sixty-forty, he reckoned, then someone voted twenty-five thousand shares with Prince, and the developer edged ahead.

"We know where this is going, don't we?" Arrington asked.

"Not yet we don't," Stone replied, busy with his pen. He looked around for a moment at the faces near him. They were tense, worried, and some had tears on their cheeks. Not a one seemed uncaring. He continued to tot up the totals.

"Where are we?" Arrington asked.

"Behind," Stone said. And then something happened that stunned him.

"The estate of Jennifer Harris," Rick called out. "I'm sorry, those shares have changed hands." He looked carefully at the page before him. "Strategic Services, twenty thousand shares."

Mike Freeman stood up. "Strategic Services votes with the studio!" he shouted, then sat down. He turned toward Stone, whose mouth was open. "It seemed like a good investment," he said.

Arrington threw her arms around him.

"And that makes it worth every penny," Mike said.

Rick made a note and continued. "James Long, Production, twenty thousand shares."

Jim Long struggled to his feet from his wheelchair, assisted by Eleanor Grosvenor. "Every share voted with Centurion!" he said, raising his voice as much as he could; then he collapsed into the wheelchair.

But Mrs. Charles Grosvenor was still on her feet. She turned and shouted at Terry Prince, just across the aisle, "Take that, you son of a bitch!" then sat down.

The other shareholders laughed and applauded.

Rick continued to call the roll, and Stone continued to track the count. "Jack Schmeltzer, Production, twenty thousand shares."

Schmeltzer stood up. "I vote with the studio," he said quietly.

"That concludes the voting," Rick said. "We'll have a final count in a few minutes." Several board members gathered around him, comparing notes. A couple of them had calculators.

"Tell me, Stone," Arrington said.

"I must have it wrong," Stone replied. "Let's let Rick tell us."

"You know," she said, "I don't think I understood

how much this would mean to me until this moment."

"I understand how you feel," Stone replied.

Finally, Rick Barron got to his feet and plucked the microphone off its stand. "Quiet please," he said. "We have a final count."

The crowd became hushed.

"Centurion Studios has received seventy-two percent of the shares voted. The motion to sell our land is defeated."

Pandemonium reigned. People embraced or shook hands, and music was rising. Somewhere in the ether, a brass band was playing "Happy Days Are Here Again."

Dino grabbed Stone's elbow. "I told you it was going to be a good day," he shouted. "My bones are never wrong, and it's not over yet." He walked away from the crowd, pulling out his cell phone.

It seemed that every person in the crowd wanted to hug Arrington or shake her hand. She stood, tears still streaming down her face, and received every one.

Finally, Rick Barron, still shaking hands and kissing women, made his way through the crowd to her side with Glenna in tow. The three of them embraced wordlessly.

Then a studio policeman made his way to Rick. "Something's wrong outside in the street," he said. "I can't make any sense of it on the radio. There's too much noise from out there."

Most of the crowd was out of the soundstage by now. Stone fell in step beside Rick. "That film was brilliant; where did it come from?"

"We shot the footage for the stockholders' meeting the year Vance died," he said, "but in the hubbub that followed, it just got shunted aside. I found the stock last Friday and edited it, put the opticals in, and got it scored over the weekend."

"I think it turned the tide," Stone said.

"I know it did. I watched Jack Schmeltzer's face at the end, and I knew he was going to vote with us."

"Did you know about Strategic Services buying Jennifer Harris's stock?"

"Not until this morning, and the name didn't mean anything to me until Glenna explained who they were."

"Then it's time you met your new shareholder," Stone said, and introduced him to Mike Freeman.

They continued out of the building, and as soon as they were on the street Stone saw what was going on. A big to-do was raging a few yards away. Terrence Prince's Bentley Mulsanne was on fire, and he could hear the studio fire engine's siren approaching.

Stone looked around and saw Jack Schmeltzer

standing across the street, a broad smile on his face.

Then Stone was surprised again. He saw Sergeant Rivera of the LAPD and two uniformed officers approach Prince, say a few words to him, then handcuff him and lead him away, him protesting the whole time.

Stone turned to Dino. "What was that?"

Dino smiled. "Rivera and I brought Carter back from Mexico yesterday. In return for immunity, he's agreed to testify against Prince for the attempted murder of Jim Long." He laughed. "Is this a good day, or what?"

Stone began laughing. "It's a very, very good day, Dino," he said.

"I told you about my bones," Dino said.

"And I'll never doubt your bones again," Stone said.

56

They watched as a police car drove Terry Prince away.

Rick Barron chuckled. "I was going to have studio security escort him off the lot," he said. "I'll give them instructions that he not be allowed to set a cloven hoof on these grounds again."

Everybody laughed.

"The exhilaration is wearing off, now, and I'm tired," Rick said. "Will you excuse Glenna and me?"

"Of course," Arrington replied.

Rick's car pulled up and they were driven away.

Stone led his party to the Bentley and everyone got in.

"I know how Rick feels," Arrington said. "I'm tired, too."

"Suspense is wearing," Stone said.

"I'm sorry to have added to it," Mike said from the rear seat.

"No, you stood up at just the right moment in the proceedings," Arrington said.

They had been back at the house for only a few minutes when Stone's cell buzzed. "Hello?"

"It's Carolyn Blaine. I'd like to see you for a few minutes, if you can manage the time."

"Come over," Stone said, then hung up. He buzzed Manolo and told him to expect a guest.

"Who was that?" Dino asked.

"Carolyn Blaine."

"She's coming over? She's a big loser in all this, isn't she?"

"Maybe not," Stone said. "I'm interested to hear what she has to say."

Manolo escorted Carolyn out to the patio.

"You've met Dino Bacchetti, haven't you?" Stone said.

"Yes, nice to see you again."

Dino nodded.

Stone offered her a drink—not to be hospitable but to get hold of her glass.

"No, thank you," she said, sniffling. "I'm not feeling all that well."

"Nothing serious, I hope," Stone said, trying to think of some other way to get a sample.

"Just the start of a cold, I think; I've already taken something for it." She took the chair offered to her. "I believe the shareholders' meeting went as you wished it to."

"It did, indeed," Stone said.

"I expect you're wondering why Eleanor Grosvenor allowed Jim Long to vote his shares with you."

"Tell me," Stone said, though he thought he already knew.

"Eleanor and I are old acquaintances," she said.

"Oh?"

"We met last year and spent some time together."

"Did you?"

"Eleanor and Jim are old and dear friends," Carolyn said. "When I told her that Terry Prince had been behind the attack on Jim in jail, she was furious. Then I told her how she could help, and she was on board immediately."

"Well, as it turned out, we would have had the votes without Jim's shares," Stone said.

"I wasn't at the meeting," she said. "What happened?"

Stone told her about Rick Barron's film and the effect it had had on the shareholders. "And beyond that, a friend of our side bought Jennifer

Harris's shares, and Jack Schmeltzer decided to go with us."

"That's very interesting," she said. "I expect Terry will be furious."

"Haven't you spoken to him?"

"Not since before the meeting. Frankly, I've been avoiding him. He'll soon find out about my connection with Eleanor, and he won't like it."

"I don't think you'll have any trouble avoiding him," Stone said, "unless he can get bail."

She wrinkled her forehead. "Bail?"

"He's under arrest for the attempted murder of Jim Long."

"They'll never pin that on him," she said.

"Yes they will. The LAPD brought Carter back from his mother's place in Mexico. They've offered him immunity, and he's agreed to testify."

Carolyn looked stunned for a moment. "That's wonderful," she said finally, and with some feeling.

"Wonderful?"

"Wonderful for me. It gets him off the street and out of my hair."

"But you told me, didn't you, that even if he lost the Centurion fight, he would still want to do the hotel project, and you were supposed to run that, weren't you?"

"I still will," she said, "even if he can't close on Friday—*especially* if he can't close on Friday."

Now Stone was puzzled. "I don't understand."

"When Terry lost the Centurion deal, he lost his Colombian and Mexican financial backing," she said.

"Does he have the personal funds to close on Friday?"

"No. Eleanor Grosvenor is, or was, his backer on the hotel deal, and she will now back out, with pleasure. That will give her almost all the revenge she wants for what he did to Jim."

"Then that means you're out of the hotel development, too, doesn't it?"

"No, Eleanor wants to proceed with the hotel. I'll run the project for her, and I'll have a lot more freedom than I would have had with Terry. Once she closes on the property I'll help her find partners for the money required to design and develop the hotel."

"You're overlooking something," Stone said.

"I don't think so," Carolyn replied, looking confident.

"Tell me, why did Prince make the initial payment from his personal account?"

"That was his money," she said. "Eleanor was to provide the rest of the purchase price, in return for a share of the project. But now Terry is out of it, and it's all Eleanor's. And mine."

"Ah, I see," Stone said.

A cell phone rang, and she rummaged in her purse until she found it. "Excuse me, Stone. I don't recognize this number, but I'd better take it. Hello? Yes, I heard," she said. "All right, I can take care of that. Call me when you can." She hung up. "That was Terry," she said, "calling from Parker Center on a borrowed cell phone."

"And what did he have to say?" Stone asked.

"He wants me to go ahead with the closing before noon on Friday. I'm to send him a power of attorney, so that I can sign the documents for him."

"So he doesn't know yet about yours and Eleanor's plan?"

"No, and the DA plans to ask at his arraignment that he be held without bail, so he's unlikely to get the full picture for a while."

"So, you plan to close, but for Eleanor, not Prince?"

"Exactly. It's poetic, isn't it? Bad people always get what's coming to them. Even if Terry beats this rap he'll be ruined by the time the trial is over, and he'll still have the Colombians and the Mexicans to deal with. They're going to want their money from the Centurion deal back, and they're going to insist."

"Yes," Stone said, "bad people always get what's coming to them. Usually, anyway."

"Can we close at ten o'clock on Friday morning?" she asked.

"Where?"

"I don't think we'd better do it in Terry's office. How about here? All we'll need is a table to sign on, and I'll bring a cashier's check for two hundred twenty-five million."

"I'll call you tomorrow," Stone said, rising.

She got up, too, and suddenly emitted a loud sneeze. She groped in her bag for a tissue and blew her nose noisily. "Sorry about that; it seems to be getting worse."

Stone held out a wastebasket for her tissue. "I hope you feel better," he said.

Manolo led her toward the front door.

Dino had sat quietly throughout the conversation. "I guess you're going to want an evidence bag," he said, digging into a pocket.

"Yes, please," Stone said, reaching for the wastebasket.

57

Stone put a note to Ed Eagle in the FedEx box, along with the used tissue, and handed it to Manolo. "Please call for pickup, and mark it for early delivery."

"Yes, Mr. Stone," Manolo said.

Dino spoke up. "Are you going to sell the property to Mrs. Grosvenor?" he asked. "Knowing what you know about her?"

"Knowing what I know about her," Stone said, "it would be safer to sell it to her than not. People who cross Barbara Eagle Keeler Grosvenor don't seem to do well. Look at Terry Prince."

"I'll give you odds Prince gets bail," Dino said. "It'll be expensive, but he'll be out."

"Didn't you just hear Carolyn say that he's broke?"

"No, I heard her say he doesn't have two hundred twenty-five million dollars to close the sale. That's a far cry from not having a few million for bail."

"Good point."

"Now," Dino said, "you should give some thought to what he's going to do if he's back on the street."

"I've been doing just that," Stone said.

"My guess is, you're going to screw him out of his twenty-five million dollars."

"No, I'm just going to let him screw himself out of it. All I have to do is wait until noon on Friday, and if he can't close—and I don't see how he can—I'll keep his money, or rather, Arrington will. I take some satisfaction in knowing that a nonrefundable deposit was his idea, not mine."

"Well, I don't think that will make him any less pissed off, do you?"

"No, I don't."

"And Stone, you do remember the things he tried to do to you when he *wasn't* pissed off, don't you?"

"I'm trying not to," Stone replied uncomfortably.

"Mind if I make a suggestion?" Dino asked.

"Not at all."

"Why don't we just get into your airplane tomorrow morning and get the hell out of here and back to New York? I mean, you don't have to be here to let Prince screw himself out of his deposit, and the relevant authorities will come get Ms. Blaine as soon as they match the DNA samples."

"You have a point, Dino, as always, but that wouldn't be any fun. I want to *watch*, don't you?"

"From a distance," Dino said.

"Listen, if you're really worried, or if you really have to get back to the precinct, then I'll drive you to LAX, and you can get the red-eye."

"Me, fly the airlines? Don't hold your breath."

"I've spoiled you, haven't I?"

"You sure have," Dino replied.

"Well, Arrington can take you as far as Virginia, and Mike, all the way to New York. You can have your choice of jet travel."

"And if I do that, who's going to watch your back?"

"There is that," Stone replied.

Arrington finished her nap in time for cocktails, and Mike Freeman joined them at her invitation.

Manolo took orders and served the drinks, along with canapés.

Mike spoke up. "Rick Barron called me a few minutes ago and asked me to join the board of Centurion," he said.

"I hope you accepted," Arrington said.

"I did. Who could resist? Are you on the board?"

"No, I didn't want that, but I've asked Rick to appoint Stone instead. He can represent my interests on the board, and eventually, Peter's."

Stone nearly dropped his gimlet. "When did this happen?" he asked.

"A few minutes ago," she replied.

"Same here," Mike said. "Something else: Rick has decided that, rather than leave his Centurion stock to his grandchildren, he'd rather sell and leave them cash."

"Is Strategic Services going to buy it?" Stone asked.

"We already have," Mike said, "pending board approval. As our counsel, will you vote for that?"

"I certainly will," Stone said.

"Then the vote will be a formality."

"Then you two gentlemen," Arrington said, "will have effective control of Centurion Studios."

Stone took a deep breath. "Whew!"

"Don't worry, Stone," Mike said, "it's just a business, like any other."

"Not like any other," Stone said.

"You have a point, I guess. Now that the issue of the land sale is settled, I suppose the next big decision for the board will be who succeeds Rick Barron as chairman and CEO."

"Rick wants to retire?"

"Do you blame him?" Mike asked. "The man is in his midnineties, and this fight took a lot out of him, I think. He and Glenna want to move up to Santa Barbara full-time."

"I don't blame him. Did he make a recommendation on who should succeed him?" Stone asked.

"He told me that Jim Long wants the job," Mike said.

Stone shook his head. "That's way too close to Mrs. Grosvenor for me."

"Me, too," Mike agreed. "Rick's recommendation is a fellow named Leo Goldman, Jr. He's a producer at the studio and a board member, and his late father, Leo Senior, was a very successful CEO."

"I know Leo Junior," Arrington said. "He's smart as a whip and a hell of a producer."

"I guess we just elected him," Stone said. "By the way, Arrington, you have another decision to make."

"Oh, no," Arrington said, "I'm all out of decisions. I've just appointed you to represent me in studio matters. You decide."

"It's not related to the studio," Stone said. "It's about what to do with the property on which we now sit, sipping gimlets."

"You decide if Prince should buy it," she said.

"Prince isn't going to buy it," Stone said, "unless he can come up with two hundred twenty-five million dollars by noon, Friday, and I hear his backing has fallen through. But there's another buyer in line, same terms." He explained about Carolyn Blaine and Eleanor Grosvenor.

"Well, I'm glad I don't have to sell it to Prince," Arrington said.

"Now you have to decide whether to sell it to Mrs. Grosvenor. She wants to build the hotel, and Ms. Blaine wants to run the project."

Mike spoke up. "Does Mrs. Grosvenor have enough money to handle that?" he asked.

"Not without other backers."

"Stone," Arrington said, "let me ask you one question. Then you can make the decision."

"All right."

"Given everything we know about Mrs. Grosvenor, do you want to be in business with her?"

"Absolutely not," Stone replied. "And I don't want to be in business with Carolyn Blaine, either." He explained her apparent background and current legal situation.

"Good God!" Arrington said. "These two women are Bonnie and Bonnie."

"They're also Clyde and Clyde," Stone said.

"Let *me* ask you a question, Arrington," Mike said. "If I could put together a syndicate of my clients to finance the project, would you like to be in the hotel business?"

Arrington thought about that for a moment. "As long as I could have a house on the property, yes," she said. "Stone, do you agree that it would be a good business move?"

"Without a doubt," Stone said. "You might even invest some of the proceeds of the sale of the land in the new venture."

"Well, then," Arrington said, "all we have to do is wait for Terrence Prince to default on Friday. The Bonnies and Clydes can take a walk."

58

Stone arrived for breakfast the following morning to be greeted with a front-page story in the *Los Angeles Times* about Terry Prince, starting with the Centurion meeting, continuing with his arrest, and finally, with his being released on five million dollars bail, cash.

Dino came to the table, and Stone tossed him the paper. "You were right, pal. Prince is on the loose again."

Dino glanced through the piece. "So he had at least five million cash. I wonder how much he has left."

"I expect Carolyn knows what she's talking about when she says he can't swing the property deal by himself. She's been his closest associate for some time, now, and I'd be very surprised if she

didn't have a copy of his financial statement."
Stone looked at his watch. "Ed Eagle will have his
DNA sample pretty soon."

"Yeah, and if Carolyn is taken out of the equa-
tion and Prince can't swing the deal, then you're
left with Mrs. Grosvenor to deal with. That's gonna
be fun."

"Don't remind me," Stone said. "Anyway,
we've now got Strategic Services to step into the
deal."

"Yeah, and you know if you get into bed with
Mike Freeman, you're not going to wake up with
his fangs in your neck."

"That's a comforting thought, Dino. I hadn't
thought of Mrs. Grosvenor having fangs, but . . ."
His cell phone rang. "Hello?"

"It's Carolyn Blaine," she said. "Have you heard
that Terry is out on bail?"

"It's all over the papers," Stone said.

"I want you to know that he will *not* be able to
close the deal."

"Well, we'll just have to wait until noon Friday
to see, won't we?"

"We can be making other plans in the meantime," she said.

"The meantime doesn't exist," Stone replied.
"Either Prince is in or he's out, and we won't know
that until noon Friday."

"But surely, you and I can come to an arrangement pending that time."

"No. I was going to call you today and tell you that. My client has a signed contract with Prince; if he can close, she's bound by that agreement. If he can't, then I can talk to other parties."

"What do you mean, 'other parties'?" she said, sounding worried.

"I mean other parties," he replied, "you and Mrs. Grosvenor among them."

"But that twenty-five million dollars you have in the bank is her money."

"The check was from Prince's personal account, with his signature on it, and that's all I need to know. My deal is with Prince. If you have some other deal with him, that's between the two of you, and nothing to do with me or my client."

"Well, when Terry can't raise the money, I'll simply get him to assign the agreement to us."

That was an alarming statement and something Stone had not anticipated. "There's nothing in the agreement allowing him to assign it."

"There's nothing in the agreement *preventing* him from assigning it, either," she said.

"I suggest we cross that chasm when we come to it," Stone said.

"Well, if that's going to be a problem, we can

simply let Terry close with our money, then force him out of the deal later."

"Carolyn, you'd better take a deep breath and consider your position. The way you're talking now will guarantee you a lifetime of litigation, and quite apart from the courts, you should consider how Prince has chosen to solve his problems in the past."

"I know how to deal with Terry," she said. "I'll see you at ten o'clock on Friday morning, as previously arranged."

"Nothing was previously arranged," Stone said, but she had already hung up. He put his phone away and sighed. "Shit," he said.

Dino was grinning at him from across the table. "Things not going as smoothly as planned?"

"Stop enjoying this," Stone said. "God, I wish I hadn't taken that twenty-five million. I let my head be turned by all those zeros."

"Don't you think that's what Prince intended?"

"I suppose you're right," Stone said. "Of course, he could still lose it all."

"Do you have any reason to believe that Prince couldn't find another two hundred twenty-five million if he had to?"

"I'm operating on what Carolyn knows about him," Stone said.

"And Carolyn is an embezzler and murderer," Dino pointed out.

"Oh, stop it!"

"I just love watching you break a sweat," Dino said.

59

On Thursday things were deceptively quiet at the Calder house. Stone checked in with Joan, who was happy with her new health plan from Woodman & Weld and with the idea of his new partnership as a source of steady income.

"It's going to be nice getting a check every month," she said. "Frankly, I'm tired of the feast-and-famine thing."

"It hasn't been as bad as that, has it?"

"You don't have to worry about paying the bills," she said. "I do."

"I suppose we're going to have to start billing our clients through Woodman & Weld," he said.

"I wondered about that," she said.

"It's a small price to pay."

"I guess you're right."

"With any luck I'll be home Saturday or Sunday, depending on how things go here." They said goodbye and hung up.

It was nearly lunchtime on Thursday when Ed Eagle called. "Hey, Stone."

"Good morning, Ed."

"Thanks for the DNA sample. SFPD is working on it. I think they had to send it away for testing, but they don't want to admit it."

"When will we know?"

"A day or two, they say. The DA here is about to jump out of his skin; he really wants an arrest in this case. I hope she's not showing any signs of doing a runner."

"None at all. There's going to be a meeting here tomorrow morning that she doesn't want to miss." Stone brought Ed up-to-date on the Bel-Air land deal.

"Well, if the hotel gets built, put me down for a regular suite," Eagle said. "I seem to be trying more and more cases out there."

Stone had barely hung up when Carolyn Blaine called, sounding frazzled.

"What's wrong?" Stone asked.

"I'm worried," she said. "I've been at the office with Terry the past couple of days, and while he's playing his cards close, I get the idea that the

Colombian and the Mexican are back in the picture. What I think is happening is that they're horning in on the Calder property deal to get their investment in Centurion back from Terry. They're scrambling around assembling cash from various sources, so that Terry can have a cashier's check ready for tomorrow."

"I thought he wanted to keep that deal for himself."

"He may not have a choice," she said. "If that happens, it will blow Eleanor's participation out of the water, but I'll still get to do the development work."

"Swell," Stone said. If you aren't in a New Mexico jail, he thought.

"I'll keep you posted; otherwise, I'll see you tomorrow morning." She hung up.

"Now what?" Dino asked, looking over his newspaper.

Stone sighed. "I just may have put Arrington in business with two drug cartels. That's who Terry Prince is raising his money from."

Dino shook his head and ducked back behind his paper.

Stone's phone went off. "Hello?"

"It's Mike Freeman."

"How are you, Mike?"

"I'm okay, and I've been talking to people

about Arrington's property. One of my clients is the majority stockholder in a worldwide hotel group, and I think he'd be a perfect partner in the deal."

"That's great, Mike, but we have a problem: it looks like Prince may be able to close tomorrow, and the source of his funds is two drug cartels, one Colombian, one Mexican." He read the names from his notebook. "Word is, they're assembling cash from what was called 'various sources' as we speak."

"Do you know what account they're using in L.A.?"

"I assume it's Prince's personal account at Wells Fargo, in his office building, because that's where the first payment came from."

"Let me make a couple of calls," Mike said, and hung up.

Late in the afternoon he called back. "I've spoken to a couple of people I know at DEA and Treasury, and they're going to be paying a lot of attention to where Prince's money is coming from," Mike said.

"Tell them they'd better pay attention fast," Stone replied. "We're running out of time here. Our closing is set for tomorrow morning."

"Where?"

"Here, at the house."

"Can you delay it?"

"Maybe for an hour, but Prince won't like it; he has to close by noon."

"Try for the hour; it could make a difference."

"I'll do that," Stone said. He hung up and called Carolyn at Prince's office.

"Yes?"

"Tell Prince we have to close at eleven, instead of ten, and that we'll be doing it here."

"He won't like that."

"I don't care if he likes it, just tell him eleven a.m. here, at the house."

"I'll tell him." She hung up.

Stone hardly touched his lunch.

"I've never seen you this nervous before," Dino said. "Relax, will you? You're making *me* nervous."

Stone finished the wine in his glass and took a few deep breaths.

Arrington appeared on the patio. "I'm going home," she said. "You don't need me for this closing."

"No," Stone replied, "and I think it's just as well you're going." He thought of telling her about the involvement of the two drug cartels but couldn't bring himself to do it.

She kissed Dino on the forehead, then came and put her arms around Stone. "Thank you for all you've done," she said.

"Don't thank me yet," Stone replied, giving her a kiss. "I'll let you know how it goes."

Arrington walked back into the house and was gone.

"So," Dino said, "it's just you and me against the bad guys."

"I hope we're enough," Stone said.

60

On Friday morning Stone managed to get down some breakfast, but he couldn't make himself pay attention to the newspapers. He called Ed Eagle to find out if there was any word on the DNA tests, but had to leave a message. He called Mike Freeman.

"Stone, they said they'd see what they could do, but I don't know what that means or if they'll do it. I wish I could tell you more." They said goodbye.

Dino looked up from his eggs. "You don't look any happier," he said.

Stone pushed his plate away and drank some orange juice to keep up his blood sugar. "I've made a terrible mistake," he said. "I'm doing business with drug dealers, and there's nothing I can do about it."

"Then don't close the deal."

"If I don't, they'll take us to court and win, and it will just prolong the whole thing."

"Stone, when you've done everything you can do, there's no longer anything to worry about."

"That's just it: I keep thinking there's something else I could do, but I can't think of what it is."

Dino sighed. "Think about flying," he said. "This time tomorrow we'll be high in the air, halfway across the country. This will all be behind you."

"I wish I were up there now." He tried to think of flying, but the thought made him nauseated.

At the stroke of eleven, Manolo announced Mr. Prince and Ms. Blaine, and the two walked onto the patio, both carrying briefcases. They sat down at the table by the pool, except Dino, who settled himself on a chaise longue with the newspapers, watching Stone warily over the top of the page.

"Everything is all arranged," Prince said, opening his briefcase and taking out a stack of papers. He began handing sheets to Stone, explaining each and indicating where Stone should initial them. Stone looked them over carefully, trying to take as much time as possible, though he wasn't sure what he was waiting for.

Carolyn seemed very nervous. She rose from

the table and began pacing up and down the edge of the pool.

Finally, Prince produced the last of the documents, the one that would seal the deal.

Stone read it through. "And the funds?" he asked.

Prince reached into his briefcase and produced a cashier's check for two hundred twenty-five million dollars.

Stone glanced at his watch: five minutes before twelve. He had lost. "Is this drawn on your personal account, like the last check?" he asked Prince.

"That's correct."

"I'd like to speak to your banker before I close the deal."

"Of course," Prince said, whipping out his cell phone and pressing a speed-dial button. He got the banker on the phone and handed it to Stone.

"Good morning, Mr. Barrington," the man said.

Stone thought he sounded nervous. "Good morning," he replied. "Mr. Prince and I are about to close a large transaction, and he has presented me with a cashier's check for two hundred twenty-five million dollars drawn on his personal account. Can you affirm that this is a proper check that will be paid on presentation?"

The man seemed to be breathing more rapidly.

"I'm afraid there's a problem," he said. "There's a man in my office from the Drug Enforcement Agency, and he has presented me with a court order freezing Mr. Prince's account. Therefore, I can't pay the check."

"I'd like you to tell your client that," Stone said, and handed the phone to Prince.

"What?" Prince said, then put the phone to his ear. "Yes?" As he listened his face slowly fell into an expression of disbelief. "That's preposterous!" he said, then listened some more. "There's nothing you can do?" He listened some more. "I'll get my attorney on this immediately." He closed the phone and looked at Stone. "I'm afraid I'm going to need an extension," he said.

Stone took a deep breath. "Denied. The deal, at your specification, was to be closed by noon." Stone looked at his watch. "One minute past, and no closing."

"What happened?" Carolyn asked. She had stopped pacing.

"The DEA has frozen Mr. Prince's bank account," Stone said. "He can't fund the deal."

A smile spread across her face. She took a step toward the table and opened her briefcase. "I'm so sorry, Terry," she said. She removed a sheaf of documents from her briefcase and handed them to Stone. "I would like to present my offer for the property," she said. "And I have a perfectly valid check for the closing amount." She handed a cashier's check to Stone. "Feel free to call my banker," she said, handing him a card.

Prince, who had been staring at her, openmouthed, recovered enough to speak. "You incredible bitch!" he said. "Do you think I'm going to let you and that woman get away with this?" He stood up, and there was a gun in his hand.

From Stone's point of view, what happened next was reduced to slow motion: Prince pointed the gun at Carolyn Blaine; she threw up her hands and turned her head away, closing her eyes tightly. Dino threw away his newspaper and clawed at his belt for his own weapon. Prince fired a single shot.

Stone saw a pink cloud explode from the back of Carolyn's head. The force of the bullet spun her around, and she fell into the pool. The water around her head became pink.

Stone dove for Prince's wrist, got hold of it and twisted up and out. Prince lost his grip on the gun and fell backward. Stone jumped on him. "Cuffs!" he yelled to Dino. The handcuffs landed on the flagstones next to him. He rolled Prince over, twisted his arm up and got one cuff on; then he looked over his shoulder and saw Carolyn floating facedown in the pool, in a patch of red water. "The girl!" he yelled at Dino.

Dino knelt on the edge of the pool and tried to reach Carolyn's left foot, but he couldn't quite reach it.

"Go in!" Stone shouted, trying to get the struggling Prince's other wrist cuffed.

Dino shucked off his jacket and jumped into the pool.

Stone left the handcuffed Prince and ran to help him. They got her out of the pool and lifted her onto a chaise longue.

Suddenly, Carolyn spat water at both of them. "What the hell happened?" she yelled, coughing up more water.

"Be quiet," Stone said. "You've been shot." He picked up a towel and pressed it behind her head, then checked it: red, but no gray matter. "Looks like it just creased you."

"But there's so much blood!" she yelled.

"Calm down," Stone said, "scalp wounds always bleed a lot. Dino, call your pals at the LAPD. Tell them we need the medics, too."

Dino got on his cell phone.

"Stone, sign my deal," Carolyn said. "Sign the papers, take the check."

"I'm sorry, Carolyn," Stone replied. "We have another buyer."

"Another buyer! Who?"

Stone was about to answer her when Manolo

walked out onto the patio and looked, appalled, at Prince, handcuffed on the flagstones, and Carolyn, bleeding into one of Mrs. Calder's good towels. "Excuse me, Mr. Stone, but there are some people here from the Santa Fe, New Mexico, Police Department. They want to speak to Ms. Blaine."

Stone grinned. "Send them right out, Manolo." He turned to Prince. "You'll have to wait for the LAPD," he said.

61

Stone was packing the following morning when his cell phone rang. "Hello?"

"Stone, it's Ed Eagle."

"Hello, Ed. I tried to reach you yesterday, but everything turned out all right. She has a slight head wound, but the SFPD showed up at the perfect moment and took her away. And now Terry Prince has a second attempted murder charge against him."

"Everything didn't turn out entirely all right, Stone," Eagle said. "The cops took her to an emergency room, where she got some stitches, and the doctor insisted on keeping her overnight for observation. They put her in a room with another patient, with a cop on guard outside her door. She stole her roommate's clothes, and while the cop was in the john, she ran out of the hospital and found a cab dropping somebody off at the ER."

"Amazing," Stone said. "Then what?"

"The cops went to her address and found the garage door open. They think she had a second car there, but they had no idea what kind, so all they could do was issue an APB for her, with no description of the vehicle. Unless the cops get very lucky, she's gone."

"I hope they fingerprinted her at the ER," Stone said.

"Nope, apparently they don't have that facility. And she still has the cash in the foreign bank account that nobody can find."

"I wonder how much she stole from Terry Prince," Stone said.

An hour later, Stone took off from Santa Monica Airport and got vectors toward Palmdale, to the east. The weather forecast was for ninety-knot westerly winds.

"We'll make Wichita on the first leg," Stone said. "Then from there, if we're lucky with the winds, all the way to Teterboro."

"Take your time," Dino said, opening a book of *New York Times* crossword puzzles, "I've got all day."

Stone leveled off at forty-one thousand feet and turned into the sun.

AUTHOR'S NOTE

I am happy to hear from readers, but you should know that if you write to me in care of my publisher, three to six months will pass before I receive your letter, and when it finally arrives it will be one among many, and I will not be able to reply.

However, if you have access to the Internet, you may visit my Web site at www.stuartwoods.com, where there is a button for sending me e-mail. So far, I have been able to reply to all my e-mail, and I will continue to try to do so.

If you send me an e-mail and do not receive a reply, it is probably because you are among an alarming number of people who have entered their e-mail address incorrectly in their mail software. I have many of my replies returned as undeliverable.

Remember: e-mail, reply; snail mail, no reply.

When you e-mail, please do not send attachments, as I never open these. They can take twenty minutes to download, and they often contain viruses.

Please do not place me on your mailing lists for funny stories, prayers, political causes, charitable fund-raising, petitions, or sentimental claptrap. I get enough of that from people I already know. Generally speaking, when I get e-mail addressed to a large number of people, I immediately delete it without reading it.

Please do not send me your ideas for a book, as I have a policy of writing only what I myself invent. If you send me story ideas, I will immediately delete them without reading them. If you have a good idea for a book, write it yourself, but I will not be able to advise you on how to get it published. Buy a copy of *Writer's Market* at any bookstore; that will tell you how.

Anyone with a request concerning events or appearances may e-mail it to me or send it to: Publicity Department, Penguin Group (USA) Inc., 375 Hudson Street, New York, NY 10014.

Those ambitious folk who wish to buy film, dramatic, or television rights to my books should contact Matthew Snyder, Creative Artists Agency, 9830 Wilshire Boulevard, Beverly Hills, CA 98212-1825.

Those who wish to make offers for rights of a literary nature should contact Anne Sibbald, Janklow & Nesbit, 445 Park Avenue, New York, NY 10022. (Note: This is not an invitation for you to send her your manuscript or to solicit her to be your agent.)

If you want to know if I will be signing books in your city, please visit my Web site, www.stuartwoods.com, where the tour schedule will be published a month or so in advance. If you wish me to do a book signing in your locality, ask your favorite bookseller to contact his Penguin representative or the Penguin publicity department with the request.

If you find typographical or editorial errors in my book and feel an irresistible urge to tell someone, please write to Rachel Kahan at Penguin's address above. Do not e-mail your discoveries to me, as I will already have learned about them from others.

A list of my published works appears in the front of this book and on my Web site. All the novels are still in print in paperback and can be found at or ordered from any bookstore. If you wish to obtain hardcover copies of earlier novels or of the two nonfiction books, a good secondhand bookstore or one of the online bookstores can help you find them. Otherwise, you will have to go to a great many garage sales.

Read on for an excerpt from Stuart Woods's
next thrilling Stone Barrington novel,

DC Dead

On sale in hardcover from Putnam in
January 2012.

Stone Barrington and Dino Bacchetti entered Elaine's on a Sunday evening, and drinks were brought to them immediately.

They took their usual table, and Elaine came over and sat down. "You two are oddly dressed," she said. "For you. What's going on?"

"Oh," Stone said, "we delivered our sons to Yale for their freshman year this afternoon, and we're dressed for humping boxes of their gear up to their apartment."

Elaine nodded. "So the boys are off?"

"They're off," Dino said.

"No wonder you both look so glum," Elaine said.

Stone looked at Dino. "Do I look glum?"

"Yeah," Dino said.

"So do you."

"You're empty nesters now," Elaine chortled. "Never thought I'd see the day."

Stone shook his head. "Nine months ago I didn't have a son, at least not one I'd ever met. Now I don't have a son again."

Elaine reached over and patted his cheek. "You haven't lost a son," she said. "You've gained a college boy." She got up and continued her rounds of the regulars' tables.

"I guess that's one way to look at it," Stone said. "Do you think he'll ever come home again?"

"Probably not," Dino replied. "You've seen the last of that kid."

"Oh, shut up. You're in the same spot."

"Nah," Dino said, "you're worse off. At least I'm not used to having Ben around the house all the time. He's been at prep school for four years, and then his mother yanked him to her place every chance she got. This afternoon, why didn't you raise the subject of visits home?"

"I thought about it," Stone said, "but I was afraid I wouldn't like the answer. After all, the kid's got the money he was paid for his film, which is more than I had a year ago, so he doesn't need me for anything."

"He doesn't just need you for buying stuff," Dino pointed out. "He still needs a father."

"You really think so?"

"Ben needs me. I'm sure of that. Why wouldn't Peter need you, what with his mother dead and all?"

"He's got Hattie. They're sleeping together, you know."

Dino laughed aloud. "No shit? What were *you* doing your freshman year?"

Stone shrugged. "Fucking my brains out, if I recall correctly."

"Actually, you continued to do that, at least until you and Arrington got married."

Stone managed a smile. "If anything, the activity increased after that."

"I'm getting worried about you, kiddo," Dino said. "You're gonna have to get back in the saddle pretty soon or you're gonna forget how."

"Yeah, I think about that a lot. It's just that . . . Well, it's like not being hungry at dinnertime. I just don't have an appetite."

Dino turned and watched as a very pretty brunette in a short skirt came through the door, took a seat at the bar, and crossed her long legs. "Doesn't that do anything for you?"

"Sort of," Stone replied. "I mean, I remember what it was like, the way you remember how you roller-skated when you were a kid, but it just isn't all that appealing."

Dino felt for Stone's pulse and looked at his watch. "Your vital signs seem normal."

"That's something, I guess."

"Look who's here," Dino said, nodding toward the door.

Stone turned in time to see a tall redhead in a well-cut pantsuit enter the restaurant. She headed for their table and sat down. "Hello, sailors," she said, leering a little.

Stone leaned over and kissed her. "Hello, Holly. What brings you to town?"

Dino kissed her, too. "Same question here."

"Agency business," Holly Barker replied. She was an assistant deputy director for the CIA. "I hope you guys remember that you're still under contract to us as consultants."

"How could we forget?" Stone asked. "Lance keeps reminding us." Lance Cabot was Holly's boss, deputy director for operations, or DDO.

"Well, fellas, you're about to get the call again."

Stone slumped. "Now what?"

"I can't tell you," Holly replied.

"Can't tell us what?" Dino asked.

"That's what I can't tell you, dummy," she said.

"What kind of deal is this?" Stone asked.

"Here's the deal: you get the daily rate specified in your contract and five hundred per diem."

"For how long?" Dino asked.

"That depends on how good you are," she said.

"Who can live on five hundred a day?" Stone asked.

"Clearly, you've been living too well," Holly replied. "If you stay at a Holiday Inn Express and eat at McDonald's, you can make money on that. Would you like my office to book you in?"

"Thanks," Stone said. "I'll make my own arrangements."

"He'll make mine, too," Dino said. "He's a regular travel agent."

"As you wish," Holly said.

"Come on, give us a hint."

"Here's the only hint you're going to get," Holly said. "I'll have a car left for you at the Manassas, Virginia, airport. There'll be an envelope locked in the glove compartment containing your credentials."

"Credentials?" Dino asked. "You think we don't know who we are?"

"Sure," Holly said, "but nobody in Washington does. You'll have to prove it, especially at the White House."

"Which White House is that?" Stone asked.

"The *only* one," Holly said. "Find yourselves hotel rooms. Then be there at six sharp tomorrow afternoon, freshly scrubbed and pressed. If you're lucky, you'll get dinner, but don't count on it."

"Is it black tie?" Stone asked.

"You're not *that* important," Holly said. "Just wear one of your nice suits."

"The blue or the pinstripe?" Stone asked.

"Your choice, sweetie. By the way, I'm very sorry for your loss."

"Thank you. I got your very nice letter. I'm afraid I haven't responded to all those yet."

"Don't worry about it."

"How are you and the boyfriend doing?" Dino asked.

"He's running a big trauma center in San Diego," she replied. "He didn't take to the Agency life—not enough blood and guts, I guess. It's been a couple of months. It was amicable."

"Let me get you a drink and a menu," Stone said.

"Love to, but can't," she said. "There's a chopper waiting for me at the West Side heliport, and I've got a briefcase full of work to keep me awake on the flight home." She stood up, and both men stood up with her.

"See you tomorrow evening," she said, then walked out briskly.

They sat down again.

"Why did you ask her about the boyfriend?" Stone asked.

"Because I knew you wouldn't," Dino replied.

*   *   *

Stone packed a bag the following morning, then, on second thought, packed a second bag. The last time he had consulted for the CIA, he, Holly, and Dino had spent a couple of weeks on a tropical isle, pursuing a federal fugitive named Teddy Fay, who gave them the slip. Who knew how long this one would take or where they would end up?

He took the elevator down to the garage and put his bags in the car; then he went to his office and wondered what to put in his briefcase.

Joan Robertson, his secretary, appeared in the doorway. "You off to someplace?"

"To Washington—for a few days, I think."

"Could be longer?"

"It's one of those things for Lance Cabot and Holly Barker. Who knows?"

"You'd better take your passport," she said, opening his safe and tossing him the document.

"I'd get my vaccinations, if I knew which ones to take," he replied.

"You don't look very happy about this," Joan said, pouring him a cup of coffee.

"I'm not unhappy about it," Stone replied. "If I'm unhappy at all, it's about Peter's being off at Yale."

"How did yesterday go?"

Stone shrugged. "Bittersweet. I'm happy for Peter, getting what he wants, but I miss him already."

"So do I," Joan said. "It was a nice change from it being just you all the time."

"You'll have Allison to talk to," Stone said, referring to the Woodman & Weld associate who had been assigned to his office, "and that means you'll have Herbie Fisher dropping by at every opportunity just because Allison is here."

"I hear on the secretarial grapevine that Herbie is already making his mark at the firm," Joan said, "working long hours, being smart. He's got the other associates coming to him for answers."

"Who knew that Herbie would turn out so well?" Stone said. "I personally thought he'd be dead or in prison by now."

"Better haircuts and suits seemed to improve him," Joan said, "and the lottery win didn't hurt."

"I hope he's still got some of it," Stone said.

The bell rang, and Joan went to let Dino in. She took his bags to the garage.

"Coffee before we blast off?" Stone asked.

"It couldn't hurt," Dino said, accepting a cup. "Has Holly called and told you what this is all about?"

Stone sat down and sipped his coffee. "Nope. I'm as much in the dark as you are."

"That used to be kind of exciting," Dino said, "not knowing what's going to happen."

"You're depressed," Stone said.

"I am?" Dino said, looking surprised.

"About Ben going away to college."

"Oh, that. Yeah. You, too."

"Yeah, me, too."

"I have an idea," Dino said. "Let's go to Washington and find out what the hell this is all about. It might improve our dispositions."

"Good idea," Stone said, putting on his coat. "Let's get out of here."

They were at Teterboro Airport in a half hour, and it took Stone another forty-five minutes to do a preflight inspection of his Citation Mustang, a small jet, get a clearance to Manassas, and taxi to the runway. Shortly, they were cleared for takeoff. Stone shoved the throttles all the way forward, waited for ninety knots, then rotated. The little jet roared off the runway like a big one. Stone contacted New York Departure and got a vector and a new altitude, and they were off.

Another three-quarters of an hour and they were settling onto the runway at Manassas. A lineman directed them to a parking spot, and someone drove a black SUV over to the airplane and parked it near the door.

"That must be our car," Dino said.

"Who would give us a black SUV but the CIA?" Stone asked.

The lineman took their bags from the forward

luggage compartment and stowed them in the rear of the vehicle. Then Stone registered with the fixed base operator (FBO) and gave them a credit card for refueling.

"I'll drive," Dino said. "I know the city better than you."

"Nevertheless, I hope there's a map in the car," Stone said.

He got into the passenger seat, and Dino got behind the wheel. "I'm going to need the car key to open the glove box," Stone said.

Dino handed him the keys, and Stone examined them carefully. There were just two: an ordinary car key and another that looked like something off the space shuttle. He inserted that key into the large nonstandard lock on the glove box and opened it. Inside he found two holstered SIG Sauer P239 9mm pistols with an extra magazine for each and a box of cartridges.

"Why do we need to be armed to go to the White House?" Stone said. "They'll just take them away from us as soon as we get there."

"Just leave them in the glove compartment," Dino said. "Is there anything else in there?"

Stone removed a thick black envelope and pulled a tab that broke the seal. He shook out the contents onto the glove box door and looked at the four plastic cards that came out.

"Okay, we've got two White House passes marked 'Staff,' and two wallets with CIA ID cards." He handed one of each to Dino, who examined them.

"Looks like we clip the White House passes to our lapels. What do we do with the CIA IDs?"

"I don't know. They've never given us those before," Stone replied.

Dino clipped the White House pass to his lapel, stuck the CIA wallet in his inside pocket, and started the car. "Oh," he said, "here's the map from the door pocket. Keep me out of trouble."

Stone opened the map and found Manassas, then found the White House. "First," he said, "drive out the gate."

Dino did so, and a minute or two later they were driving north on the interstate. "Hey," he said, "I forgot to ask where we're staying."

"At the Hay-Adams," Stone said. "Sixteenth and H Street."

"And how do I get there?"

"It's across Lafayette Park from the White House."

"And how do I get there?"

Stone consulted the map. "Straight ahead. I'll let you know when to turn. This is your local knowledge?"

"Right. You give me directions," Dino said, "and my local knowledge will get you there."